A Perfect Mother

A Perfect Mother

Patricia Fawcett

ROBERT HALE · LONDON

© Patricia Fawcett 2007
First published in Great Britain 2007

ISBN 978-0-7090-8453-2

Robert Hale Limited
Clerkenwell House
Clerkenwell Green
London EC1R 0HT

www.halebooks.com

The right of Patricia Fawcett to be identified as
author of this work has been asserted by her
in accordance with the Copyright, Designs and
Patents Act 1988

2 4 6 8 10 9 7 5 3 1

Typeset in 11/13pt Times New Roman
by Derek Doyle & Associates, Shaw Heath
Printed and bound in Great Britain
by Biddles Limited, King's Lynn

To Lewis and his 'little ladies'
Meg, Ella and Daisy

CHAPTER ONE

PANIC OVER

Dᴬᴰ was home, recovering after the emergency admission to hospital, following his faint and fall. Frances phoned to tell her the news, having already informed Diane, managing somehow to convey the fact that it was no thanks to either of them that he was alive and well and back to being his usual irritating self.

'Thank goodness for that,' Maggie said, as relief flooded through her. She understood now what they meant by the term 'her knees gave way'. She sat down abruptly for she had got herself into a bit of a state, thinking all sorts of worst-case scenarios for the last few days, ever since the phone call from Frances announcing that he was in hospital again. Even though Frances had told her to stay put, she had her bag packed ready for the off, not quite trusting the hospital's view that he was going to be just fine or however they put it in their veiled terms. Ridiculously, she had been making plans for the funeral, determined that Frances and Diane were not going to have it all their own way. She would make damned sure they played some of his favourite music somewhere along the line.

Squashed in the middle of the Troon family, Maggie sometimes felt battered on both sides by her sisters. All right, so maybe she was being a bit macabre thinking of funerals, particularly as Dad was not quite sixty, but men dropped dead far younger than that.

'I'm coming over at the end of the month,' she said, interrupting

Frances's long-winded explanation of what had happened. 'I'm just working my notice out.'

'Coming over? For how long?' Frances could not have sounded more surprised if she had suddenly announced she had grown a second head. Surprised and not entirely pleased at that.

'For as long as it takes. The thing is, I've decided to come home.'

'Home? For good?'

'Yes, and you needn't sound quite so put out.'

'Oh, sorry, you just took me by surprise. What's happened? Has Dave left you then?'

'We left each other.'

'Gracious, I thought he was the love of your life?'

She decided to ignore that. 'I've been thinking about coming home for a long time, ever since Dad had the first little do last year, but this has only made me see that I'm doing the right thing. It's not fair to expect you to deal with things all the time. I've given notice at the flat.'

'That's very commendable of you but what about your job? I hope you've thought this through, Maggie, and you're not acting on impulse. Jobs don't grow on trees.'

She had her big sister voice on and, as always, Maggie was rattled by it. Frances always treated her as if she was dippy. 'I have thought it through,' she said. 'My job's sorted. I've got a transfer. If you don't mind, I'll live at home for the time being. I can help you with Dad. It's high time I did.'

'You can have your old room,' Frances said, trying to put on a bright voice. 'It will be like old times.'

'Yes . . . will Dad be OK about it? Should I have asked him first?'

'Whatever for? It's your home too. He'll be fine about it. I'll mention it, though.'

'Is he in? You can put him on if you like.'

'He's out. He's driven off somewhere.' Frances's disapproval was evident. 'I'm not sure he ought to be driving in his state but he insists. What if he faints again?'

'He won't.'

'He never says where he's off to and I feel I need to keep tabs on him.'

'He won't like that.'

There was a moment's silence. Over-protective sprang to Maggie's mind. They might be worried about him after the health scare but they must not start trying to wrap him in cotton wool and it sounded as if Frances was trying to do just that. It was just as well she was going to be there to balance things out because Dad had a short fuse where Frances and her fussing were concerned.

'Well, what a surprise,' Frances said, again too brightly. 'It's all happening. Guess what? Diane's popping up, too, for a few days. It isn't often we find ourselves all under the same roof, is it?'

'What's *she* coming up for? And how can she spare the time? She holds that company together, doesn't she? Without her, it will collapse like a pack of cards. In fact, the entire advertising industry might very well implode.'

'Don't be sarcastic, Maggie. She's trying to do the right thing, I suppose.'

'But you've just said Dad's on the mend. There's no need for her to start panicking.'

'She seems to want to come up. She said she needed a short break away from the family and she wants to see Dad.'

'I hope he won't think you've called the two of us over because he's on his last legs?'

'Oh no. He's fine. Flirting with the cleaner, would you believe? I caught him gazing at her the other day with this idiotic look on his face. Fortunately, she doesn't seem to notice. I really don't know who he thinks he is sometimes.'

Maggie was smiling as she replaced the receiver.

She had been stupid to think of funerals. Her father was made of sterner stuff. And, now that Mother was gone, he was her sole parental prop and all this had made her realize how much she needed him.

It had been on the cards for some time, the break-up with Dave. It came to a head at Christmas, which had been a disaster. Their steady relationship started to nose-dive when, with three whole days together and nothing to do but supposedly make merry, they had finally begun to realize they had nothing in common. They had all warned her it wouldn't last; her colleagues at work, her neighbour Pamela, even Frances, who had never met him and whose own experience of men was virtually nil.

Dave was your original charmer, the mix of boyish charm, success and helplessness an utter winner. At ease with women of all ages, he had a smile that would cut through the most cynical female heart but he didn't want to grow up, responsibility a dirty word, and playing the eternal engaging schoolboy was only for the likes of Peter Pan. Maggie had made the mistake, that age-old one, of thinking that, given time, she could change him, make him the man she wanted him to be rather than the man he was. It was doomed to fail, of course, and she had been a fool for trying.

No matter. Breaking up might be hard to do but it was also an opportunity to break out of a rut, to do something different, although at first she would not have bargained on going to these extremes of changing jobs *and* moving back home. It was time for a fresh start, a reappraisal of her wardrobe for a kick-off, which consisted largely of a couple of suits for work, boring black trousers and snazzy tops. How many pairs of black trousers did she need? Dave liked a bit of sparkle and she couldn't believe some of the stuff she had bought to please him – middle-age cruise-wear. It was wonderfully therapeutic to dump the lot in the recycling bin. Being single again was a great excuse for some retail therapy and she fancied a younger image.

She and Dave had been together for eighteen months – a record in his book – and, at the beginning, it had been idyllic and she could even tolerate the times apart when he was on his trips abroad to wherever the English cricket team was playing. Being apart had its compensations, for the reunions had been bliss.

The problems began and ended with money, Dave being one of those hopeless cases, and maybe it was petty to argue about his contributions to the daily running expenses but when they dwindled to practically nothing it became annoying because he earned substantial fees as a sports reporter. Could she live with a man whose wallet was glued to his back pocket? Could she live with a man whom she suspected was in serious debt and in denial about it? Never mind that he was handsome and sexy and that they had had great times together, the crux of the matter was that, if they stayed together, she would spend the rest of her life trying to prise money out of him for whatever reason. Or worse, she might be expected to provide the financial prop.

Also, she could not pin him down about long-term plans, about his intentions, honourable or otherwise. It became increasingly obvious that she would have to let it go, that it wasn't going to work, that she should shoot it all in the foot sooner rather than later. She was in her middle thirties now and she would have to get her skates on if she was to achieve all she hoped for in the home and family department. When he had flirted with all and sundry at the last party they had gone to as a couple, when she had come very close to throwing her drink in his face, when she had seen the sympathetic glances shot her way, she had known she was losing the battle.

Annoyingly, she had waited just that fraction too long, still giving him the benefit of the doubt, and then Dave had made the decision for her by deciding to go off with Emily. It was a bolt from the blue and she was still suffering from the sting of it. There was no way she was going to admit that to Frances, although she had told Diane about it – not that she had been that sympathetic either but then she had enough of her own concerns to sink the *Titanic*, as she was fond of saying. She did say, however, that Rupert had not liked the idea of Dave traipsing off for weeks on end.

'What on earth has it got to do with him?' Maggie had asked, deciding it was just as well that the two men had never met.

'Nothing at all. But you know us. We've never been apart for more than a few days at a time in the last fifteen years.'

Quite. Her sister had the dream marriage.

Maggie was determined not to rush into another relationship. This time, next time, she would take her time. The man of her dreams, this elusive Mr Right they all talked about, had to be out there somewhere and maybe she would have to settle for somebody less than perfect.

Too true she would.

11

It was all very well fancying a man but she was beginning to real-ize there had to be more to it than that. She had to like him and she wasn't even sure now that she had liked Dave. She had passionately loved him, adored his lean, male, gym-toned body, his voice, his easy smile, but had she liked him? He was a great talker but never listened. And, as for the cricket ... could she live with a man who lived and breathed the game?

Now that it was too late to back out of moving, she was starting to have a few regrets. She would miss Pamela. She would not miss the flat or Newcastle particularly, and she certainly would not miss Dave but she would miss the little chats with Pamela. Pamela was her very own agony aunt, a good neighbour in the true sense. She was a plump curly-haired blonde in her forties and, watching from the sidelines, had seen it all coming. Pamela had the bottom flat in their small block and happily did the gardening, which consisted of looking after an assortment of potted plants and troughs filled to the brim with seasonal flowers, a vibrant mix of early summer bedding plants now. Before Pamela came on the scene it was all sadly neglected but she had been out there with her trowel and a little sack of compost almost before the removal men had gone.

Pamela was at her usual vantage point, on her knees, messing about with her secateurs, when Dave left for the very last time. Maggie was not actually wringing her hands in despair but just stand-ing there as he fussed around cramming his belongings into the sporty car he could in no way afford and, as she stood there, it suddenly occurred that it was a pathetic thing to be doing – watching him leave like this. They had already said all there was to say upstairs and there was no need to wave him off.

She had followed him downstairs automatically and now seemed to be rooted to the spot. How many times had she waved him off in happier circumstances as he set off for the airport? They had been tearful goodbyes and then it would take a few days to settle to life without him but then there had always been the coming home to look forward to. There would be no more of those.

Getting into the driving seat at last, he then had the cheek to wind the window down, wearing his cute little-boy expression, intent, it seemed, on having a final word.

'Look, Maggie, no hard feelings, eh? Sorry it's turned out like this.' To her amazement, she saw him waving money, a few twenties, in his hand. The nerve of the man! Was she expected to take it? Did he think this was the appropriate moment to give a financial peace offering, to chip in at last to the housekeeping? Emily wasn't there in the car with him – he had some sensibilities left – but she might as well have been, in her flame-haired splendour. She remembered being introduced to her a few months ago, remembered, too, the flutter of dismay as she took in her wild and wonderful hair, which was a blaze of colour.

Looking at him waving the money, she heard him say, through a thin haze of disbelief, something about a contribution to the gas bill.

'You can stuff your money, you bastard,' she heard herself saying, appalled at the tremor in her voice.

'Suit yourself. I've offered.'

As he roared off, she muttered an embarrassed apology to Pamela, who could not have helped but overhear although, in her unflappable way, she took it in her stride.

'Cup of tea, flower?' she asked, in her lovely sing-song accent, whipping off her gardening gloves and clambering to her feet. 'You look like you need it.'

So, a little later, it was tea, tissues and sympathy sitting at Pamela's newly installed breakfast bar with Pamela's husband Martin despatched with a single glance as he unknowingly came whistling through.

As she confessed to Pamela over a slice of Asda's luxury lemon meringue pie, it was the humiliation that did it. Knowing that Dave was living with her, in her flat, enjoying all the comforts, both domestic and sexual, and all the time he had been in a relationship with Emily, who was everything she was not, tall and voluptuous, a fellow journalist.

'I never liked the idea of him disappearing for weeks on end,' Pamela said, echoing her brother-in-law's misgivings. 'You need to know where your man is so that you can keep your eye on him. Men are too easily led, aside from my Martin, and he knows which side his bread is buttered,' she added with a little confident smile.

'What is it with me? Every man I've ever known has left me for a redhead,' Maggie said. 'It's very odd but I can even remember a little redheaded girl when I was at junior school. She was called Tania and she had gorgeous curly hair and she took Trevor Lodge from me. I still have the class photo. He was a lovely little boy and we used to play together before she came along. And then, in the sixth form, there was Mark Broughton. I liked him. The trouble is all the other girls did too. He was the best looking of a sorry bunch.'

'Don't tell me he went off with a redhead?'

'You bet he did. A girl called Trisha,' she said, recalling her in a vivid blaze of irritation. 'She was the class bad girl.'

They laughed. 'There's always one of those,' Pamela said. 'You wonder what happens to girls like that in the end, don't you? Do they stay bad girls for ever?'

'And then there was another Mark at college. He joined a quiz team and then went off with Belinda who knew *everything*. She was a redhead too. I tell you, Pam, I'm beginning to get a complex about it.'

Pamela was smiling at the indignation.

'But the worst thing of all—' She hesitated and decided not to say it. There were some things best kept to herself. 'Should I dye my hair, do you think?'

'No, you should not. It's a lovely colour as it is. I used to have dark hair, too, once upon a time. In fact, I wish I'd kept it that colour.' Pamela touched her overly blonde locks and smiled, taking hold of Maggie's hand and giving it a little squeeze. 'Let's face it. You've been unlucky. You've just picked the wrong men. He had a wandering eye, that one, and he was too full of himself. You deserve better than that. Martin fancies you, if that's any consolation. I don't suppose it is. And keep it to yourself. He'd die if he thought I'd told you.'

Martin was rotund and bald but he was a nice man and it was a consolation, sort of.

'I'm at the end of a phone if you ever need to speak to me,' Pamela had said, when Maggie was stuffing the last of her things into the car, prior to her departure a few weeks later.

'Thanks.'

Awkwardly, both of them knowing that it was extremely unlikely they would ever see each other again, they hugged. As she drove off, seeing Pamela standing there, waving her goodbye, Maggie had to hold back tears. Sometimes, daft or not, it was as if Pamela had stepped into her mother's shoes. In fact, Pamela had been a good deal more sympathetic than her own mum had ever been. She would miss her.

Passing the Angel of the North, which always provoked a reaction – love or hate – it occurred to her that she had been living in the northeast for a very long time now, since her stint at Durham, and at one time she had imagined she would stay here for ever. It was bitterly cold over on the Northumberland coast with the North Sea winds lashing it, even in summer, but she liked the people up here, cheerful, chirpy and cheeky, and the accent never failed to amuse her. Even though it wasn't that much of a journey home, just a hop over the hills, she regretted that she hadn't made the effort more often, but Frances was such hard work. Frances was such a worrier. Goodness knows what her pupils at school made of her and Dad wasn't exactly tripping over the moon either when she visited. She loved him; had always run to him when she was little, rather than her mother. Diane had been Mother's little girl, the one most like her, and with her arrival, she and Frances had been pretty much left to their own devices.

Once again, Maggie had waited just that fraction too long to arrive at the decision to go back home and now it looked as if she was doing it only because of what had happened to Dad.

Now that it was too late, she was having second thoughts about all this. It felt as if she was running home with her tail between her legs. She couldn't make it out in the big world so she was returning to her roots, to safety, to the family nest, to her dad's solid and comfortable presence.

It made her feel like a complete and utter failure.

CHAPTER TWO

THE PRODIGAL DAUGHTERS RETURN

MAGGIE and Diane's expected arrival had sent Frances into one of her famous flurries. Thank heavens for Mrs Latham, for at least this time Diane wouldn't appear with a fluff of dust on the end of her finger, looking accusingly at Frances. She had a cheek. She never lifted a finger domestically either and yet it seemed as if she expected Frances to wear herself to the bone.

In anticipation of her sisters' homecoming, Frances rushed out to buy some new bed linen, and towels for the bathrooms, and even remembered to buy some cut flowers for the house. Normally, she could not be bothered with elaborate floral arrangements indoors but she knew that Diane would comment if there were no flowers around. The arrangement, bought at great expense from the best florist in town, was on the hall table where Diane was sure to notice it as she swept in. It was perfectly positioned for maximum effect, a strawberry-vanilla mix of pink and cream roses, which was daft because she could have popped into the garden and picked them for nothing.

Opening the windows wide, Frances let the morning air rush in and wished that she had had some notice of all this. She could cope with one sister but two was a bit much and she was determined she was not going to be relegated this time to some sort of skivvy, waiting hand on foot on Diane. Maggie was more willing to give a hand but she was a touch cavalier in the kitchen and she didn't know where they kept anything although, to be fair to her, other people's kitchens were always a nightmare.

This room, Maggie's room, was lovely with large windows on two sides, one of them looking out towards the hills, but in all the years Maggie had been away, Frances had never been tempted to move in here. It was Maggie's room and that was that and now that she had grown used to the idea, it was rather nice that she was coming back permanently. Thinking about it, Maggie's reasons seemed sound enough, although Frances still worried that she was impulsive and being ditched by Dave – as had surely happened – could be a step too far. Frances was well aware that she herself could never be accused of impulsiveness because she weighed everything up to the nth degree, although she still managed to make horrendous mistakes. "Just go for it" was not a maxim that sat easily on her shoulders.

The last time Maggie lived here at Park House was eighteen years ago, just before she went off to university. She was offered a place at Lancaster and although they lived on the wrong side of town, well on the way to Carnforth, it was an easy enough commute straight down the M6; but she had opted for Durham instead, saying that she preferred the course offered. Frances had known the real reason was that she wanted to be a proper student, live in student accommodation, to stretch her wings, to have that important bit of independence, just as Diane would do a year later.

After her own college course down in Cheshire, a course she had enjoyed even though homesickness had been a real problem, Frances had elected to return home, being lucky enough – or perhaps unlucky enough – to secure a post at a local school. It was not the school she had attended as a girl so it wasn't as if she had gone in a complete circle but it was a school she knew and it did seem unadventurous to say the least.

As expected, Maggie had never come home in the permanent sense, gaining a modest degree before taking a job as a charity fundraising organizer up in the north-east and seeming to settle there. Frances had visited her various grotty bedsits and flats from time to time but it was usually an uncomfortable experience, particularly if

Maggie was with somebody. A visiting shy older sister was not exactly flavour of the month then.

At the last count, she was living with this man called Dave, whom Frances had never met and now never would. She had spoken to him in passing on the phone before he passed it over to Maggie, and he had called her Fran, which everybody who knew her knew she hated. It somehow said something about him.

Poor Maggie had a knack of picking the wrong men. Frances had just known that Dave would go the way of all the others. Frances might be the big sister, three years older, but sometimes she felt twenty-three years older. She just didn't have a young outlook, never had had, and being forced into the position of staying at home and looking after Father had only underlined that. As the eldest daughter she couldn't shake off this annoying feeling of responsibility. If she didn't do it, who would?

In the old days, in one of Jane Austen's novels, for instance, she would have been referred to as Miss Troon, the eldest daughter held in some esteem. In her more depressed moments last year, just after Father was ill for the first time, she could see the years stretching ahead: Father getting ever older with her continuing to be house-keeper-cum-general-dogsbody-cum-nursemaid eventually and still, most importantly, *Miss* Frances Troon, spinster of this parish.

Such thoughts were not worthy of her. She was head of the history department now and very good at her job and that had to count for something. She was of the no-nonsense school of teaching, siding with all the old hands, which was not terribly fashionable but it worked for her. She was passionate about her subject, desperate to invoke the same enthusiasm in her pupils, although, on occasions, flogging a dead horse seemed most apt. She liked to think the children respected her and she also liked to think she treated them fairly. As to whether or not they actually liked her, well, that was debatable but she didn't see herself as being in some sort of popularity contest. She liked to retain a certain formality and was reluctant to take fancy ideas on board, which sometimes made her unpopular with the head-mistress. This made her elevation to head of department all the more surprising. She must be doing something right.

It was just life generally that didn't always seem fair. Diane was the youngest and she was the one who had it all. Sailing effortlessly through school, she had a first-class degree from Cambridge, creamed off even before she graduated as a potential high-flyer. Now she held an executive post with an international advertising agency, and, if she could be believed, she very nearly ran the whole outfit. She also had a devoted husband, four children and a gracious home in south-west London. It went without saying that she was always beautifully turned out, too; a woman with style. For Frances, who had none, that really grated.

Diane was one of those rare women who seemed to have worked out how she could have it all. She had cornered the ambitious genes from the Troon family pool, Maggie had reaped the prettiest ones and Frances had been left with all the mediocre ones, the sober, worthwhile, dull ones. Diane was surely Dad's favourite and after all Frances did for him that hurt, that really hurt. She yearned for praise from him but it never came. As for her mother . . . well, it was Diane she called out for at the last, even though it happened to be Frances who was holding her hand.

'Mrs Latham?' She caught the cleaner before setting off for work. 'Would you please run the duster round Maggie's room and would you put fresh linen in the blue guest room for Diane? I've left the sheets out for you. Oh, and could you freshen up the flowers? We can't have them dying on us just yet.'

'Right you are, Miss Troon.' Wendy Latham smiled the smile that made her whole face crinkle. 'That will be nice for you, having your sisters back home for a while. I'm quite excited about it.'

'Are you?' Frances could not imagine why, for, frankly, she had no business being excited about it, but she did not prolong the conversation. She was awkward with staff, uncomfortable at the idea of employing anybody, not sure how to deal with them, and she had learnt that there was no such thing as the perfect cleaner. They were either useless at the actual job or too familiar and Wendy Latham was certainly the latter. She tended to chat too much if she got the chance and Father did not help by condoning it, sitting drinking tea with her, for heaven's sake, when she was being paid by the hour. Cleaners were a law unto themselves and Frances hoped this one would last the course. She was paying her more than the going rate in the hope that would keep her happy. In Mrs Latham's favour was the fact that the house was looking better than it had looked for years. Frances felt vaguely ashamed, knowing how horrified her mother would have been to see standards slipping. Horrified but hardly surprised because she had always considered Frances to be sloppy, constantly telling her to tidy up. It had not worked and, even today, she often closed the door to her own room with a little shudder. As for the state of her car, well, that beggared belief.

Frances set off for school, trying to put her domestic problems aside. It was the last week of term and things were flattening out as they always did, with everybody, staff and pupils alike, desperate for a holiday.

She sat a moment in the car, letting her thoughts settle.

It was close to the end of the road with John and this coming weekend was the crunch. For an affair, it had been short-lived, she thought, as she drove to school. It had been wonderful while it lasted, as if she had indeed been lifted lightly onto cloud nine, but hadn't she always known it could not last for ever? She wished now she had kept it strictly to herself but she had blabbed to her colleague Polly and she would have to be told when it was all over.

When she got home later, Maggie would probably have arrived and Diane would be due soon. It did not augur well, cheerfulness very low on the agenda, what with Maggie's relationship breaking down and Diane's recent miscarriage. At least she had Rupert to console her.

Good old dependable Rupert.

Polly veered to the 'all men are bastards' school of thought but even she was finding it difficult to blame this one on John. She did not actually say that it was all Frances's fault but she might as well have done. Frances did not need to be told anyway. She knew what the score was.

The day dragged with nobody, staff or pupils, having the stomach for it. Frances left with indecent haste, stopping off for some shopping. None of them could cook with any degree of competence, so it promised to be an interesting few days. At least at this time of year they could survive on cold platters.

As she turned into the drive at home, she saw that Maggie had arrived.

CHAPTER THREE

I<small>T</small> was late when Rupert and Diane finally sat down to supper together. The au pair had given the children their tea but they had taken some settling tonight, which had played havoc with Rupert's schedule, leaving the meat overcooked. It was annoying, particularly as he had taken some time choosing it at the butcher's.

It was a balmy summer evening and he had left the French doors open in the dining room, so that they had all the benefits of dining alfresco without the disadvantages. He had taken some trouble with the table this evening, setting out the cream china and pink candles, and in the centre of the table he had placed a tiny bunch of mixed sweet peas. It was meant to be a little romantic meal before she departed but, for all the notice she took of it, he need not have bothered.

He was trying to keep relaxed about it. It was like that these days. Diane seemed to be in a little world of her own and was taking even less interest in the children than was her norm. He supposed it was something to do with the recent miscarriage. Ever since then, it was as if there was a little protective shield round her and it could not be pierced, not by him anyway.

Her bags were out in the hall, packed with enough clothes to stage a fashion show, and she planned to set off directly after an early breakfast tomorrow. He could tell she was anxious already to be off but he would do his best to dissuade her if she took it into her head to travel up tonight. She could hardly keep her eyes open as it was.

Her sudden announcement that she was going home was a surprise, even if he was used to Diane's continual torpedoing of the smooth running of the house. Charging up to her dad's on a whim was a bit of a facer, though. She had never done that before. Usually, it was he who had to persuade her to visit. She was lukewarm so far as her family went. Having no family of his own here – his parents had gone off to be with his brother in Australia – it peeved him that she could be so cavalier.

'Did Frances ask you to go up?'

'Not exactly.' Diane put down her fork, dabbing at her mouth with her napkin. 'I just think I ought to. I know it was difficult with me not being well either but I never visited him this time in hospital. . . .'

'He was only in for four days whilst they did the tests.'

'I know but that doesn't stop me feeling guilty. I'm worried about him. He could have bled to death.'

'No, he couldn't. I think Frances exaggerated the amount of blood. A little blood goes a long way. Look at Roger when he gets his nose-bleeds. You'd think we were in a slaughter house. Anyway, your dad's got the all-clear, hasn't he? It was just a blip. The pills will sort him out.'

She nodded, pushing her half-eaten plate of food aside. 'Sorry, darling, that was delicious,' she said. She looked tired but then she always did these days. It was more than his life was worth to suggest she take it easier. She had gone back to work far too soon after the miscarriage but she had insisted she was fine so he had gone along with it. As Maggie had said on the phone when he worried her with it, a swift return to the office might be just what she needed to take her mind off it. Whenever Maggie rang here, Diane was always in a tearing hurry and, after a few brief words, she would pass the phone to him so, as a result, he talked to his sister-in-law more often than she did. He liked Maggie. Maggie would listen and, if prompted, offer advice. He rarely took the advice because he reckoned he knew Diane better than she did.

Or did he? Rupert wished Diane would talk about it, tell him how she was feeling but, emotionally, she could be a closed shop sometimes. He wanted to comfort her but she wasn't letting him do that. Putting on a brave face came to mind and he loved her so much for the sadness she must be feeling. Being pregnant again had come as a shock but he had seen the way she was coming round to it, as she had done before, and losing it had come as an even greater shock. They did not do miscarriages in the Buckman family; they did carefree, uncomplicated pregnancies with healthy babies at the end.

Her difficult mood was enough to put him off his own meal and, for a minute, he felt that keen cook's irritation that his efforts had come to naught.

What's the matter, sweetheart? Come on, you can tell me. Is it work?' he asked, taking their glasses of wine out onto the terrace. He loved summer skies and, looking at this one, found his artistic eyes riveted by the swirls of colour gathering there. Diane followed him out and they stood there, looking onto the long narrow garden. He wasn't into gardening, not much, but he liked it to look good, as did Diane, and he liked the slightly moist night smell of it. He particularly liked the feel of cool grass under bare feet but he wasn't about to go charging off just now.

In this neck of the woods, this larger than average garden was an oasis they coveted and, from a purely practical point of view, it would add thousands to the price of the house if they ever decided to sell. Following the redesign of the garden when they moved in, Diane had found a man to look after it. He wasn't cheap but at least he knew his daffodils from his onions. The colours were subdued, as per Diane's instructions, but sometimes Rupert longed for a blaze of orange or a splash of yellow.

Rupert handed Diane her drink, as they sat on the still warm stone bench on the terrace.

'Why don't you wear shoes?' she asked, a little irritably. 'Your feet get so dirty.'

'I wear them when I have to,' he replied, not being drawn into an argument about it. 'It feels good barefoot against the stone. Smooth yet gritty. You should try it.'

'No, thank you,' she said, putting out her foot and admiring the elegance of her house-shoes. In the distance, a siren blared but it was easy enough, after all these years, to shut out city sounds.

'I've had a pig of a day,' she said with a shudder.

'Who is it this time? Piers or Candida?' he asked, naming two of her current adversaries, wanting to get to the bottom of what was bothering her. For no sane reason, Rupert actively disliked Piers, who had an even grander-sounding job title than Diane, whilst Candida was the new girl on the block.

'Piers is just an incompetent, I can cope with him. It's Candida.' Diane managed a smile. 'Oh, so many things. She does come up with the ideas, I grant her that, but I can't keep track of her, Rupert. She's undermining my authority bit by bit, taking full advantage of the fact that I've been preoccupied of late.' She pushed at her hair, the gesture not having so much impact now that it was brutally short. 'As for Piers, well, he just stands there, poised to go in any direction. She puts on such a confident show that people are uncertain, starting to hedge their bets as to whose side to be on. The workplace is all about plots and counter-plots and she's devious.'

'So are you,' he reminded her. 'It's just a case of being one step ahead of her the whole time. And she's not the only one with the creative ideas. That's why companies keep on coming back to you.'

'But for how much longer? It's a competitive business and you're only as good as your last advertising campaign.' Diane sighed and he looked sharply at her, for it was unlike her to be so negative. 'At the moment, she's still the new girl. And that's another thing. She's supposed to be twenty-nine but I wouldn't bank on it. She's easily as old as me.'

He laughed at that. 'You're only thirty-four. It won't make much difference. And I would have thought she'd lie upwards, if you know what I mean. In her position, it might be better if she was older. *You* are considered far too young by some people, aren't you?'

'That's different. I'm brilliant at the job so age means nothing,' she said, perfectly at ease with the self-praise. 'It's the principle, Rupert. Lying about her age now when it hardly matters is very disturbing. And just to make matters worse, I've only just found out that she's distantly related to Harry.'

Harry, now an American billionaire, was the advertising genius who had founded the company in the sixties. He was a huge man in all respects, whom Rupert had met on a couple of occasions, and he led a lifestyle that befitted his status and his money: private jets, chauffeur-driven cars and what have you.

'Related to Harry?' There didn't seem to be much to say to that but it did put a different complexion on things.

'Not surprisingly, she kept it very quiet,' Diane continued. 'It makes my blood boil because I've had to work so bloody hard to get where I am and she just comes swanning in like she owns the place. Single and sexy and carefree with a mind like a double-edged razor.'

'Does she have the qualifications?'

'Oh yes, she has those,' Diane said. 'From some American university,' she added with a sniff.

Well, then, perhaps it's all above board.'

'You would say that,' she said, looking at him irritably.

Rupert sighed. He got all these office shenanigans second-hand from Diane but the workings of big business never ceased to fascinate and appal him at the same time. He was just thankful that he needn't be a part of it. It wouldn't be his scene at all. 'Where is Harry these days? I haven't heard you mention him for ages.'

'He's spending more and more time in the States in an effort to drum up more business – as if we need more clients when we're run off our feet. He never lets up,' she said with a slight smile. 'And while the cat's away, Candida irritates the hell out of all the women but the men won't hear a word said against her. It's so blatant.'

Rupert sipped his wine, a carefully chosen Chilean red which he would certainly try again. He had never met the mischievous-sounding Candida but he could picture her because Diane had given him a feature-by-feature account of her in such detail that she would be applauded if she were a witness in a crime. He wondered if his wife quite appreciated her own considerable charms. That alabaster skin of hers, for a start, and those eyes, an interesting but infuriatingly difficult dark mix he had tried and failed to reproduce on canvas.

'Now, come on, darling,' he said. 'Don't tell me you haven't used your own sex appeal at work when it suits you?'

Diane gave him a look, before turning away in a vain attempt to hide a yawn. He was worried at the idea of her driving up north in her present state, even after a night's sleep. He knew she was not sleeping well, aware of her fidgeting in the king-size bed they shared. He could sense her lying there, awake, staring up into the darkness. He had tried the gentle cuddling approach but it hadn't been a big success so he was trying his damnedest to be patient. He would have preferred to go with her tomorrow, share the driving, but it would mean leaving the children and he saw that perhaps she needed to be on her own a while.

Poor Diane.

The pregnancy had been unplanned but so had two of the others and they had got through them and would have got through this one, too, if it had gone ahead. It wasn't the right time yet, far too soon, emotions far too raw, but they would have to have a chat and decide what was to be done next. Just now sex was off limits. In fact, it had been a bit iffy for the last few months, with Diane so distracted by work problems. As often as not, she had snubbed his advances in that subtle way of hers. That's why he had been so thrilled when she was pregnant again. Thank God. She could take some time off, even though, if last time was anything to go by, it would be the absolute minimum. She needed some breathing space, to direct her mind to other things. He couldn't get her to see that. Out of sight, out of mind, out of a job was her philosophy.

What happened next would be Diane's choice. He would love another baby but even he had to admit that five kids was pushing it and he was ready for the snip if that's what she wanted.

The evening air was cooling rapidly and, seeing her shiver, he followed her indoors, shutting out the night. They went through to their sitting room where she collapsed on to a chair, settling back and closing her eyes.

Ah well, a cat-nap was better than nothing. Looking at her, he felt the stirrings of desire but he would have to play that very cool until she was ready. He had fallen in love with her the first time he saw her and that was before he saw her gorgeous hair because she had just washed it and it was wrapped in a towel. A woman had no idea how sexy she could look with no make-up and a towel wrapped round her head.

He had been there, at the house, as Maggie's boyfriend, but once he had set eyes on Diane it was curtains so far as that relationship went. Maggie had been remarkably OK about it but then, their relationship had been only at the starting-up stage and he didn't think it would have stood the distance. As soon as he saw Diane, he knew it had to be her and only her.

The children never set foot in this room, the adults-only sitting-room on the first floor. Diane had insisted on employing a top interior designer, paying what Rupert considered to be well over the odds to come up with something he could have done himself for nothing. Catching a glimpse of the absurd amount the designer charged for his efforts had spurred him into doing the design course he was nearing the end of. Quite what he would do with his qualification was another matter. He was, he cheerfully admitted, unbearably lazy.

The result of the designer's manic efforts was pleasant, he had to admit, if a little bland, a palette of cream and light wood. The sofas were the softest leather, the few accessories carefully chosen and on the walls there was an ever-changing display of his paintings, providing the only splashes of colour. Being big bold canvases they certainly made an impact but sadly up until recently they had not made enough of an impact for him to make a decent living out of it. He was under no illusions. Very few artists made it in that sense. They always had to compromise, go into some related field. Diane thought it was because he was too self-effacing about his work. Aim high, she told him, with a degree of impatience. These people won't touch a painting unless it costs a bomb. Most of them don't know a thing about art either. It's all about investment, darling.

That could be termed a cheap dig on her part but he was relaxed enough not to mind. Diane did not know a thing about art herself. Their household money came in and went out at an astonishing rate

28

and they never had any spare cash, not your actual money-in-the-pocket cash. As of this moment, Rupert had no idea how much money they had. Diane dealt with it all and there were numerous accounts and stocks and shares and so on. Financial matters left him cold and he was more than happy to leave it to her.

He could be called a kept man, Rupert thought with a frown, although by God he more than paid his way in looking after the kids. He had help in the lumpy shape of the au pair – a dour East European – and there was a woman who came in to clean three times a week and somebody else to do the ironing but he did *all* the cooking himself. Diane hadn't the time to spit, not that somebody as elegant as Diane would ever do that.

'I could kill Enid Blyton,' Diane said suddenly, opening her eyes. 'Those excruciating Noddy stories. I want to wring his pompous little neck. And as for Big Ears. . . .'

'Alice loves them.' Rupert smiled. 'And she loves Mummy reading them.'

'I know. And I have to finish a huge tome for next month's book club. Five hundred pages of complete crap.' Diane yawned again and ran fingers through her hair. 'How some of these people get published is beyond me. I might have to get Shirley to do a précis. The others are so intense that I have to be seen to make an effort and make some pertinent points.'

'What possessed you to join a book club? You're always saying you haven't got time for hobbies.'

'Hobby? You must be joking. I joined because of the contacts, Rupert. Never underestimate the power of the social acquaintance. It's essential for networking.'

He had no patience with some of this. She brought it on herself. 'You should be taking it easy,' he said, irritated enough to mention it now, aware of the little dig about networking. She had always maintained he could sell his paintings if he put himself about more but he still thought of himself as an artist rather than a marketing man and he didn't have her skill in social chit-chat. That did not worry him in the slightest, for most of these people were not worth knowing and certainly not worth kowtowing to.

'Taking it easy . . . I ask you.'

'Remember, darling, you're still recovering from losing the baby.'

'Don't talk about that,' she said abruptly, standing up and slipping her shoes back on. 'I'm going up. I need an early night. There's no need for you to do the same,' she added quickly, too quickly for his liking.

'Must you drive up tomorrow?' he asked, voicing his concerns. 'It's a long way. Why don't you take the train? You can relax on the train.'

'I like my own transport and, believe it or not, driving soothes me,' she said. 'I'll be back as soon as I can. I'm taking a huge risk in taking time off work, Rupert. Candida might well stage a coup in my absence.'

He laughed.

He wasn't sure if she was joking or not.

When she was gone, he went up to check on the children, realizing that Diane had not done so.

Philip and Roger, ten and eight respectively, bunked in together from choice and they were both flat out. Little Freddie – their poor little Freddie – was also flat out, clutching a soft toy, and Rupert sighed as he looked at him. Diane had her head in the sand where Freddie was concerned but, sooner or later, she would have to accept they might have a problem. Learning difficulties . . . a hushed word in these quarters.

He stood over Alice's bed a long time, smiling down at his daughter. It was a very feminine room with a pretty pink theme. Diane had asked yet another interior designer – a specialist in children's rooms – to decorate it. It was almost unbearably smug, the room of a very fortunate child. Gently, Rupert leaned over and removed Alice's thumb from her mouth. She stirred a little grumpily but settled down again and he straightened the duvet with its fairy pattern. Unable to resist, he touched her hair, smoothing it down.

She, of all the children, had inherited her mum's glorious red hair. Lucky child? That was debatable, he thought, as he closed her door. The so-called quality time Diane spent with her was hardly that. He could not understand why Diane showed so little emotion when it came to the kids. She liked them as babies but seemed to grow bored with them as they grew older. She was one step back, all the time, and he felt sometimes as if he was doing both jobs, being Dad *and* Mum.

They had to talk.

CHAPTER FOUR

T HE circumstances in which Frances met her John were not the least romantic. It was the previous wet and windy January, actually her favourite time of year because it took the least effort. She liked winter clothes because they were so easy. Monochrome for school, a couple of long, dark, wool skirts and several grey and black jumpers, and some jeans and brighter tops for home, plus a heavy coat, generally saw her through. She had a collection of opaque tights, which hid her legs nicely so that she didn't need to be bothered with constant waxing. Smooth legs were lovely but an unnecessary indulgence, unless she was expecting to be whisked off to bed by a good-looking man. As that was a non-starter, she didn't bother with waxing. Her legs, even with the aid of cosmetic tanning cream, never looked right in summer. She had what could be called sturdy legs and her large feet looked much better in boots. Boots for a woman with thick ankles were an absolute godsend.

For a while, blaming it on the damp weather, Frances had been suffering from aches in her neck and shoulders, tolerable but a nuisance. She chose to suffer in silence rather than have her father ply her with cures from his overstocked medicine cabinet. She tried applying a rubbing cream, which made her eyes water and, even with a generous spraying of perfume, the unpleasant medicinal smell of it still lingered. Also, apart from making her feel as if she had put a hot iron on the affected area, it did not help that much. Then, as the ache started to shift and spread downwards to the top of her right arm, settling obstinately there and becoming slightly more than a nuisance, when she found herself eyeing the bottle of pain-killers, she knew it was time to do something about it.

On the recommendation of one of her more sympathetic colleagues, she booked in for a session with an osteopath.

The complementary healthcare clinic was in a big, well-cared-for Victorian house. There were two osteopaths, a physiotherapist and various other therapists offering a range of services to sort out every ailment under the sun, the whole brought together with a cosy seating area and a low, glass-topped table on which sat a few copies of *Hello* magazine and the obligatory *Reader's Digest* as well as some glossier offerings.

The weather had turned bitterly cold overnight and the first snow of the season was forecast for later in the day. It was certainly in the air as Frances had hurried in. Spotting her reflection in a corridor mirror, she saw she was now red-faced, startlingly so, not in any way that could be construed attractive. This ability some women had of blushing attractively had never been her forte.

A few people were waiting, talking gloomily of the impending snow, of which a foot or more was predicted, enough anyway to bring everything to a surprised standstill. The children at school would be delighted if they got a couple of days off and it would be a relief for Frances, too, if she didn't have to struggle through it with the car. She would, she decided, hide her father's car keys or he would be out in it for the sheer hell of it, just to annoy her, slipping and sliding all over the place.

Frances, given the choice of Mr Jefferson or Mrs Butterfield when she telephoned, had opted for the woman for two reasons. One, because she thought she might be more sympathetic and two, because she would have to strip off to a certain extent. She was shy about such things in front of strangers, medical professionals or not. She always felt such a lump.

Leafing through *Lancashire Life*, she felt an anxiety churning in her stomach, hoping to goodness that this lady could do something to ease what was now an unpleasant, persistent throb at the top of her arm. It was making her feel a little sick and very snappy and last night her father had told her off which, ridiculously at her age, had upset her. If he had known she was in pain he would not have done so but she had opted not to tell him because she did not want to worry him. After all, Mother's problem had started with a little persistent pain and look where that had ended.

She had tossed and turned last night and she felt like death now; she would have taken a couple of pain-killers but she had not wanted to arrive in a dopey state. A door to her left opened, voices, and then a tiny elderly lady appeared, followed by what must be one of the osteopaths, a man in dark trousers and a clinical-looking white cotton jacket at any rate. She found herself sitting up straighter, the magazine on her lap, as she took him in. She heard and liked his voice first of all. Medium pitched, it was a firm voice, full of authority, and she imagined he would be rather good at controlling an unruly class without the necessity of raising it. He was around medium height, slim build, early forties, dark haired, and he was being very gentle with the old lady, who was twittering in a delightfully flustered fashion.

Before she could be accused of eavesdropping, Frances averted her gaze, picking up the magazine and determinedly turning pages. It had not taken long to form a pleasing impression but then she was like that and it worked the other way round too. She knew straight off if she would never get on with somebody. She almost wished she had booked an appointment with him instead because she could have joked with Polly about him.

Another door was opening and a middle-aged woman with bold black-framed spectacles and short silver-blonde hair appeared, consulting a list and calling her name.

Frances replaced the magazine on the table, gathering her things together – handbag, scarf, gloves, umbrella, kitchen sink – and followed her into the consulting room.

However, without acknowledging it, she could feel his eyes on her.

The snow dutifully arrived in a silent downpour and it was heavy as promised but short-lived. It was beautifully soft and clean for a few days, making the garden look like a fairy tale, but it soon turned to slush and Frances had to buy a new pair of thick-soled wellingtons because she did not want to give the children at school the delight of seeing her doing a graceless skid on the school playground, which was like a skating rink.

'This bloody weather!' Polly smiled as Frances, looking like a polar explorer, entered the staff room. 'I hate it. Give me sunshine any day. I sometimes think I'm solar powered,' she added, stifling a yawn. 'I have heaps more energy in summer and simply grind to a halt this time of year. I need my shot of sun. It's eighty-five degrees in Melbourne. Lucky beggars.'

Frances, unravelling herself from her outdoor clothes, peeling off her soggy gloves, had to agree that a bit of sun would not be unwelcome just now. She and Polly, a relative newcomer to the area, had begun to meet socially over the last few months. Polly, who taught modern languages with a frenetic zeal, was in her late forties, separated from her husband, and she and Frances had gone to the cinema a few times and been on a couple of day trips last summer up to the Lakes. It was nice to have company on these occasions and they shared an interest in the theatre and historic buildings.

Then rather abruptly, it had stopped.

Puzzled at what was a distinct cooling on Polly's part, worried that she had somehow done something to offend her, Frances had eventually rooted out the problem. It had taken some time to make Polly spew up the unpalatable truth but, apparently, rumours had started up about them and Polly was mortified that some of the older children had jumped to the conclusion that she and Frances were a couple.

Frances's first reaction was to laugh. Although she herself had never been the giggling variety of teenage girl, she understood them very well. All girls of a certain age went through this sort of fantasy and naturally enough it was the female members of staff who bore the brunt of such silly ideas. It had upset Polly, however, who was quite pink at the thought.

'I've been accused of some things in my time but never that,' she said. 'And because it's just rumours, we can hardly issue a public denunciation, can we?'

'Gracious, you shouldn't let that sort of thing bother you,' Frances told her. 'Can you believe those girls? We both know we'd get married like a shot if we met somebody.'

'Speak for yourself,' Polly said with a wry smile. 'I've been there, done that, and now I'm happy on my own but why does nobody believe that? It would take a very special man to tempt me and I'm really not on the look-out for him. I have my own place and I'm free to do what I want when I want. I can wear comfortable clothes for bed – be hanged to sexy nighties – and I can fart to my heart's content without worrying about destroying the romance.'

She had a carrying voice and Frances shushed her as one of the male teachers glanced their way with a frown. Polly's irreverence was one of the things she found endearing about her but the outspokenness did not always sit happily with some of the other members of staff.

Undeterred, Polly gave him a cheerful wave. 'I'm seriously think-ing of buying a sweet little cottage somewhere deep in the bowels of France and one day I shall retire there. It will be bliss. No need for smart clothes,' she added, looking down at her suit, for she rated as one of the better-dressed members of staff. 'As for kids—' She shud-dered. 'I have enough teaching them, thank you very much, without having any of my own. Perish the thought. What about you, Frances? Do you have any thoughts in that direction?'

'Gracious, no, I'm pushing forty,' Frances said. 'I might have entertained the thought a few years back but not now. It's never been a big deal. I couldn't face it. My sister in London has four.'

'Four? Whatever possessed her?'

Frances smiled. 'I have no idea. She admits two of them were mistakes. Considering she's so intelligent, I can't understand why she can't get that part of her life together. She's not particularly maternal either, if you can believe that. My other sister is but she's not married and is very unlucky in love.'

'Aren't we all? What about you? Is there anyone?'

Frances shook her head. 'I envy you living alone, Polly. Even if I wanted to conduct an affair it's not so easy with my dad around all the time. I wish I had my own place but what can I do? Dad needs somebody around and there's only me.'

Polly smiled. 'Cheer up. Something or somebody will turn up. You're right about the rumours,' she said. 'We shouldn't let a bunch of snotty-nosed kids put us off going out occasionally so long as we don't make a habit of it. Fancy the cinema next week?'

She agreed, although less enthusiastically than Polly, because, despite her show of bravado, it had got to her a bit. She knew who they were, the rumour spreaders, and felt like taking the three know-ing-eyed girls aside in her next lesson and explaining that she had actually had sex with men, strange as it might seem to them, and it was just bad luck that she had never found the right man, the one she wanted to share the rest of her life with. Sex had always been a let-down and the earth had definitely stayed put where she was concerned but it was a necessary part of the equation. She was sure that, with the right man at her side, as in the idyllic pairing of Diane and Rupert, it would all be wonderful.

Diane despaired of her and she knew she did herself no favours by having no style. She had made a few expensive mistakes over the years. She was shorter than she would have liked, short with big feet, which didn't make sense, but she was only a fraction overweight. It was proving hellish to shift those sticky extra pounds, though.

The massage and manipulation had helped her physical problem but she would need a few more appointments until it was sorted completely. At £30 a session it was proving expensive and she did not tell her father because she just knew he would pour scorn on it.

Mrs Butterfield had asked if she could remember a moment when her body twisted and yes she could. She had slipped going up the garden and jolted herself but it had not hurt at the time. That was probably it, Mrs Butterfield said with a nod of satisfaction, an actual muscle injury, a pull that would heal perfectly given time and patience. Although it was good for business, she sympathized because she of all people knew just how painful muscle spasms were.

Frances liked and trusted her but the day before her next appoint-ment was due she received a phone call from the receptionist to say that Mrs Butterfield was ill and had cancelled her appointments but that Mr Jefferson, John Jefferson, could squeeze her in if that was OK. Mrs Butterfield, who tended to chat as she worked, had mentioned him in passing. Poor Mr Jefferson, she said. His wife had walked out, leaving him with three little girls. Such a shame and he coped so well. He lived in a house very similar to this one, beautifully situated on the edge of Williamson Park, all alone with the children. Mrs Butterfield, sensing her indiscretion, had shut up at that point but she had said quite enough. So far as Frances was concerned, his domestic arrangements ruled him out in her search for Mr Right. She was not becoming involved with a man with baggage and three small girls counted as excess in her books. Best forget him, even if she had caught several glimpses of him over the weeks and he was still as attractive to her as ever.

Pure fantasy land.

'Four-thirty tomorrow with Mr Jefferson, Miss Troon? Shall I book you in?' the receptionist asked.

She hesitated but, with her shoulder twitching in sudden alarm at the thought of abandonment and with Mrs Butterfield ruled out for the next fortnight at least, she was loath to give up on the treatment just yet when things were on the mend and so, reluctantly, she agreed to see him.

'Try to relax your shoulders, Frances,' John Jefferson said, his nicely warmed hands moving across her bare skin to the base of her neck, where he continued the rhythmic rubbing movements. 'Hmmn. There's a lot of tension collected here. Is that OK? Give me a yell if it hurts too much. I can tell it's very tender.'

'That's fine,' she said, sitting on the edge of the treatment table, her jumper off, but her bra, her big white cotton 34E M&S bra, very much on. She wasn't showing much flesh, less than she would if she was stretched out on a beach, and he was acting very professionally, as indeed he should. He had quietly asked permission to lower one strap as he worked on her shoulder muscles. It was just that she felt awfully vulnerable sitting here with her bosom hanging out. Half dressed like this was worse than being naked.

'Take a deep breath,' he said, placing her arm across her chest. 'And then, as you release the breath, relax. . . .'

Easier said than done because she now knew exactly what was coming – a manipulation that should and would release a whole lot more tension. Even though she closed her eyes, she could sense his nearness, smell his subtle aftershave and, for a mad moment, it took all her concentration to stop from falling against him.

Steady.

Treatment over, she dressed as he dealt with the paperwork. She touched her dark hair, wearing it fastened up as she always did for the sessions, hoping that it and she looked all right. She felt hot and bothered and flushed but that could be the treatment. It was surely not his nearness that flustered her. She hoped it was not as obvious as that.

'It all feels a lot better,' she told him, worried that he might suggest another appointment and not sure if she could cope with that. A schoolgirl crush at her age was just plain stupid and she needed to stamp down on it. 'Mrs Butterfield did say another couple of sessions should do it and it's certainly not bothering me enough now to need pain-killers.'

'Good. I'm pleased to hear that. In that case—' He swivelled round in the chair, waving a pair of reading spectacles in his hand. When she dared look at him, she noticed how kind his eyes were. And how blue. 'In that case, Frances, I think we'll just leave it for the moment and see how it goes. Of course, if you have any more problems, get back to us. In the meantime, do the exercises Mrs Butterfield gave you and try to avoid too much heavy lifting. You don't lift the children at school, do you?' he asked with a smile.

'Good gracious, no, we're not allowed to touch them at all,' she said, smiling back and handing him her cheque. As she did so, she noticed the framed photograph on his desk, an unmistakable school photograph of three dark-haired girls.

'My little ladies,' he said, catching her gaze. 'Seven, six and four and a half. The little one's just started school.'

She caught the proud father look and told him they were sweet as she was expected to do.

And, leaving it at that, she really did not expect to see him again.

The February weather was no better than January and so wet that Frances had invested in a roomy black mackintosh that billowed round her legs. It had not been cheap but somehow it didn't look quite as good on her as it did in the advertisement that had drawn her to it – the slinky, sultry girl modelling it could have something to do with the discrepancy. As an umbrella was impossible in the near-gale-force conditions of late, she had resorted to wearing a pull-on waterproof hat, a bit reminiscent of a lifeboat man's sou'wester.

Very chic.

She was in the supermarket car park, hoisting shopping from the trolley into the boot of the car, fully absorbed in the task in hand, when she heard his voice.

'Hello, Frances.'

She whirled round, one of the heavier bags, the one with the two four-pint cartons of milk, in her hand.

'Caught in the act,' she said, seeing him looking at it. 'Sorry. I know I shouldn't be lifting this. I might as well go in for weight training.'

'Exactly.' He tutted but smiled. 'You're going the right way about setting your problem off again. Let me help.'

'Thanks.'

Guilty, she let him lift the remainder of the bags from the trolley. She didn't think her father had set foot in a shop since Mother died. He was remarkably vague about any kind of shopping, particularly grocery shopping, shuddering at the very idea of surfing through such an establishment, more than content for the supermarket fairy to fill up the cupboards at home.

By the time the last of the bags was stowed away, she had taken off the awful hat, her hair whipping round her face, quickly damp from the rain. Oh well, she knew she looked a fright so it was all too late. She had come straight from school and had not even bothered to refresh her make-up, let alone put on some perfume. How was she to know he would be here?

'Nice to see you again,' he said as the rain gathered pace. They grimaced up at the sky and, to her surprise, he seemed every bit as embarrassed as she was. She struggled for something interesting to say but couldn't think of a thing. How pathetic was that? 'Sorry I can't stop but I have to pick the girls up from their after-school club in a few minutes,' he said, taking her trolley and offering to whisk it away. 'Take care then.'

Slamming her boot shut, she was not sure what to make of it. She had not noticed him before he spoke so he could have got away with not speaking. Instead, he had chosen to do so. Did that mean something or was he just being polite?

Meeting him had flustered her, though, and she sat a moment in the rapidly steaming-up car thinking about the chance encounter. He hadn't asked her out, heaven forbid, so she was surely reading far too much into it. She hoped she hadn't blushed as she feared she had because that was terribly unbecoming in someone of her age.

She was no good at this. Never had been. Diane could flirt with the best of them, had always had the boys fluttering round her. Funny that because Maggie was, in theory, prettier. Rupert had been Maggie's boyfriend, just briefly, but that was before Diane got her hands on him. Frances always thought that had been a bit off. She wouldn't have done it. But then she had never had the chance.

She had never been in the business of chasing after a man and she was not about to start it now. In any case, there were his little ladies to consider and she really wasn't up to taking on a ready-made family. It was bad enough coping with Diane's children when they visited. She liked them but she did not know them at all. Freddie was a slow learner and might need help but she dare not suggest such a thing to Diane. Little Alice was sweet and so like her mother, at least in looks. Let's hope she turned out to have a gentler nature. Diane was like a whirlwind and everybody knows that sooner or later whirlwinds blow themselves out.

If John wanted to see her again, he had her number. And, if he did, she had a worrying feeling that, despite her doubts, she might well say yes.

CHAPTER FIVE

Park House, the Troon family home, was full of nooks and crannies and a bugger to keep clean and they had gone through a lot of cleaners over the years, Mrs Latham being the latest in the line. Harvey guessed it was because Frances rubbed them up the wrong way. She could be a touch hoity-toity when she liked. It was like that with teachers. She treated him sometimes as if he was in her class at school.

His eldest daughter was a great worry to him. Frances was an earnest sort of girl, dull as dust if he was honest, and she didn't have much of a sense of humour so far as he could see – and he knew that men appreciated that in a woman. He certainly did, although Angela's own brand of dry humour had fizzled out pretty damned quick, becoming a vindictive sarcasm when the children started to arrive. Looking back, she had been far too fastidious a person to cope with babies and all the mess they brought with them but had obstinately refused to employ anybody to help. The children were her problem, she said, and she was not going to palm them off on somebody else. She bucked up a bit when Diane arrived, either because she was more into the swing of it by then or, more likely, because Diane was a mini-replica of her mother and that had delighted Angela.

He had tried his best to assist but he had never been a hands-on dad in the way that Rupert was. Perhaps it would have been different if his children had been boys but missing out on sons had never bothered him. For some reason, he found it difficult to admit how proud he was of his little girls . . . big girls now, of course.

He wished Frances would get herself married off but that was look-ing increasingly unlikely. Although it was absolutely none of his busi-ness, he did not think she was a virgin still. At her age, he hoped to God not. There had been a few boyfriends, particularly when she was at college, and she had once brought a man home for Christmas, a guy he had actually liked. That relationship, such as it was, had died a thousand deaths eventually and when he had enquired of Frances where Jim was these days, she had come over all snotty and snapped, 'How on earth should I know?'

Her features, OK separately, did not however hit it off together, and she was also a touch dumpy, always had been, and that had been a constant irritation to her mother. Her family were all slim, as was his, so where on earth had Frances got the fat gene from? She is not fat, he used to say, shushing her in case Frances overheard, just nicely rounded.

Men married plain-looking girls so that shouldn't be a problem and she had a nice smile when she could be bothered to use it. Frances seemed to have got it into her head that he needed looking after and he could not understand where she got that from. He would be happy on his own and he certainly didn't need her fussing over him. It was getting worse and this last little hiccup had not helped. Admittedly, he would not have wished that on his daughter. Coming home and find-ing him comatose in a pool of blood – all right, a little puddle then – had been enough to set off a great to-do. He only had a vague memory, quite pleasant, of the trip in the ambulance, and he wondered if that was how it would be when you were dying, a not unhappy sense of simply slipping away. Angela had looked peaceful enough at the end but, just like her, she had waited until he was out of the room snatching them – himself and Frances – a cup of coffee, before she gave up the ghost completely. By the time he got back, Angela was gone and Frances was in a terrible state.

Hands up. He had nobody to blame but himself for this last little episode. His blood pressure was a bit iffy following his mini-stroke last year and he was prescribed pills to take care of it but lately, feeling as fit as a fiddle, he had been lackadaisical about taking them. Frances put them out for him at breakfast time, all neatly there in a little egg-cup beside the glass of water. She kept an eye on them, reordering his prescription for him and collecting it, and he was surprised she didn't go to the trouble of standing over him while he took the bloody things. She did not, so, as often as not, he tipped them in the bin when she wasn't looking. It had been a very silly rebellion, he now realized, but he hated being reliant on pills. He had every kind of pill in his medicine cabinet but they were for show. He only took them if it was absolutely necessary. Having them there, the whole caboodle, was a great deterrent.

So, not having a clue what his blood pressure was, even though Frances had insisted he have a do-it-yourself BP machine and he was supposed to check it a couple of times a week, he had been unaware when it dipped so dramatically that he had a dizzy spell and fainted. He was alone at the time and as he fainted – no memory of that, of course – he had been unlucky enough to bang his head on the edge of a low table. An inch to the right and he would have hit the hearth and could have killed himself. As it was, it had knocked him out cold and he had undergone some investigations to make sure there was no sinister reason for it. Nobody had asked if he had been taking the prescribed pills and he had not volunteered any information, although he had felt a bit guilty. Frances would go spare if she knew.

In the privacy of his bedroom, Harvey Troon, naked, surveyed himself in the full-length mirror. Frankly, he had had to steel himself to look. Well, it could be worse. It could be better – he could be twenty years younger – but it could definitely be worse. For his age, sixty about to knock on the door, he was just about holding it together. His build fortunately veered to the tall and slender and he had a flat stomach still and thank God he had managed to hang on to his hair, which had stayed darkish with just a fleck or two now of grey. Many years ago, a woman – not his wife – had told him that he looked like Cary Grant. He admired the man, liked the debonair streak, and he reckoned he had been a decent actor, remembered some of the films.

Cary Grant, eh? Immensely flattered, he had laughed it off, said never in a million years, and then he had gone home and seen that maybe she was right. In a certain light, catching him at the right angle, there was a distinct resemblance. Cary Grant in his prime, that was. Poor guy, he was dead now, but he had aged gracefully, silvery hair and still a twinkle in his eye in his eighties, just as Harvey intended to do.

What did Mrs Latham – Wendy – really think of him? The fact was he'd fallen in love with the woman as soon as she walked through the door that first morning. Amazing because he'd never felt like that with Angela. With Angela there had never been a defining moment, a this-is-it moment. He remembered being attracted to her, of course – her flowing Titian hair particularly had been a gigantic turn-on for him – but theirs had been a gentle easing into love. This time, with Wendy Latham, it had been instantaneous. He did not know what had hit him and it had very nearly taken his breath away. He must have looked a fool, standing there like an agonized teenager, muttering whatever it was you muttered when you met somebody for the first time. Frances, completely unaware of the bombshell she had dropped, had promptly whisked her away and he had been left standing in the hall, hoping that Frances would decide she was suitable for the job. Frances was very fussy when it came to cleaners and he reckoned word must be getting around because the applications for the job had apparently been thin on the ground.

He could hardly believe that this bright, smart, gorgeous little lady with sparkling blue eyes and a lovely smile was applying for the job. It didn't seem right then and it most certainly did not seem right now.

He was deluding himself in thinking that she would be interested in him so he had best forget it. The truth he had to face up to was that he was a man close to sixty years old who had had a health scare last year and whose belief in his own body had been shattered as a result. It was as if the last remnants of his youth had puffed out in that instant his brain had a little stutter. As a man who had been rudely well all his life, it had come as a shock and he had lost confidence, damn it, confidence that he was only slowing regaining. The episode had left no outward signs, or very few, but mentally it had rocked him and that had been the hardest thing to cope with. You put a plaster on a cut finger but what do you do about a bruised brain? He had to get on with things, put aside the nagging doubt that it would catch up with him sooner or later.

What on earth had he to offer a woman like Wendy, aside from a nice house and a bit of money? She was nearly ten years younger and he must seem incredibly old to her. When *he* was young, deep in his Cary Grant prime of life mode, he was rather adept at attracting the ladies – pulling the girls, they now called it – although his ridiculously early marriage to Angela had put paid to that. She had been eighteen, a mere girl, and he only two years older, still studying and in no position to support a wife. They were mad even to think of it but, deliriously happy at first, it had been a challenge they had been delighted to take. Ignoring some tutting from some quarters, they vowed to show them, those doubters, that their love was no fickle thing.

He had no wish to stray in the early days but later she was always there, suspicious of him. He supposed he ought to have been flattered by the jealousy which bordered on the insane but he had been merely irritated. She used to check on him, popping into the office at odd moments with the prime purpose of catching him having it off with his secretary. As if. . . . It had been perfectly ludicrous. Although he hoped his daughters had been unaware of it, he and Angela had been on the brink of separation when she was diagnosed with her final illness and then it seemed churlish to leave her in her hour of need so he stayed put, although he got precious little thanks for the gesture.

The truth was hard to face. They had married far too young, more or less forced into it with Frances on the way. Happy enough, they had seen nothing but a rosy future stretching ahead but he might have known that a kind of resentment would eventually poke its nose in, an uncomfortable awareness that they had somehow trapped each other.

'I think I might have outgrown you, Harvey,' Angela once said to him, stopping him in his tracks. 'If we hadn't got married then, when we did, I don't think we would have lasted long together.'

Knowing her very well, he had protested vigorously, saying that he would never have outgrown *her*, which was the right thing to say. Living with Angela had been like standing in a minefield and you never knew when you would step into trouble.

Sighing, he got dressed and went downstairs to his study, hearing Mrs Latham pottering about in the kitchen but not disturbing her. At the moment, until he worked out quite what to do, he felt he ought to keep his distance. Mrs Latham did not touch this room. He kept it tidy himself with his unique filing system. He was in the middle of writing a book about Lancashire architecture, which even he was finding tedious, and there were a lot of papers and stuff that must not go astray. He had taken to the computer like a duck to water despite his daughters' dire predictions to the contrary. They seemed to think that as he neared sixty it was a turning point, somehow pressing the old-man button. Diane had given him a sober-looking cardigan for his birthday, admittedly a cashmere one, but he had never worn it. She would be buying him a flat cap next. Since Angela's death, he had prided himself on developing a new style, going in for the casual look that Angela had so despised. As he recalled, one of the first things he had done as a widower was buy himself a pair of jeans.

The truth was, he did not feel old, give or take the blasted little do. Granted, it was a set-back, but he was raring to go again. He had even asked Dr McGowan if he could have sex again – making a joke of it – and he had laughed, too, and said by all means provided he didn't swing from a chandelier. He had sweated buckets about that nonchalant question even though he had known Donald McGowan for years and Donald had surely known it was purely rhetorical as, at the time of asking, it had been. Just to make it absolutely clear, Harvey had added that chance would be a fine thing, making Donald smile.

The little do last year had nudged him into early retirement, which he had been planning anyway. He missed some of it. He missed the daily drive into town, the buzz of the office, the camaraderie, and not least the work itself. There was something very satisfying about designing industrial units although Angela had wanted him to do property design, thinking that much more glamorous. He could not make her understand that design was design. He missed it but the little do had scared the pants off him and he had to leave some time to finish this book, which was proving to be more of a challenge than a pleasure.

Returning to his desk, he sat down, finding himself staring at the photograph of Angela that faced him. It was awkward that, looking at a picture of your late wife when you were thinking so much now about another woman. It was Angela at her best at that, her beautiful grey-green eyes staring at him openly with no trace then of the disapproval that frequently settled there when she was older. She had, at the last, even before the illness struck, a very discontented look. He hoped Diane wouldn't develop that too. There were worrying traces of it already.

He had spent a lot of time in this garden, with Angela, relaxing under the oak tree. The old romantic in him remembered those days well. They were blissful summer afternoons, always summer, and they would have upmarket picnics, scones and jam and cream and a big pot of tea from the silver pot with white napkins. That was in the balmy days of their courtship before she was pregnant.

Although it was a secret he would carry to his grave, she had seduced *him*. She wasn't a virgin either, which had surprised him, and she had been quite confident that nothing would happen, a confidence that was misplaced because Frances had happened. The mythical shotgun had not materialized, not quite, for Angela's parents had also married very young and her father in particular seemed happy with that.

'If it's the right girl, Harvey, age doesn't matter,' he said. 'Might as well get yourself married sooner rather than later.'

And so they had.

He was overawed by Park House when he first set eyes on it and it had pulled him up sharply, emphasizing what he knew already, that they were poles apart on the social spectrum. His own parents were not exactly paupers but Angela's were bloody rich. It hadn't mattered to Angela, not then, because she imagined herself to be head over heels in love with him. He would never forget her father's firm handshake, the steely look in his eyes when he offered his congratulations.

Harvey knew that the fact that he was an architectural student of some promise, a few glittering prizes in his hand already, had swayed it with him. It would seem that Angela's future, even without their helping hand, would be secure.

'You've been a fool getting her pregnant but we look forward to being grandparents,' Angela's father had said with a rueful smile. 'Don't you let her down, Harvey.'

The thing was, looking back, he had. Somewhere along the line, it had all gone belly up. He had disappointed her and he didn't know to this day quite why, and that was hard.

CHAPTER SIX

OCCASIONALLY, Maggie had to attend seminars run by the charity, usually held at the same hotel in London, and when that happened, she made time to pop over to see Diane and the family. It always felt like a duty visit, although she loved to see the children. Sometimes she felt that, were it not for them, she might forget to mention she was coming down, for it was most unlikely she would bump into her sister by accident.

The last time she had visited was middle January when she was trying to get herself back into the swing of things after Christmas. It had been a disaster of a Christmas rather than the cosy one she had envisaged with just the two of them. She had wished at one point that she had taken up her dad's offer of going over to him and Frances. Anything was preferable to trying to cheer up an increasingly depressed Dave. He was a real misery when it came to Christmas.

Dave was now abroad with the cricket team and, for once, she had welcomed having some time to herself. With the north-east coated in a chill drizzle for weeks, she looked forward to the short trip to London, although, as ever, she was not particularly looking forward to seeing Diane. Diane could stop a bullet in mid-zing with one of her famous looks.

Diane and Rupert's house was what they would call in her neck of the woods a real belter. It was graceful Georgian, beautifully proportioned, which suited Diane perfectly, the front pale yellow, the interior practically unrecognizable nowadays after all the changes they had made. Diane had a good eye and had seen that the basement could be opened up and used to great effect and, although getting planning permission for a modern extension to a listed property had been challenging to say the least, she had not been put off and the gorgeous open-plan basement kitchen area at the rear of the property was testament to her perseverance.

'Great to see you, Maggie.' Rupert drew her into the hall, kissing her on both cheeks before helping her with her coat, a heavy coat bought for the biting northerly winds back home that was making her feel too warm down here. London always felt sticky and sludgy to her, whatever the season, in a way that Newcastle never did. Bracing it might be but the cold blew the cobwebs from your brain.

'I've brought some sweets for the children,' she said, handing them over. 'If they're allowed them, that is.'

'In small doses,' he said with a smile. 'But don't tell Diane. She acts as if sweets are cyanide pills.'

'Isn't she here?' Maggie slipped her boots off, not wanting to leave a dirty trail on the beautiful black and white tiles of the hall. As she put her boots by the door, she saw her big toe peeping through her barely-black tights and cursed silently. Diane would notice. As if that wasn't enough, the burgundy toenail polish was chipped as well. Oh well, in for a penny, in for a pound.

'I can find you some slippers if you like,' Rupert remarked with a grin, noticing of course. 'You take the same size as Diane, don't you?'

'Does she wear slippers?' she asked, returning the smile. It was a rhetorical question. She knew damned well her sister would not wear slippers – well, certainly not the fluffy type.

'Flat Italian suede pumps,' he said instantly. 'Cheap at a hundred quid a pair. She bought half a dozen pairs, all the colours, so that they tone with whatever she's wearing.'

'I won't bother, thanks.'

The hall had not long been redecorated and a fresh paint smell lingered. The red carpet on the stairs certainly made for a traditional look but it suited this grand house to perfection. As with everything that Diane did, the accessories were carefully picked, the flowers on

51

the hall table chosen to tone in with the decor and obviously professionally arranged. Maggie always felt a bit of a fraud in this house, as if somehow she ought not to be here. Rupert seemed comfortable enough but then he was the sort of man who fitted in wherever he was. He was, of course, not wearing shoes of any kind, far happier with his feet bare.

'She won't be long. She sends her apologies. There's been a bit of a cock-up at the office.'

'Another of those, eh?'

'It's hell there at the moment. Don't get her talking about the office, for God's sake. She hasn't been getting back until very late. If she's not up to her eyes in work, she's entertaining clients. It's meant three very expensive new frocks.'

Maggie laughed. 'Any excuse.'

'You know her; she's very keen on projecting the right image.' He pretended indignation but his eyes told the truth that he loved his wife to bits. She could get away with murder where Rupert was concerned. 'She's working specifically on a big television campaign just now and that's taken over. Eleven o'clock the other evening. She hasn't actually seen the children, not when they are awake, for days.'

'That's not good.'

'I know. Please don't mention it. She feels very guilty but there's not much she can do about it just now. She'll make it up to them later.'

Maggie frowned, none too sure. Expensive gifts were one thing but one day, Diane would sit back and wonder where the years had gone and by then it would be too late. At the risk of being profound, Maggie reckoned that time, not so-called quality time, just time, was the most precious gift you could give them. It was more than her life was worth to make any comment about that. 'Where are the children?' she asked.

'Philip's at his violin lesson.' He grimaced. 'I know, don't tell me, bad choice of instrument but there you are. Just because the music teacher says he has promise, Diane instantly sees him as some sort of violin virtuoso. And Roger's at his extra French lesson. Freddie's upstairs with the au pair and Alice is having a nap. That's everybody accounted for, isn't it?'

'I'll go and see Freddie in a minute. How is he, Rupert?'

'OK.' He managed a smile but a shadow passed over his face and she was quick to notice it. 'Diane won't have it that there's anything wrong.'

'Maybe there isn't. Some children are late starters and he is only six. He's still only a baby in a way. You shouldn't panic.'

He gave her a knowing look. All right, she wasn't a parent herself and had no business giving him advice but they knew each other well enough.

'Come on through. Can I offer you a drink? You are staying for supper, I hope? I've done your favourite bread and butter pudding.'

'Have you? You're a star, Rupert. Thanks.'

'How's the seminar going?'

'Fine. All the usual stuff.'

'Do you like the job?' he asked, pouring them each a generous gin and tonic.

She nodded. 'I like meeting people and, in a way, I even like the travelling. I think I would be bored staying put in an office all the time.'

'It's a big area for you to cover.'

'You bet. Northumberland is huge. It doesn't pay very well but charities don't. They don't like to be seen spending vast sums of money on staff salaries when it could be put to other uses. It's debatable, of course, that they risk not getting the best staff as a result. I think they should start competing in the business market but don't get me started, Rupert, or we'll be here all night.'

Rupert passed her drink over and she took a seat on the sofa. This house was city chic and stylish, cottage frills reserved for the weekend property in the country. Maggie had no idea what Diane earned but it must be an awful lot to keep her living this lifestyle. It was as if sometimes Diane didn't know what to spend her money on next. Maggie had fretted about what to wear tonight; uncomfortably aware that whatever she chose would be criticized. Diane had a personal image consultant who helped her choose her clothes each season and on Maggie's last visit she had been unlucky enough to be introduced to the woman. She was called Justine and had given her a quick once-over before sighing deeply. As Maggie had been wearing her best muddy-brown velvet jacket at the time, the one she had bought at Bainbridges in Newcastle and thought fantastic, it was a smack in the face.

'Not your colour, darling,' Diane had quickly explained after Justine, with a final despairing glance her way, left. 'She gets terribly upset about people choosing the wrong colours.'

'She can talk. She looked as if she was wearing army surplus.'

'Khaki is very in. Didn't you know?'

Diane's wardrobe, as in personal dressing room attached to her bedroom, was colour coded, colours that of course worked for her, seasonally arranged, work clothes one side, casual wear the other. Where Rupert put *his* clothes was a mystery. As to the shoes . . . Diane could start her own shoe shop with the number of shoes and boots, all beautifully clean. When they got scuffed, she threw them out. As Diane never walked anywhere, she did not actually need walking shoes but that did not stop her having an impressive selection to go with the leisure outfits that equally rarely got an outing because Diane did not do leisure either. When they visited the country cottage, she zonked out, she told Maggie, leaving Rupert to do invigorating and educational walks with the children. They wanted a dog, a big goofy retriever, but she was resisting that strongly. Dog hairs were an absolute no-no, according to Justine.

'Why do you have a country place if you don't like it?' Maggie had asked. 'What's the point?'

'Because everybody else has one. It's an investment,' Diane told her bluntly. 'Mind you, I should have thought twice about a period cottage. Quaint, yes, practical, no. Rupert has permanent concussion from banging his head on the ceilings. The worst thing is it's so bloody quiet, until the cows start, that is. The farmer moved them into a different field for some reason and they mooed all night long right outside our window. If I'd had a shotgun, I'd have shot the lot. And then, we had a crow pecking at the window at its reflection. It's a nightmare frankly.'

Maggie had no sympathy.

And as if that wasn't enough, on the help front, Diane had a little lady who came in twice a week to do the ironing. All she had to do was reach for the hanger and retrieve a crisply ironed blouse, slip into one of her suits that were regularly cleaned and pressed and bingo. . . .

It made you sick, although Maggie was not sure she would swap places with her given the chance because it was just too frantic for words. Her own life was not exactly easy but at least she made sure she had her shot of chilling-out time.

Going home that time after the safari through Diane's dressing room, Maggie had seen her own clothes afresh, despairing of the motley collection, crammed and jammed somehow into the self-assembly pine wardrobe. The flat did not have one when they moved in and they had got fed up with heaping clothes on chairs, so they had bought their own from IKEA at Gateshead, struggling to fit all the pieces into Dave's car and then struggling even more to assemble the wretched thing when they got it home. After much cursing and giggling, Dave, screwdriver in hand and instruction book in the other, had become increasingly wild-eyed. They had abandoned it after two exasperated hours and opened a bottle of wine, toasting each other in a bubbly bath before going to bed.

'How is Diane?' she asked Rupert now, watching as he sat down in the chair opposite. He was still incredibly graceful, long-limbed and agile. 'Is she still acting as if there's no tomorrow? I suppose there's not much point in asking her to slow down a little, is there?'

'Not a hope. You know Diane.' He smiled the same smile that had jolted her heart years ago, although it had been a lost cause from the moment he set eyes on her sister. Maybe that was another reason she avoided too much contact. She wasn't the first girl to have her boyfriend stolen by her sister and she wouldn't be the last and there was no earthly use thinking about what might have been because for all sorts of reasons it might never have happened. Nothing had gone on between her and Rupert, nothing of significance, because she had been playing it terrifically cool, taking her time, but she saw the way his eyes very nearly popped out when Diane sauntered into the kitchen at Park House, snacking on a sandwich, face shiny, her hair newly washed and caught up in a towel, wearing an old dressing gown that she had outgrown to great effect for it showed a wonderful expanse of newly smooth leg.

'Oh sorry,' she said at once. 'Didn't know you were entertaining, Maggie. Excuse me—'

'Is *that* your younger sister?' he asked when she was gone.

'Yes, that's Diane,' she said, knowing then as she saw the adoring-puppy-dog look on his face that it was a lost cause.

Her brother-in-law was perfectly cast as a struggling painter down to startling azure-blue eyes and the fair hair tied back in a raggedy ponytail. He was thin, too thin, looking as if he needed a good meal although, as he was a cook of some consequence and enjoyed his food, that clearly was not the case. He and Diane were long married but it was sometimes an embarrassment that they still acted like teenagers in love, dreamy-eyed, constantly touching in passing and smiling silly smiles. Rupert was on her wavelength, easy to talk to, whilst she could not talk to Diane about anything of importance. She wondered why their marriage seemed such a success because they had nothing in common.

'How's life treating you, Maggie? Dave OK?'

The question was casually put. 'Fine,' she lied, unwilling to let him in on her worries about him. The two men had not met and she had a funny feeling they never would. Dave would not like Rupert. He would think him airy-fairy in the extreme, having no patience with artistic beings and, being culturally challenged, he would not understand Rupert's modern paintings either, one of which had just caught her attention. An arresting picture of blues and greens, tipped with pure white, dipping and swirling, it could ostensibly have been done by her niece Alice who, at her tender age, showed the same uninhibited zeal for shape and colour.

'I haven't seen this one before,' she said, going over to have a closer look, realizing as she did so that it was best viewed from afar.

'It's called "Ocean". It's going in the exhibition next month,' Rupert told her, unable to hide his excitement. 'Did Diane mention it?'

'Yes, I think she did,' Maggie said, not willing to admit that Diane had said not a word. Diane supported Rupert in his artistic endeavours but in a way that was vaguely condescending. Whether or not his paintings were technically good passed Maggie by but she liked the big bold colours, the shapes and, from a distance, they were indeed eye-catching. Like the man himself, it was as if they would fit beautifully into any setting, be it office, modern apartment or gracious family home like this.

'It's at a small but supposedly influential gallery,' he went on, his underlying excitement sizzling. 'It belongs to one of her many contacts. Diane's organized it and we're having a reception . . .' he pulled a face.

'You'll have to dig out your suit,' she told him with a smile.

'I most certainly will not. I'm allowed a little eccentricity,' he said, returning her smile. 'I hate that sort of thing but if it's what it takes to flog them then I'll have to go along with it. There are some Americans coming along, keen collectors apparently, on the look-out for up and coming English artists, so we shall see. Diane's put triple the price tag on them that I was going to charge. She says I have to have faith.'

Diane seemed out of sorts. She was probably worrying about work, Maggie thought, as they ate the delicious meal prepared by Rupert. As she was family and it was therefore informal, they ate at a large table in the basement kitchen, the meal suitably rustic and wholesome. Nursery food, Rupert said with a laugh as he dished up the bread and butter pudding. Diane ate like a sparrow, taking one mouthful then putting it aside. Maggie, tucking into hers, eyed her with a disapproving frown. Surely she couldn't be worried about her weight?

'Did you know Frances has engaged another cleaner?' Diane asked at last, making a belated attempt at conversation. 'That makes four in the last year. I know I have had problems with staff but Frances has no idea how to tackle an interview. Did you know she's paying almost double the usual hourly rate? For somebody who's supposedly intelligent, she is hopeless at times. If she had only thought to ask me, I'd have put her straight. You have to start as you mean to go on.'

'It seems to be working out this time,' Maggie said, seeing Rupert raise his eyebrows but not responding. 'This Mrs Latham is very efficient, according to Dad.'

'What does he know? He spends all his time in his study writing that ridiculous book.' Diane played with the cheese and biscuits on her plate. 'I don't want him letting the house go to pot. Is this woman keeping it up to scratch or is Frances letting her off with things? She's not exactly the tidiest of people herself, is she?'

'She's hopeless,' Maggie agreed.

'You have a very poor opinion of your sister,' Rupert commented, pouring them more wine and looking hard at both of them. 'I've always thought she was very efficient.'

'Efficient maybe but she's also soft,' Diane said. 'As a result, people don't know where they stand with her. That's why she's not got herself a man.' Rupert exchanged an amused glance with Maggie, but, undaunted, Diane carried on, in full throttle now. 'As to the cleaner, I would have insisted on references. There are a lot of valuable antiques at the house and Dad wouldn't miss the odd vase, would he?'

'Honestly.' Maggie laughed uncertainly, more than a little shocked. 'You have to trust people, Diane.'

'Why? It isn't as simple as that. You have to be careful when you let people loose in your home. The temptations are huge and I've had more than my share of light-fingered staff so I know what I'm talking about. You're as bad as Frances, Maggie, far too gullible, but then you've never employed staff, have you?'

'No. Why would I do that?' Maggie sipped her drink, pleased to see that, despite the edgy conversation, Diane was beginning to relax at last, smiling now and not so tense. Rupert had said it took a few hours to unwind before it all started up again.

'Why, indeed?' Rupert was on her side although she was aware that he had eyes only for his wife. She seemed to thrive on the stress of her job, although tonight for some reason she seemed pale and listless. Spending a fortune on her appearance had to help and the grey dress fitted like a dream, a broad black belt accentuating her slim waist, her hair cascading down her back, smooth and sleek. Even though Maggie was wearing a new outfit, bought for the seminar, she still felt like somebody the cat had dragged in, the hole in the toe of her tights not helping. Diane had, of course, commented on it, telling her that if she bought good~quality tights that would not happen. She recommended Wolford.

Maggie glanced at Rupert. She was damned if she was going to say she could not afford them or an envelope would arrive next week with a couple of pairs tucked in. Diane was generous but that sort of thing rankled.

'We must take a drive up north, darling,' Rupert said, addressing Diane and relieving a sudden awkward silence. 'It's ages since we were up.'

'I know. I couldn't face traipsing up there at Christmas,' Diane said. And I do feel guilty that I haven't seen Dad for such a long time but it's time pressure. We never have the time.'

'Nor do I,' Maggie admitted. 'But Rupert's right. I feel we're loading all the responsibility onto Frances and it really isn't fair, is it?'

'She chose to stay up there,' Diane said with a shudder. 'So don't start on that. She's like a frightened dove with clipped wings, only happy in her own environment.'

'Oh, come on.' Rupert frowned. 'There's nothing wrong with wanting to stay put. Sometimes I wish I had. And why are you thought to be lacking something if you decide to do that? Flying off, searching for new roots, isn't always what it's cracked up to be.'

'Meaning what?' Diane asked icily.

'Meaning nothing,' he said with a shrug. 'I was just pointing out that staying put shouldn't always be regarded as a bad thing, the easy option.'

'The jobs are here,' Diane told him, thawing a little and smiling at him. 'The jobs that matter and you would never be recognized for your talent up there, darling. I know life is a bit hectic but that's why I bought the cottage so that I can unwind.'

Maggie noted the first-person usage. Significant, she thought.

'I love the cottage but we never get the time to go there,' Rupert murmured. 'We've put three visits off already this month. What's the point?'

'The point is it's too much bloody hassle getting everything together. Once we get ourselves organized better, we can go every weekend.'

Sensing trouble brewing, Maggie turned the conversation to the happier subject of the children, although, noticeably, Diane changed the subject deftly when Freddie was mentioned. Maggie had no idea whether they ought to be worried or not. He was a lovely little boy, very like his father, opening his arms at once to her for a cuddle when she had gone up to see him this evening.

Maybe he was a bit short on cuddles from Diane.

CHAPTER SEVEN

T HE garden was at its very best in summer and an easy distraction for Harvey as he tried to do some work on his book. He was no gardener, never had been, for that had been Angela's passion, which she had passed on with varying degrees of success to Frances. Her gardening urges came in small energetic doses, when she worked miracles helped by a keen lad who came in two afternoons a week to mow the lawns – no mean task – and help with the heavier stuff. Frances's approach was to bung in as much as possible in as many different colour combinations as possible, an approach sniffed at by Diane, who had called it vulgar.

It was a nice day today and he would take a stroll in the garden later, get some sun on the old legs. Whenever possible, he lived in shorts as soon as June burst forth, possessing a couple of pairs of faded ones and a pair of ancient floppy sandals. No socks, of course, as per Diane's terse instructions. Angela would have never allowed it. Men's legs, she had once said, are better hidden.

Harvey liked summer, never mind that Frances was constantly complaining directly the temperature hit the hot mark. Something was up with Frances and he couldn't yet put his finger on what. She seemed different, distracted, but he wasn't too worried because she couldn't hold onto secrets for long, if it was something she was keeping from him. He hoped it wasn't something to do with him, something the medical team had told her and not him. He didn't quite trust those hospital doctors. The last one he had quizzed had told him he would probably live to be a hundred but he hadn't looked him in the eye as he said it and maybe he had one of those blasted clots that was, at this very moment, lazily circling his body just waiting for the right time to strike gold.

Bit of a worry, that.

Outside the room, the vacuum cleaner started up with a thundering crackle, reminding him of the presence of Mrs Latham. The TIA, officially a transient ischaemic attack – he preferred not to think of it as a true stroke – had made him look at life afresh. A cliché it may be but looking potential death or serious disability in the face gave you a significant jolt. It hadn't made him have a sudden religious experience, nothing like that, but it had made him live for the day, that sort of thing. And the way he saw it, his life was by no means over. He and Mrs Latham could have twenty very happy years ahead of them, travelling into their dotage together. He wasn't cut out for the bachelor, or rather widower, life. He needed a woman to share things with, to talk to, and to wake up beside.

His daughters, when they got wind of it, would think him an old fool for they wouldn't let him forget he was getting on. He liked to remind them that some rock stars of his generation were still going strong, strutting their stuff on stage, getting off with women young enough to *be* their daughters.

He had tried to tell Frances something of his feelings for Mrs Latham – sounding her out, in other words, telling her how much he looked forward to the little lady's visits – but she had shot him down in flames with a stinging rebuke.

'Father!' She only called him that when she was really upset. 'For goodness sake, don't you dare do anything to embarrass her! What's got into you? The last thing I want is for her to take the huff and leave. Promise me you won't say anything to her?'

Thoroughly irritated that she should consider it *such* a preposterous idea, he had promised, scout's honour, but that was just to shut her up and he had never actually been a scout. He had no intention of keeping such a ridiculous promise.

Fiddle to Frances. What the hell did she know about the finer workings of a man's heart? Where was her man? Harvey smiled, fussing a moment with the items on his desk top, moving Angela's photograph so that she did not stare at him quite so prominently. Why he still kept it there he had no idea but moving it would seem faintly traitorous. The desk was mahogany, bought locally many years ago and stamped Gillows of Lancaster. It was a magnificent desk with a hinged reading slope and, on it, in addition to Angela's photograph, there was a Regency bronze inkwell and a modern paperweight given to him last Christmas – in lieu of a personal visit – by Diane's children. Neither Diane and co. nor Maggie and her man had bothered to come last Christmas and, although he and Frances had tried to make it special, it had turned out to be a bit of a damp squib.

Harvey swivelled his chair.

The study had, like Maggie's room immediately above it, views to both back and side of the house, which was at the very heart of the village. It was a soft grey stone house close to the road with just a frothy collection of tall plants, a short paved path and smart railings separating it from the pavement. From the front, it was rather plain and small-looking but, once inside, it was a veritable Tardis.

The drive was off to the side, curving round in a loop to the back of the house where all the land was. The road itself was nothing more than a village lane but it had grown busier over the years with the addition of a small estate built in a worryingly soggy spot by the river. Building on a potential flood plain? What were the builders and architects thinking of? And how on earth had it got the go-ahead from the planners?

Harvey did not mind the comings and goings the new estate had brought with it, although it was just as well Angela had not been around when they were seeking planning permission because she would have been up in arms, raising objections galore, rustling up petitions, not content until she got her way. She would have been a bloody pain in the arse for the builders whereas he had been more or less happy to agree to whatever they proposed. Presumably they had done their homework to minimize the risk of flooding so good luck to them. *C'est la vie.*

He enjoyed the contrast the house offered because it was a different world at the back, a haven of tranquillity, an escape. The garden sloped gently down to the woods and eventually, via a little bridge, to the river but the boundary of his land was vague and it appeared simply to merge into the open countryside, looking to the wood beyond the river.

Blessedly, the new housing estate was hidden from view in a dip.

Park House was a one-off. He and Angela, after years in a poky town house, had moved in here shortly after Maggie was born and Harvey's love of the house had continued long after his love for his wife had sadly gone. The house was a gift to Angela from her parents, who had escaped into a smaller property over in the Lakes, downsizing long before the word was so popular. They were both gone now, within a couple of months of each other, neither of them ever getting over the loss of Angela, who had been their only beloved daughter.

Harvey, ever guilty that he had made Angela pregnant when she was a mere child, had felt the burden of marrying a girl with money of her own, a legacy she came into on her twenty-first birthday. He was aware of his in-laws' concern and it had given him a determination to show them, to make a go of things. He had built up his own business gradually and, give or take the usual problems as the girls were growing up, not helped by his wife's volatile nature, family life went reasonably well until shortly before Angela's death. He had never asked his girls the question – afraid of the answer – but he hoped they would say they had a happy childhood.

Who knows whether he and Angela might well have toddled on through troubled times to this very day, neither of them having the stomach for a divorce? Angela might well have mellowed as she grew older but now he would never know. Angela, though she had threatened otherwise at one point, had left him the house, her beloved collection of antiques he could frankly take or leave, and, the icing on the cake, a couple of terraced properties down by the canal over in Lancaster, properties he let out, via an agency, to students. It made him very comfortably off.

This house was too big but he didn't care for the alternative and he must not forget that it was Frances's home, too, and she showed no signs of leaving. He was worried about all three of his daughters for very different reasons; Maggie because she flitted about too much and could not settle, Diane because she tried to do far too much and would run out of steam before long and Frances because she was so hopeless. She had no social life so far as he could see, although she had been out and about a bit more these last few months, probably with that bloody terrifying woman from school, Polly somebody. She had eyed him up, no two ways about it, but presumably found him lacking because she hadn't been back since. Thank God for that. She wasn't his type.

Frances had to put herself about a bit more if she was ever to get off with a man and he was certain she was up for the idea. She was shy, that was her real problem, and shyness such as hers could come across as snootiness or even snottiness. As for looks, well, they didn't mean a thing. At least they ought not to mean a thing although he knew they did. He was a vain old sod himself, always looking in the mirror, generally liking what he saw. He could give any man of his age a good run for his money.

Whenever her private life was touched on, Frances blushed like a teenager and clammed up. He knew she wasn't having one of those biological clock panics because she wasn't keen on kids, obvious whenever Diane's brood came up. Surrounded by the Buckman clan, Frances looked almost scared and he had seen the littlest one, Alice, eyeing her aunt up from a distance with a distinctly wary look.

With a sigh, he opened the door of his study and, after a quick word with Mrs Latham, who was enthusiastically dragging the vacuum cleaner in the direction of another plug, he went upstairs. Aware she was watching, he took the steps vigorously, although to his chagrin he had to pause at the half landing when he was out of sight to catch his breath. Once up, he stood rooted to the carpet, trying to bring to mind the reason for his being there. Bloody hell, he knew precisely what would happen. He'd get himself back downstairs and then he would remember. It was damned annoying but he wasn't too concerned because people younger than him complained of the same thing. He certainly was not in the market for going senile, which is what his daughters seemed to be thinking. And it definitely was not another little do.

What the hell had he—?

'Found them, Mr Troon. . . .'

He looked down, saw her triumphantly waving his glasses, which he really should have strapped to his person because he was forever mislaying them. How did she know he was searching for them? Could she read his mind? He hoped not for he was having some unfortunate lustful thoughts regarding this lady. He had thought just for a minute of pinning her against the wall and kissing her, going for it, as they might say, but he had dismissed that idea at once as perfectly daft. He had to attack this with a bit more subtlety than that. She had been a widow for years, bless her, and he didn't want to frighten her to death. On the other hand, they were neither of them teenagers and she would not appreciate him acting like a nervous schoolboy.

It was like walking a tightrope.

He went back downstairs, more slowly, taking the glasses from her, smiling his thanks. She was a very smiley lady and that was a relief after suffering years of pursed lips and sharp intakes of breath. Wendy Latham wore her light brown hair pulled gently off her face and fastened up with a velvety hair thing, a style he much admired although he was not quite so admiring of the shapeless pants and baggy tops she wore for cleaning; hiding what he knew was an excellent figure. Angela would not have been seen dead in clothes like that. In fact, she had been seen dead in one of her smart tailored dresses, looking so well as she lay there in her coffin that it had given him quite a jolt. He had half expected her to sit up suddenly, look him in the eye and say, 'And another thing, Harvey.'

Thinking about Angela brought him up sharply as it was apt to do. Wrong moment, of course, but Angela still lurked in this house.

'I'd like a word, Wendy,' he said, closely avoiding tripping over the cable. 'Have you a moment? Leave that,' he added as he saw her finger poised over the switch.

'I can't leave it in mid-Hoover, Mr Troon. I'll just finish the hall and then I'll make us a pot of tea.'

'Let's take advantage of the sunshine. We'll have it outside under the oak tree,' he said, going into the garden to wait for her. It was a bad choice, the oak tree, for all the old memories seemed to be lodged there. But he had been buggering about with this idea for too long now and he had to come out with it before he completely lost his nerve. She could only say no. He hoped she would say yes please but he had a nagging worry that it would be no.

They were, in his opinion, ideally suited. She was a cheerful, friendly, uncomplicated woman who seemed to get on with every-body, and, after Angela, he needed that. She loved this house and surely she would love living here as mistress of it rather than its cleaner. She had had a tough old life, although the snippets of infor-mation were slow coming. There was a limit as to how much you could find out about somebody in fifteen-minute intervals and she was very precise about how long she took for her break.

The way he felt just now he was of a mind to change his will and leave her the lot, whether or not she said yes. It might cause a stink but he rather liked the idea of that. His girls did not need it. Diane had more money than she knew what to do with. Frances and Maggie had only themselves to look after and they were both independent women.

He saw Mrs Latham – Wendy – approaching across the lawn and felt his heart hammer, suddenly remembering his promise to Frances.

Frances would go daft if he caused Wendy to leave but it was a chance he had to take. It was now or never. He squinted into the sun, moving the garden chairs around so they were in the best position. From this angle, the house looked superb, the stone taking on a pink-ish hue. Unfortunately, sitting under the tree like this held too many memories and he had half a mind to say he had changed his mind and could they go back indoors.

But she had gone to the trouble of carrying the tray out and it would make him look like an indecisive fool.

Which he was.

67

As Wendy drew near, he saw to his surprise that she had put some lipstick on.

Why? he wondered.

CHAPTER EIGHT

MARCH came in like a lamb and, reluctantly, Frances shook off her boots and winter skirts and riskily bought herself a few new lightweight clothes and booked herself an appointment at the beauty salon to start the saga of the summer leg wax. She and Polly were back to going out occasionally, lunches and the cinema. After a slow start on the personal front, Polly was opening up about her former life and ex-husband.

'No wonder you left him,' Frances said sympathetically, trying to picture the house in the Scottish borders where Polly and her ex had lived. 'Although it was a shame you had to leave such a nice area.'

'Yes, I do miss it but I had to get away. I just took the first job that came along.'

'You didn't specially choose here, then?' Frances asked, aggrieved that, for Polly, this was all second best.

'It's as far south as I wanted to go,' Polly said diplomatically. 'It's fine for the moment and, more important, it's affordable. I need to watch the pennies after Eric cleaned me out.'

She lived in rented accommodation in the middle of town. Frances had been invited over for tea and, after the briefest hesitation about deepening their friendship outside of school, she had accepted.

Polly showed her round. It wasn't bad for a rented cottage, the bold colour schemes maybe not to everybody's taste. 'I know it would make sense to buy something,' Polly said when they were back in the little sitting-room. 'But it doesn't pay to rush these things. And I still have my dreams of France. I can see the cottage. Miles away from anywhere with all that rustic charm that is typically French. I would enjoy the simple pleasures of life.'

They exchanged a smile. Dreams indeed.

'I'd like my own little place too,' Frances said. 'But there's Father to think about and he needs me.'

'Does he? Are you sure about that? He's not that old?'

'No, it's nothing to do with age. He couldn't manage on his own. I suppose he's never had the chance to try since Mother died. He can't cook, can't shop, can't do anything to do with looking after a house.'

'You underestimate him. I'm certain he could manage if he had to or, if not, he could get a housekeeper,' Polly said with some exasperation. 'He looks pretty businesslike to me. For goodness sake, Frances, you must stop thinking you're indispensable.'

She nodded. 'He wouldn't relish the thought of paying for a housekeeper. He's tight as a drum with his money.'

'Has he never thought of remarrying? Then he could kill two birds with one stone.'

'Why? Are you offering?'

'Oh, I don't know.' Polly smiled. 'I thought him very attractive when you introduced us. So, if I *was* on the look-out for a man. . . .'

'But you're not?'

'No.' Polly seemed very sure on that. 'How old were you when your mother died?'

'Twenty-five. Grown up but it still felt very young to lose my mother. It all happened so quickly, one of those invasive sorts of cancer. Maggie and Diane were even younger but they were both finished college and starting on careers. It was a difficult time though and now Dad's illness has frightened us again.'

'Poor you. Having no immediate family is an advantage sometimes. On the other hand, there's nobody to tell me if I'm making a complete hash of things.'

'I don't take much notice of what my sisters tell me,' Frances said with a smile. 'Particularly Diane. Just because she's top of her profession, she thinks I've wasted my life going into teaching and has a very poor opinion of teachers generally.'

'That gets my goat,' Polly said. 'They should try it before they start complaining. It's like banging your head against a brick wall most of the time and then . . . just sometimes, there's a little glimmer of light on the horizon. That's why we do it, of course. It's hardly for the money, is it? And it certainly isn't for the prestige any more. Once upon a time, teachers were thought to be somebody. Now we're looked on with pity.'

'I would miss it, though,' Frances reflected. 'If I had to give it up, that is.'

'I don't think I will. I can't wait to retire.'

'You've a long way to go yet.'

'Oh, I don't know. I have plans. No way am I soldiering on until my sixties.'

'How will you afford it?'

Polly pulled a face. 'At the moment, I never will. The thing is, Frances . . . I may be coming into an inheritance soon. I don't want my Aunt Jenny to die, bless her, but she is in her nineties and not at all well and it would be a blessing, as they say. Do you think me dreadful to be thinking of it?'

'No, not at all. You have to be pragmatic about these things.'

'It will mean I can retire sooner rather than later. I shall think about it but it's nice to have the option, isn't it? I could have my dream. I could buy a little place in France, soak up the sun and just while away the days. Potter in the garden, pop along to the patisserie, have a little conversation with the locals, be thought of as the mad Englishwoman, no doubt.'

'You would be bored stiff.'

'Maybe . . . I wouldn't mind trying it, though. I could always come back to teaching.' She sighed. 'Nothing's guaranteed. She's a feisty old soul and she might very well leave the lot to a cats' home and, if she does, so be it. I'll spit on her grave but there you go.'

The accompanying smile was meant to imply she was teasing but Frances was not so sure. She envied her the secret plans even if there was something distasteful about waiting for a relative to die in order for it to come about. Escaping from here was not on *her* agenda, because she was thinking about John Jefferson quite a lot these days and whether or not there was to be a future with him. After what Polly had told her about her own unsatisfactory marriage, she wondered why John's wife had left *him*. There had to be a very good reason. You just didn't up and leave your husband and children, did you? It was either an extraordinarily brave or a very selfish thing to do.

It made her realize how little she knew about him. Instinctively, she liked him but that was dangerous. However, there was no reason either to assume that he was a madman in disguise or a wife-beater. He was just a man she had taken a shine to and, if circumstances had been different and he had been single, then who knows? There was a little spark between them. She had felt it and she suspected he had felt it too.

She steeled herself for what she felt was an inevitable further meeting. She needed to resolve it in her mind anyway and get him out of it if possible. Brooding about him was no use if nothing was to come of it. She had, rather to her irritation, mentioned him to Polly, who had seized gleefully on it and told her to go for it. Polly had told her to fake a sore shoulder but Frances knew she would never get away with that.

In the event, they met by accident. It was in a shop in town, where she was buying some stationery for her father for his book. Why he couldn't do it himself was beyond her but he had this aversion to shopping and she was daft enough to volunteer.

'Hello. It's Frances, isn't it?'

She whirled round. Why did he always catch her by surprise?

'You're standing better,' he said. 'Not so stiffly.'

'Am I?' She was not aware that she had been standing badly but took his professional word for it. 'My father's writing a book,' she said, seeing him glance at the ream of paper, the notepads and the pens. 'He used to be an architect and it's about the hidden architectural splendours of Lancashire. Something like that. He's being secretive about it.'

'Sounds interesting.'

'Do you think so?' She laughed. 'Sorry, but he admits to having a very plodding style.' She was glad that this time she was looking her best. She was wearing a classic cream dress she was fond of, her waist – one of her good points – accentuated with a wide coppery-coloured leather belt Diane had given her for Christmas. Diane only bought the very best and she dreaded to think how much it had cost. She would bet on much more than the dress itself, of course. John had noticed, having given her a quick appraisal, a very male glance at that, one that had made her breathe in and stick her chest out. The dress had a scoop neckline but she did not care to show cleavage; it was scooped enough but not too much.

'Have you time for a coffee?' he asked, glancing at his watch. 'I was just about to take a break.'

'I'm sorry. I have to get back. But. . . .' She waited for him to suggest another time, hoping he didn't think she was giving him the brush-off. The niceties of this lark had always been a mystery to her.

'It's a bit awkward with the girls and everything,' he said. 'But now that you are no longer a patient, I can ask you out. Would you like that?'

'Well, I—' She stared, struck dumb, wondering if he had somehow engineered this meeting. If he had, then she was extremely flattered.

'I thought we might manage lunch sometime,' he asked. 'How about this Friday? If you're free, that is.'

She accepted, not into delaying tactics, but afterwards, as the warm glow slowly dissolved, she found herself worrying about the wisdom of it. This could be one big mistake. What was she thinking of? There was no future for them. His three little ladies would not go away. She might have coped with one child at a pinch but three . . . the thought of becoming a substitute mum to three children was just too awful to contemplate.

But then, she told herself, come on, Frances, it wasn't as if he had proposed marriage. She was getting ahead of herself here. They were only going out for lunch, for heaven's sake.

One step at a time.

*

'Here we are, Mr Troon. . . .'

Wendy had carried the tray from the kitchen, through the sitting room, onto the terrace, down the steps and across the lawn to the table and chairs that nestled permanently under the oak. 'That was a bit of an obstacle course,' she said with a smile.

'Sorry. I should have helped,' he said, feeling discourteous to be sitting here like the lord of the manor whilst she did the lot.

'No, you take it easy, Mr Troon. You must get yourself fit again after your little scare,' she said, whipping out a little white cotton tablecloth before bustling around with a plate of biscuits. 'I found some chocolate digestives, the milk chocolate ones you like.'

'Sit down, Wendy, and stop fussing.'

She sat down, looking hot and bothered, and he didn't think that was because of the sun, although it was at its dazzling height and the dappled shade under the tree was most welcome. It was a still day and he could hear the river in the distance. Harvey closed his eyes momentarily, enjoying the warmth on his face. When he opened them, Wendy was looking at him, blushing as she caught his amused glance.

'Angela and I used to take a glass of wine out here on a summer's evening. She loved the garden,' he said, wondering why he had mentioned his wife. He hoped she was not listening in, wherever she was, because this was a bad enough ordeal without her shaking her head and clicking her tongue in exasperation. 'Act your age, Harvey,' he could almost hear her saying.

'I'm not surprised. It's a lovely garden to sit in,' Wendy commented, looking round with pleasure. 'You've got a border to be proud of there,' she added, indicating the wide one beside the wall. 'I know they're not very fashionable just now but you can't beat an herbaceous border, a proper one. And I like the mixed colours. My Tom always said that you should never be able to see the soil and you can't in that one. And I like the different heights, too. You should never be worried about putting taller plants at the front. . . .' She was

74

prattling in her nervousness and this was developing into a horticultural lecture.

He stirred. Time to get this show of his on the road.

'How long have we known each other, Wendy?' he asked when she paused to draw an agitated breath. It was quiet, noise from the lane subdued in this sheltered spot, just nature sounds, water, birds, bees and what have you, the air hot and sweet and sticky, smelling of summer.

Face flushed, Wendy moved slightly in her chair and he wished once more that they were sitting indoors. This place, under the tree, held too many memories suddenly. Somehow, they seemed to congregate here, to this place, for all the urgent stuff. And it was here, ten years ago, that Rupert Buckman had spoken to him about wanting to marry Diane. It had surprised him because he thought Diane was hellbent on a career and he didn't have her down for getting married at a relatively young age, certainly not to Rupert. It brought back his own bloody awful meeting with Angela's father and, remembering that ordeal, he held his tongue about Rupert's artistic hopes, which struck him as singularly dodgy. The guy, for all his faults, made Diane happy and that's all that mattered although, on the painting side, Harvey's misgivings had unhappily been proved right. Being creative was all very well, to be applauded, but it sadly did not bring in the readies so it was just as well Diane provided them.

'I can see why you like to sit under this tree, Mr Troon,' Wendy said, looking up at the leafy ceiling. 'It's a lovely tree, a very good shape. It's surprising how few trees are perfectly shaped.'

Rather like people, he supposed, although he reckoned Wendy was as good a shape as any.

'I like trees,' she went on cheerfully. 'My husband Tom was pretty much an expert. He had to help with the felling on the estate and it always pained him to destroy a tree. Of course you have to accept that they are living things and they get past their best.'

He stopped himself, just in time, from saying 'like me and you', which would have been most ungallant. He followed her gaze, looking into the distance, time splintering suddenly so that he could hear

Maggie playing here whilst the adults had tea. There had been a slide and a swing and a little Wendy house, which Maggie had taken charge of as he remembered, Diane taking no interest in it or the teddies that Maggie constantly and very carefully carried about. Funny when you think that it was now Diane who did all that for real, houses and children. He would deny having a favourite child, parents always did, but Diane had without doubt been Angela's and Maggie his. Maggie was like him, still on the look-out for true happiness, which Diane, for all her hectic lifestyle, seemed to have found with Rupert.

'Let's take our tea under the tree, Harvey,' Angela had said, after her ill-fated visit to the hospital consultant. 'I have something to tell you.'

Jolted from his reverie by a little cough from Wendy, he turned to face her, recalling he had asked a question but forgetting now what it had been. She'd been on about the bloody tree for the last few minutes.

'I've been working for you for nine months now,' she said, answering his forgotten question, the china cup rattling a moment in the saucer. She had small hands with stubby fingers, her narrow wedding band still very firmly there. Her hands had none of the elegance of Angela's but then she had never cleaned other people's houses for a living. They had always been beautifully manicured, nails shining with a pearly pink polish. 'I hope you are satisfied with my work, Mr Troon?'

'Good God, yes.' He sighed, returning to the matter in hand. He couldn't mess about in an indecisive fuddle for much longer. 'The situation you and I find ourselves in, Wendy ... both of us being widowed, I mean, is a sorry state of affairs, isn't it? My wife's been gone for fifteen years now and I expect you miss your Tom, don't you? Or was he Thomas?'

'Everybody called him Tom,' she said. 'He was christened Thomas but nobody called him that.'

'And my late wife was Angela but nobody dared call her Angie,' he said with a smile, which she nervously returned.

'I did meet Mrs Troon once,' she said to his surprise. 'She gave a talk on flower arranging for the WI I used to belong to.'

'Ah.'

'I remember she was a very smart lady,' she said, a faint show of colour on her cheeks.

'Oh yes. She was certainly that.' He straightened up. Enough of this. Out with it, Harvey, or he would regret it. 'How about the two of us getting married? You and me. What do you think?'

She set the cup down and stared at him. 'Is this a joke?'

'No. It's a great idea. You love the house, don't you?' He waved a hand towards it and, as if knowing it was on show, it did look its spectacular best today.

'Well, yes, I love the house but—' She frowned. 'That's no reason to get married. You get married because you love each other.'

'That too,' he said, worried that this was going wrong. 'I like you a lot,' he added, not able to bring himself to say he loved her. Declarations like that were for film stars on the screen. 'Will that do for starters?'

'*Like* me?' she bristled, her smile gone, sitting as upright with indignation as she could in the garden chair. 'You're not supposed to like me. I'm your cleaner. You pay me to do the cleaning, Mr Troon.'

'Harvey, for God's sake. Call me Harvey. I know I pay you and don't think I'm asking you to marry me to get out of that. I'm asking you because I like you, Wendy. All right then, dammit to hell, I do love you. I loved you as soon as I saw you. And I think you are lovely. You must have been beautiful when you were younger,' he said, regretting the back-handedness of the compliment as soon as he uttered it.

She made one of those little feminine 'humph' sounds but he knew she was pleased. However, she would not look at him directly, gazing at a point somewhere beyond his right shoulder.

'You cheer me up,' he went on, undaunted. Now that he'd started on this he had to carry on to the bitter end. 'And I need some cheering up with my daughters acting as if I were at death's door. I look forward to the days you come over, Wendy. Isn't that as good a reason as any?'

'It's no reason,' she said, picking up the tray and starting to clear away when they were only just started, still avoiding looking at him. When she started back hurriedly across the lawn, he had no option but to follow her.

'Give me the tray,' he said.

'No. I can manage it myself,' she said, holding onto it as he tried ridiculously to wrestle it from her. 'I don't think you should be talking like this. I can't marry you, Mr Troon. What would your girls say?'

'It's bugger all to do with them,' he said. 'Sorry, but it really isn't. It's just me and you.'

'Mr Troon. . . .'

'Harvey, please. How many times have I to tell you?'

'That's not right,' she said. 'Not when I'm working for you.'

'But you needn't be. Marry me and you needn't slave away like this. We'll get somebody else in. You can put your feet up.'

She paused on the terrace, tray in hand, and gave him a very womanly look, reminding him unfortunately, for an awful moment, of Angela.

'Look—' He was getting desperate. 'If you're worried that it's going to be some sort of loveless arrangement then, believe me, it won't be. I'm not asking you to marry me because I want a companion or a housekeeper. I'm asking you because I love you, Wendy. We would be together in every way, if you follow what I mean.'

He heard her sharp intake of breath, cursed himself for rushing things . . . too soon, too soon.

'We could leave that side of things until you feel ready but there would be no problem there if that's what's bothering you. I've got the all clear to—' He stopped, realizing he was getting into ever deeper water with every word.

'I'm sorry, Mr Troon.' She stepped into the kitchen with the tray and placed it on the table. 'I really can't have you talking to me like this. I'm going to have to hand in my notice to Frances if there's any more of it. I'll make some excuse. Don't worry; I won't land you in it.'

'Please don't leave,' he said, running a weary hand through his hair. 'I'm sorry if I've offended you. I didn't mean to.'

'I'll just do these dishes, then I'll get off,' she said, rolling up her sleeves.

'Leave them. Frances will stick them in the dishwasher later.'

'Not these china cups she won't.'

'Leave them anyway. I'll do them myself. I'll drive you home now.'

'No need,' she said stiffly. 'I can get the bus.'

'I will drive you home,' he repeated, watching as she slipped into some sort of horrific-looking lightweight anorak. He wanted to give her money so that she could buy some new clothes. He wanted her to live here in this house with him. He did not want her going home to the little house she lived in down in town, quite near to the ones he owned, in fact. She had a bit of a trek to get here and she did not drive so that made him feel guilty, thinking of her standing around waiting for the damned bus in all weathers.

'No, thank you. I can catch the bus.'

He followed her into the hall, snatching up the car keys in some hope that she would change her mind but it was not to be. Stubborn then. . . . Ah well, it was no bad trait.

'I'll forget what you said, Mr Troon. After all, you are a bit over-wrought just now. There are plenty of cleaning jobs going begging but I've found one I like and I don't want to give it up. I still want to work for you but there's to be no more mention of that little matter. Do you understand?'

Harvey wished he had the nerve to give her a good kiss, there and then, and to hell with what she might say, and looking at her, at her flushed cheeks, her bright eyes, he had a sudden feeling that it might be a good idea to do exactly that. Tiptoeing round the subject had not worked. The ladies liked a bit of fire, a show of bloody enthusiasm.

You could not win, that was for sure.

CHAPTER NINE

SHAKEN by a lorry cutting in on her, causing her to brake hard, Diane pulled off the motorway at the next services. Switching off the engine, she sat a moment, taking a few deep breaths to calm herself down. For a few seconds, back there, she had stared tragedy in the face. They always said these things happened so quickly you had no time to react. A few more inches and that would have been that.

The newspaper report, probably tucked away somewhere insignificant, bottom of page five maybe, flooded into her head. A brief report of the actual crash and then: 'The victim, pronounced dead at the scene, was named as 35-year-old mother of four Diane Buckman, a senior executive with MGC Marketing. Senior director, Leo Fitzgerald, 42, paid tribute to Diane saying she had been a valuable asset to the company and her expertise would be sorely missed. Her husband Rupert, 41, an artist, was too upset to talk.'

Leo would get his oar in, that was for sure, putting on his sober face, trying to moderate the southern American accent that he seemed embarrassed by when most people, including her, thought it charming. And her long-suffering, ever-patient Rupert would be gutted, as the popular press might say. As for the children . . . Diane got a grip on herself, reaching for her bag. The description 'mother of four' sat strangely on her. She rarely had time in her busy day for the motherly stuff and sometimes, shame on her, the children would seem just another chore, something else to slot into a day that never had enough hours in it. The children would miss her, she hoped, but the worrying thing was they would get on very well without her. They did most of the time already. Sometimes, she felt like a stranger just passing through. Her PA Shirley had volunteered to keep a home diary for her as well as her business one, reminding her of the various activities her children were engaging in, so that she would not miss the important ones. She checked on it weekly in order to surprise Rupert with how up to date she was. The fact that he normally *represented* her on these occasions was a sore point but it was impossible to be in two places at once and with four children, there was always something on the school agenda. She had never yet managed to catch one of the Christmas concerts, having to rely on Rupert to fill her in on them.

Brooding on it did no good. If she could cut herself into two bits, it would make life a lot easier.

A cup of tea to steady her nerves, that's what she needed before she went any further. She didn't suppose a motorway café would have such a thing as herbal tea but anything hot and sweet would do. For a moment, she really did not want to leave the cosy comfort of her car but driving off immediately, as she was tempted to do, was clearly not an option. She needed a breath of fresh air.

Carefully, she locked the car behind her, knowing the very flashiness of the top-of-the-range soft-top would appeal to a car thief. This was her car, a totally impractical two-seater, with Rupert and the au pair sharing the heftier one for city driving. Living in London, she did not get to drive her vehicle very often and relished the time she did. At least she normally did but the near-miss had brought her up sharply. Driving in the fast lane needed concentration and she was sadly lacking in it these days.

Her heels tapped as she walked across the tarmac and, even here, further north than she had been for some time, the sun was at its glorious best, the warmth having built up steadily during the month. In London, the sun had been so relentless that it had soaked into the very pavements so that it felt as if the whole city had under-floor heating. She felt uncomfortably sticky after being cooped up for so long. She had been anxious to make a good stab at the journey before she took a break, driving a fraction longer than was safely recommended. In fact, she might well have dozed off back there, just for a second, a second that could have proved fatal.

She was wearing cream linen wide-legged trousers and a gorgeous little olive-green silk top, a cashmere wrap thrown round it, and, catching sight of her reflection in the glass doors as she went inside, she knew she stood out amongst such dire competition as frequented motorway service areas. Where did they get these people from?

She freshened up first in the ladies' powder room, which surprisingly was clean and sweet-smelling. Emptying her make-up bag on the little counter top and taking up all the room as a result, she slowly and methodically redid her face, the shock of the near accident beginning to fade. She had to look her best because her father had this habit of peering at her before telling her she looked exhausted. Only fathers could get away with that. Rupert never dared to say that, not exactly, but then Rupert had always had a misty-faced romantic vision of her. She often thought she did not deserve someone as perfect as Rupert. He was a wonderful husband, frequently buying her flowers – with her money, actually, but the thought was there. He adored her and the babies and their coming along at regular intervals had always thrilled him rather more than it had her. He was a great dad, too, bonding easily with all of them. His sons adored him and Alice was very much Daddy's little girl. Where did that leave her? Neglecting them as she knew she did, she had no business to feel remotely miffed.

She never remembered her own father being as approachable, always a bit of a mystery, and as for her mother . . . well, she had been neurotic, making no secret of the fact that Diane was her favourite child. What must it have been like for Frances and Maggie, whom Mother barely tolerated? Maggie was much more like their father in appearance and that seemed to have peeved mum and as for Frances . . . Frances was plump and rosy-faced even as a child.

'You work much too hard, Diane. You have to realize you're not expected to do every damned thing, not with four children,' her father would say before launching into another of his lectures about her not taking family life seriously enough.

Good grief. She could clock him one for that remark. She did take her responsibilities to the family seriously and she was lucky in that Rupert was such a hands-on dad. She sometimes forgot that he had to find some time in the day to potter about in his studio but that's why they employed an au pair and a cleaner so that he could do just that.

She applied a final top coat of the brownish lipstick, ignoring the loud sigh from a woman beside her who was trying to find some space for her own belongings. Not giving an inch, Diane shot her an annoyed glance. Tough. She was here first. She quickly ran her fingers through her hair, cut very short these days. She thought the look, the elfin look, suited her but she knew Rupert hated it.

Standing next to the blessed Candida recently in the ladies' powder room at the office, she had been all too aware that, with no family responsibilities on her shoulders, Candida looked good and hassle free, her skin as smooth as Alice's. In fact, if she was honest, the woman had the guts and determination to get on with or without a leg up from Harry and it was a well-known fact that the people at the top were not necessarily the ones with the most ability but certainly the ones with the most drive. You only had to look at her boss Piers to see that. It was ridiculous in this day and age that, in her opinion, Piers had got where he was largely as a result of string-pulling and name-dropping. He had also developed a technique of hiding behind others and never shouldering the blame when an idea flopped as, sometimes, it did. Whenever they were faced with the exciting prospect of preparing a presentation for a new client, Diane would gather the team together for a creative brainstorming session and Piers predictably ducked out of those, simply because, contrary to the impression he liked to promote, he was utterly devoid of ideas. Diane usually delegated the responsibility of the presentation itself to her creative team but she liked to keep her hand in and occasionally took one on herself. When she did that, she insisted her team be present so that they could see how exactly it should be done, a master-class if you like. It was a very English thing to understate your own abilities and she was having none of it. She was bloody good at her job and proud of the fact.

Unlike Piers, Candida had some ability, Diane had to own to that, and she also had charisma by the bucketload. It was a nagging worry to Diane that lately, with her domestic problems mounting, she had let things slip just a tad and Shirley, bless her heart, had stepped in to save her from making a colossal balls-up on a couple of occasions. She would trust her PA with Alice's life but Candida was not to be trusted and her thoroughness in ferreting out unpalatable truths was a worry. Carrying the enormous burden of her secret, Diane was getting very jumpy.

Sighing, she reached for her perfume, spraying it lavishly and causing the irritated woman beside her to give a theatrical cough.

Voilà!

That would do for the moment and she could retouch her lipstick after having her cup of tea. Clipping her bag shut, she walked out, hearing somebody say something about 'some people'. She felt no guilt. It was every woman for herself in the workplace and she had worked herself to the bone for the company and, despite what some people might think, she did not keep having children so that she could milk the maternity leave system dry.

If only. . . .

She had asked for papers to be sent into the private maternity hospital where Alice was born and was back full-time within the month, so nobody could accuse her of that.

Sipping a green tea – surprise, surprise – she tried to forget work, thinking about meeting up with her sisters again. It was a surprise that Maggie was moving from the north-east but maybe it's what she needed to do after Dave. A new start. With no encumbrances, it was easy enough for her to do that. As for Frances . . . Diane was not looking forward to Frances. Frances was a pain in the neck. The children were almost frightened of her. She was a teacher, for God's sake, and you would think she would have some sort of way with them but she did not. She most certainly did not rate highly in her children's list of favourite aunties. Even the auntie in Australia was placed higher than poor Frances.

She had not been strictly honest with Rupert recently. In fact, she had not been honest with him for a while now. The real reason she was coming up here was nothing to do with her father, not really. Chats on the phone would normally suffice there, particularly as he was no longer in any danger of dying. No, the reason was that she needed to get away from her husband for a while, to think about things without him being there clouding her judgement.

Walking back to the car, she was relieved to find it was still there. She must stop this business of thinking everybody was out to get one over on her; it was beginning to be a problem.

Before she set off again, she checked her mobile.

Rupert was not going to contact her for the next few days unless there was an emergency so that she could have some breathing space. And she certainly did not want anybody from work contacting her.

She switched it off.

CHAPTER TEN

B Y the time April was over, they had done a few lunches, Frances and John, casual lunches but very pleasant for all that. She found she was looking forward to them more and more. They were getting on famously and she had skilfully changed the subject whenever the little ladies, Victoria, Isobel and Eleanor, were mentioned. More happily, they had a lot in common. He, too, was interested in medieval history and they had some fascinating chats about it.

These assignations were becoming important to her.

'Lunch again?' Polly would say with a broad smile. 'My, my. . . .'

It was always obvious. She bothered with lipstick, which she didn't always, and a touch of blusher, although she had to be careful with that. And perfume, of course. Just a little of the precious, very expensive scent Diane had bought her for her birthday. For all the preparations, however, it was remarkably solemn and sedate, hardly feeling like a lovers' tryst, although John had taken to giving her a little kiss on the cheek when they met and when they left the café. It was always the same café, in a smart side street, and so far they had not met anybody they knew.

Frances almost wished they would. She was proud of him and wanted to introduce this handsome escort of hers to one of her colleagues, although how on earth she would introduce him was a minor worry. Just a friend, probably. She could hardly call him a boyfriend at her age and she did not want them jumping to the conclusion that he was her lover. She knew the other members of staff thought her a little dull. They were all partnered up, to a man and woman, with the exception of Polly.

In fact, it was all proceeding a little slowly for her liking. In her limited experience, in the couple of relationships she had engaged in at college, it had all happened by now. What was he waiting for?

She wanted John to make a move but, for reasons of his own, he seemed happy to be taking it slowly and it was not in her nature to take the initiative. Sexually, though, it was becoming a bit frustrating. A few of her dreams lately involved her finding herself naked, trying desperately to cover herself up because she was standing in front of 4H. It must mean something but she had no idea what, other than the obvious.

All she need do for the moment, all she could do, was be there for him. Was it possible that he just thought of her as a friend? Polly thought not. Polly was eagerly awaiting the outcome, convinced it was just a matter of time.

Daft as it seemed, Frances knew she was falling in love. It had never happened before. She was cautious, of course, and had listened intently when he talked at last about his wife, searching for clues as to why she had left him. He needed to clarify the situation, he said, but he wouldn't bring up the subject again unless there was a reason to. He didn't want to slag Julia off because she wasn't here to answer back but, after the initial shock of her leaving, he was not sorry that it had worked out this way, that she was more than happy to leave the girls with him, that she had effectively heaped all the responsibility onto his shoulders.

Julia kept in touch from her new base abroad but it was a haphazard arrangement and she let the children down as often as not. In a way, he wished she would just let it go because after her promised visits failed to materialize, they were confused and upset. It concerned him greatly that her neglect of them would have a profound effect on them in later life and he was doing his best to make sure it did not cause major problems.

Frances hated all this for obviously she had to take his side but it made her feel uneasy. Part of her really did not want to become involved but it was too late and she was. It made her feel as if she had stepped onto a slippery slide and couldn't get back up. There was nowhere to go but down, swiftly and easily. It was no surprise when eventually the lunches became an invitation to dinner. She enlisted the help of Polly, who helped her choose a simple black jersey dress, a coup d'état, according to Polly, for it pulled her in and pushed her out in all the right places.

'You'll knock him for six,' Polly said as she tried it on for the umpteenth time.

'I'll have to wear my mac over it. It might be cold when we come out.'

'You'll do no such thing. You'll spoil the effect. You'll just have to shiver.'

In the event, Polly relented, lending her a lovely wispy wraparound shawl, so fine that it fitted neatly into her bag to be produced if the chill evening air bothered her too much.

'Off out?' her father asked, stating the obvious as they bumped into each other in the hall where she was about to check her make-up before she shot off. She was spectacularly bad with make-up; could not seem to strike a happy medium. She had very nearly poked her eye out with the mascara wand and even now the lashes looked uneven.

'I am.' She popped her lipstick in her bag. 'Do I look all right, Dad?' she asked, twirling round for him.

He took a careful look. 'You brush up quite well when you make the effort, sweetheart,' he said, which she took as a compliment.

The dinner was all she might have hoped for and afterwards John drove her home and, for the first time, kissed her properly, stroking her cheek and then, as she opened her eyes, she saw that he was look-ing at her with a tenderness that very nearly overwhelmed her. The thought hit her hard. This man, for better or worse, loved her.

Getting out of the car, neither of them wanting it to develop into a teenage frantic snogging situation, she drifted indoors feeling warm and loved, closing the door quietly but not quietly enough, for her father appeared at once.

'You look flushed,' he said, peering at her. 'Are you sickening for something?'

She was not sure if he was joking for he had that twinkle in his eye but with her heart still thudding and her breathing only just returning to normal, you could say that. Afraid he might ask for more details, she went on the attack, asking if he had taken his night pills.

'Night pills?'

'Oh, Dad—' Sighing, she went to sort them out. She would have to start standing over him as he took them because she had become suspicious lately that he was throwing them away. If she ever caught him doing that. . . . Honestly, what could you do with him? He was always protesting that he wasn't yet in his dotage but sometimes he acted as if he was.

Afterwards, she had a leisurely bath, forcing herself to look at her body as if through John's eyes for, after that kiss, it was heading one way only. He knew she was lumpy, nothing could disguise that but, to her relief and delight, he still looked at her with eyes that shone. She really ought to set the record straight before it went the final step. Tonight, with the meaningful kiss, they had reached a turning point and there was only one way to go. It was just a question of when and where.

The problem being that, as soon as she told him about her luke-warm attitude to children in general, she worried that it would be goodbye Frances and thanks for the good times. He might love her although he had not said so as yet, but his children were very high on his list of priorities. As well as a new wife, he would be looking for a mum for them and there was no way she could do that.

First, though, before he left her, she so wanted him to take her to bed.

Wendy Latham had the energy of a woman half her age, passionate about keeping herself in trim because, in her opinion, nothing aged a woman so much as excessive weight. Her job, all that bending and twisting, provided an excellent work-out and she reckoned she had no need to go to the gym even if she could find the time and money for such extravagance. On her way home, she stopped off at the newsagent's-cum-general store at the top of her street to pick up a few essentials, her mind still in a whirl from the conversation she had had with Mr Troon.

Would you credit it?

He was a one and no mistake.

She had nearly missed her stop on the bus for thinking about it, staring at her reflection in the bus window, holding onto such a secret as that. She felt like shouting it out loud, telling the world that, at the ripe old age of fifty, she had just received her second proposal of marriage from another handsome man.

Absurdly, she felt like telling Tom.

Under the circumstances, with her heart and head bursting with excitement, feeling like a young girl, it was probably unwise to risk a conversation with Moira at the shop. Picking up anything from the shop was not for the faint-hearted for if Moira was in, you could not get away without a bit of a natter or third degree, whichever way you looked at it. In the last couple of years, Moira had single-handedly turned the fortunes of this shop round and it was particularly popular with the many students who lodged round here. She made sure she stocked all the stuff they needed and nothing was too much trouble. Moira had once been a Samaritan – were they supposed to tell anybody that? – and had not lost the knack of listening and making you say more than you intended. She had proved to be a welcome shoulder to cry on just after Wendy moved in and told her about losing Tom. Moira's husband was also dead so she felt qualified to offer advice, which was to forge a new life for herself but to give herself a bit of time to grieve first. A year, she said, and then you could think about moving on although, personally, there would be no more men in Moira's life, one being quite enough.

Wendy might not have signed the Official Secrets Act but she did feel a certain obligation not to divulge too much about the people she worked for and the Troons were no exception. On the contrary, Moira liked to talk about her own family in great detail. She had a son who was a consultant gynaecologist over in Swansea. He was married with twin boys and she never stopped boasting about him.

'If you have any problems . . . down there,' she once told Wendy when they were alone in the shop, 'ask me first and I'll have a word with my Paul before you need go bothering your doctor.'

Needless to say, Wendy had not taken up the offer, not that she had any problems down there anyway. She and Tom had never had children, reasons why unclear, but, after the initial disappointment, they had decided not to pursue it further and at the last it had not mattered to them. The funny thing was it had never mattered much, not having children, but it mattered now that she had no grandchildren and Moira's constant harping on about hers did not help.

She got out of the shop as soon as she decently could, tempted but managing not to say a word about it to Moira, who had instantly sussed that something was up.

You look like the cat that got the cream,' she said. 'What's happened? You haven't won the lottery, have you?'

'No such luck,' she said with a laugh, although, thinking about it, it was worth far more than a lottery win.

She could tell from the start today that Mr Troon had something on his mind but she hadn't bargained on that. She smiled to herself as she let herself into her house. It was a long time since a man had said she was lovely and that he loved her and a woman needed to be told that now and again. Tom had always been embarrassed by stuff like that and had never actually said it as such.

Mr Troon – Harvey – was different altogether, more sophisticated a man. He, too, had seemed reluctant to say the word love but he had said it anyway. And as to the suggestion that he was prepared to wait for that side of things . . . she didn't know what to make of that. She was walking a fine line between being flattered and offended. Who on earth did this man think he was and who on earth did he think she was? She hoped she was not the female equivalent to him of a 'bit of rough'. No, she couldn't be or he wouldn't have asked her to marry him.

Had she been subconsciously sending out vibes? Thinking back, she had brushed her hair and put on some fresh lipstick before taking the tray out today, feeling a need to look her best for him. In fact, she had been toying with the idea of wearing something more flattering to do the job. She had a nice bum and some tight jeans and a plain T-shirt would look a lot better than the sweatpants and loose top that flattered nobody.

The truth was, although she did not love him, not in the way she had loved Tom, she did have a bit of a thing for him, realizing that as soon as she met him.

'This is my father, Mrs Latham,' Frances had said, forced to introduce them as he had suddenly appeared in the hall. 'Father, this is Mrs Latham. She has applied for the cleaning job.'

They shook hands but he seemed barely interested in her, simply nodding and smiling. He was a handsome man, young-looking for his age, but then men who kept their hair had an advantage. And he didn't have a paunch either, which was another off-putter. She had caught the odd look from him and . . . oh, come on, Wendy, she knew exactly what that look meant. She had been genuinely concerned when he had his faint and fall and ended up in hospital although it wasn't really her place to visit him there. She had sent him some grapes and a get well card via Frances and he had looked a little shaky on his return.

He was no longer shaky.

She thought she had handled it very well today, doing the right thing in seeming to be affronted by it, for she had a horror of appearing too easy a conquest. Men didn't like that. They liked to have a bit of a fight on their hands. It would do no harm to have him sweat it out a little whilst she considered things.

She dumped the shopping in the kitchen, made herself a cup of coffee and took it through into the little sitting room. It was a rented place, this, and the only thing in its favour was that it was clean and warm and not damp. At short notice, it was the best she could do. To be honest, she and Tom had not thought things through properly, not been prepared for tragedy, but then you never assume a premature death, do you? They had been making plans as usual and, although he had been complaining of feeling a bit breathless, it hadn't been enough to bother the doctor. She had a thing about bothering the poor doctors when they were rushed off their feet. Tom had only mentioned the odd twinge in his chest in passing and she hadn't thought it important. But then for Tom to mention a twinge at all ought to have alerted her that something was up.

If only. . . .

It meant she had to leave the tied cottage and there had not been much sensitivity shown there. Tom's ashes were barely cooling when that employer of his, not even in person but sending his agent, was round enquiring as to when she would be vacating it. Of course it was nobody's fault but their own. Tom had always known that would happen if he were, as he put it, to snuff it unexpectedly. They would appoint somebody else to help on the estate and the cottage came with the job. So, she had known the facts and that was that. They had always assumed that, by the time he retired, they would have put enough by to move on. They had modest hopes, nothing too fancy.

There was a bit of money but not much and she was not qualified for anything. She had been a member of the cleaning team up at the big house on the estate but she had always thought that job had only come about because she was Tom's wife and it was convenient. She couldn't face staying on after he died and, in a great huff, annoyed at their insensitivity, she had handed in her notice before she could think about it. After that, she had thought briefly of shop work but cleaning appealed to her more, although she only earned a pittance. She cleaned for Mr Troon and an office in town four early mornings before she went to him. It was hard work but hard work never killed anybody. A dodgy heart did.

She remembered the interview at Park House, sitting in the formal drawing room, wearing her dark grey suit, the one she'd worn for Tom's funeral and rarely since, smart black patent leather high-heeled shoes that pinched her feet, and as a finishing touch the beautiful pearl choker she'd got from Tom's mother when she died. She had worn her hair in a top knot and some neat gold earrings, worrying then that she looked like she was applying for a better sort of job. Frances Troon, whom she had spoken to on the phone, turned out to be a worried-looking round-faced girl wearing hipster jeans and a low-necked turquoise blouse with her bra straps showing, a black bra at that. She had shoulder-length straight hair, clean shining hair, the sort you saw in shampoo adverts. The hair did her proud but the blouse needed a good iron, Wendy noticed, aware of her own crisp one.

After introducing her to Mr Troon, Frances took her into the drawing-room and asked her to sit down. Wendy's expert eyes had already taken in the fact that the room needed a thorough going over and the windows were a disgrace. She wondered what had happened to the last cleaner but she could hardly ask and it didn't look as if Frances was going to enlighten her. She was a teacher, she knew that, and that was enough to make her nervous.

'My father had a mini stroke recently and, although he's recovered quite well, it has made him a little forgetful,' Frances explained. 'And, as such, I would like you to keep an eye on him, Mrs Latham, when I'm not around. I'm really not keen on him driving.'

'Oh well, I don't know about that,' she said, wondering how she would stop him if he had a mind. He had a firm handshake just now when she was introduced to him, a firm handshake and a nice smile. She would be the cleaner not his keeper.

'I know it's not strictly part of your job description but you will be here and often I won't and, if he has another little episode when he's driving, goodness knows what will happen,' Frances went on.

'Has the doctor said he shouldn't drive?'

Frances gave her a look. 'No, not exactly.'

'Well, then. . . .' She remembered the firm handshake, the clear gaze, and knew that if he had a mind to drive his car then she wouldn't be able to stop him, Frances or no Frances.

She thought she had burnt her boats then, daring to challenge Frances, and she was sorry because she really wanted the job. This was a beautiful house but Frances obviously never lifted a finger. The floors were dried out and needed a good polishing. She could tell just by looking at them that the skirting boards would be no strangers to a film of dust and she dare not imagine what the kitchen would be like.

Strange though it might seem to most women, she enjoyed cleaning and this house would provide a right old challenge to bring it back to its glorious prime. In fact, she was hard pressed not to roll up her sleeves and make a start, there and then.

'Well. . . ?' Frances asked, cool eyes searching her own. 'Can I rely on you, Mrs Latham?'

'You certainly can, Miss Troon,' she said, and that was that.

She considered the proposal now, half watching a repeat *Antiques Roadshow* on television. She enjoyed the programme although she didn't go in for antiques herself. There were a few special items at Park House that Frances had felt fit to point out.

'Take extra care, Mrs Latham,' she had said, scaring the living daylights out of her because she knew that would make her nervous handling them and she wouldn't like to face Frances if she broke one of the ornaments.

The ornaments in this room could be classed as cheap and cheerful, a job lot from Homebase, and the room itself was stuffy because she couldn't get the windows to open. The landlord took security seriously and all the windows were double-glazed with fiddly locks. The trapped air felt stale and warm. She thought of the spacious rooms in Park House; plenty of windows to fling open there. Imagine if it belonged to her? Some of the rooms needed a lick of paint but she was a dab hand with a paintbrush – if he would ever let her, that is. She knew he would not, that he would get somebody in, and the thought delighted her.

She ought to say no to Mr Troon because she did not love him. She liked him well enough and they had a laugh together so was that enough? And what he was offering was a good sight better than this. He was offering her a bit of security and that mattered at her time of life. What would Tom think? She suspected he would tell her to go for it. Why not? As for the sex, well . . . she would worry about that if it happened. She and Tom had always had a healthy sex life and she couldn't really see herself with another man although Harvey was not exactly obnoxious and given the right setting, the right mood, who knows?

Could she marry for reasons other than the one that mattered most? What sort of woman would that make her?

She reckoned she could put off 'that side of things' indefinitely. He was a gentleman was Mr Troon and would be patient with her.

Mrs Troon. Mrs Wendy Troon. She would never get used to being that.

She thought of the other Mrs Troon, Angela.

She had not gone down well with the WI, sweeping in, done up to the nines, talking down to them, making sure they knew that she was a member of the well-known Ashburn family, dispensing her smiles as if they cost a fiver each.

She would turn in her grave if she knew her husband was contemplating marrying his cleaning lady.

CHAPTER ELEVEN

THE first time John cooked for her at his home, the little ladies were elsewhere being baby-sat. It would be a cosy dinner for two, promising so much that she had been in a dream for the last few days, a fact noted by Polly. It had taken all her concentration this morning to produce a lively lesson for 3B, a good class with a few potential high achievers. A session with them always gave her a fillip. Polly was right. Teaching could be the very worst of jobs but sometimes it was the very best.

Polly caught up with her in the staff room. 'OK, spill the beans,' she said. 'You seem very distracted. Don't tell me your sex life has taken off at last?'

'Polly!' Frances glanced round hurriedly. 'No, it has not.'

'What's wrong with the man?' Polly clicked an exasperated tongue, thankfully lowering her voice to avoid broadcasting it to all and sundry. 'For crying out loud, you've known him long enough. I thought it was three dates these days and then wham, bang.'

'Maybe it is for some people,' Frances said, all too aware she was being unbelievably prim. 'But not for us.'

'Maybe that's why she left him,' Polly said. 'Not enough zip.'

'It's nothing to do with that,' Frances said, although the thought had crossed her mind. It was driving her mad, in fact, but she was confident he had passion enough in him. The way he kissed her had proved that but she wasn't about to give details to Polly.

'How's your Aunt Jenny?'

Polly smiled at the abrupt change of subject. 'She's not so good. She scarcely recognized me on the last visit. She's retreated into a little world of her own.' Polly had the grace to look ashamed. 'I feel awful about it. I like her, Frances, and I am the only person in the whole world that vaguely belongs to her. Isn't it sad? Sometimes I think I'll end up exactly the same. There won't be anybody to grieve for me either. I might have to ask you to plant a red rose on my coffin. Would you do that for me?'

'Polly!' Frances joined her in a laugh to lighten the mood but it was a sobering thought, nonetheless, and she took it with her to her next lesson, which, in contrast to the previous one, proved to be a soul-destroying exercise trying to interest a class of excitable and bored eleven-year-olds in the complexities of nineteenth-century life.

For the dinner date with John, she was wearing new clothes from knickers up, taking on board Polly's cheery and cheeky 'be prepared'. She took her time doing her make-up properly for a change and she wore her hair up, as he liked it, but not pinned up too frantically so that, if he wanted, it wouldn't be too much of an effort to disengage it and have it tumble softly over her shoulders as in the manner of many a seduction scene on camera.

Oh, these romantic dreams.

It was a prosperous-looking street, all the houses up to scratch, the gardens well cared for. In fact, John's garden alone left a bit to be desired. She frowned as she took a look at it going up his path. My, my, if she could get her hands on this, she would soon sort it out.

John drew her inside, kissing her on the cheek and calling her Fran. He had taken to doing that and, for once, from him, she did not mind. In the brief time she was in the hall, she took in the church pew, mirror above it, and a grouping of floral prints in black frames. She didn't know quite what she had expected from the interior but its very tidiness from the hall inwards worried her because she knew that with her help, it would soon lose that pristine look.

John invited her to have a browse round whilst he was busy with the meal and, avoiding his bedroom, she wandered into the large room that the girls shared. They didn't need to share, John had pointed out, for the house had five bedrooms in all, but they wanted to at the moment. Frances could never recall sharing a room with either Maggie or Diane, even when they were small and, with them, she didn't see how it could have worked. Sharing with her sisters would have been a nightmare.

There were three distinct areas in this room with three little beds as in the Goldilocks story. It was pretty and feminine with a pink and lilac colour scheme with patchwork quilts. There were white book-shelves and three toy boxes and plenty of space in the middle to play. It was a lovely room, very well thought out, the children's original artwork pinned on a big board and, looking round, she was suddenly moved almost to tears by the way John was coping alone. She loved him for that too.

One area, she was pleased to see, was delightfully, happily, messy with toys, crayons, building bricks and so on spread all over. Dropping to her knees, she found herself picking up a pile of nursery books and putting them back on the bookshelf. A blue bunny with a torn ear stared at her from the pillow of this bed. She picked it up, held it close. It had remains of chocolate on its mouth as if someone had been force-feeding it.

'There you are.' John came in, smiling.

She put the bunny back quickly, pulling the quilt up a fraction to keep him covered, and turned round, smiling in turn.

'Nice room,' she said casually, catching his amused glance.

Following him downstairs to the sitting room, she knew one thing and one thing only. She so wanted this to work out. How, she had no idea, but if it didn't, it would break her heart. His, too. Melodramatic it might be but she felt that this might well be her last chance at love and marriage. If she blew this, then she might just as well forget it.

The sitting room had two long narrow windows with simple blinds, the walls a surprising deep red. John had done it himself, he told her, proudly adding that he wasn't just a pretty face, although he did know his limitations and the original cornices had been professionally restored by a decorative plasterwork specialist. The focal point of the room was a gracious fireplace with a large gilt-framed mirror above it. There were a couple of comfortable sofas, low tables, and there you had it. It was not a bachelor's pad but then John was no bachelor. The pretty cushions and accessories suggested a feminine touch but obviously not from Julia as she had never lived here. The whole, while pleasant, had a slightly fussy feel to it which worried her a little. She had never thought of John as being a finicky sort of person but then she had to remind herself that she was only at the getting-to-know-him stage. She hoped he wasn't going to turn out to be somebody who was constantly and rather obviously clearing up after her.

'Don't worry. I'm not obsessive about tidiness,' he said with a grin, reading her mind. 'It's just that I don't use this room much so it doesn't get messed up. My mother always said you should keep one room tidy so that you have somewhere to entertain the vicar or the Queen if they pop in unexpectedly. I have some special cups and saucers, too, just on the off-chance.'

She laughed, relaxing a little.

'As you can see, the girls don't play in here,' he went on. 'It's a no-go area for them. We've more than enough rooms so it isn't a problem and I thought I'd start off as I meant to carry on when we moved here. So, we have house rules. If children are presented with a set of rules, they are OK about it. They like to know where they stand. But then, of course, you know that.'

'You'd be surprised, John. I only know about children in a classroom situation,' she pointed out. 'It's not quite the same at home. Children often present a very different face at school. Parents are surprised to be told their children are very quiet or shy or what have you when they are the opposite at home.'

'You must be a good teacher, Frances.'

'Oh, I don't know. . . .' She was pleased, however, for praise of any kind was a bit thin on the ground in the teaching world. Criticism was flung at them from every quarter but praise was something else.

They smiled across the room at each other. This, this cosy togetherness in a home setting, had lifted their relationship to a different level and they knew each other well enough by now to recognize that.

They had talked a lot over their lunches and dinner and she had told him about herself, her sisters, her dad, losing her mother, her career, all the important things, and he in turn had told her about his work, his interests and life after Julia. He still hadn't explained the real reason why Julia had abandoned her children, just kept saying she had her reasons. Her curiosity was growing. She wanted to know why. It seemed important to know why.

'You'll have to ask *her*,' he said, which was reasonable enough. 'She knows why. I don't.'

And, as meeting Julia seemed a very unlikely prospect, that was as far as she got.

'You can tell me about her, you know,' she said, having another go at it, standing at the kitchen door as he completed the preparations for their meal. She had offered to help but he had refused. He liked cooking; proper cooking, that is, when fish fingers and Mr Men yoghurts were not on the menu. Just as well. It was a cook's kitchen at that, putting their own kitchen at Park House to shame.

'Julia? I've told you all you need know,' he said, sounding surprised. 'It's history. I admit that, for a while, I closed down where women were concerned. When somebody walks out on you, it knocks your confidence.'

'Surely you must have guessed it was going to happen?'

'No. Call me naive but no. I did think at one time she might be having an affair but it never occurred to me that she might actually leave us. Looking back, she tried her best to prepare us for it. She began working late. She would pick the kids up, give them their tea and then go back to the office when I got home. She said later that she thought we would all adjust to it, get used to her not being there. Once she made up her mind, she didn't hang about. She packed her bags in secret and went.' He shrugged and, seeing the sudden pain in his eyes, she wished now she hadn't reminded him about it. 'The way I saw it, she might leave me but not the children. It's not natural, is it? Men have always been the one to walk away.'

'Leaving the woman to pick up the pieces,' Frances said. 'It does seem, on the face of it, to be a very selfish act, but who am I to criticize? I don't have children. I have no idea what it's like to be a mother.'

'I always told myself that, after Julia, I would never again be swayed by good looks,' John went on, suddenly very busy, chopping and slicing. 'You've seen her photograph – she was a stunner.'

'I haven't actually,' she said, noting the back-handed compliment and not liking it one little bit. 'Seen a photograph of her, that is.'

'Do you want to see one?'

'Not particularly,' she said, tight-lipped. 'So you decided you would go for Miss Plain next time?' she asked, unable to keep the edge out of her voice. 'And, boy, do I fit the bill! Homely, I think they call it.'

'Hey—' He put down the knife, wiped his fingers on a cloth, hurrying over to her. 'That came out all wrong. No, look at me, please . . . I think you're fantastic, Frances. You're everything she was not. Oh God, that's not right either. What I mean is that you're an old-fashioned girl, shy and vulnerable and, believe me, with today's modern women that's like finding a rare diamond.'

'Oh, come on. . . .'

'What have I said now?' He drew her towards him so that her head rested on his shoulder. Her body was stiff and unyielding, annoyed at him. 'Now listen to me,' he said, voice muffled. 'When I said that thing about looks, what I meant was that Julia was beautiful but, ultimately, there was no substance there. It's all very superficial with her. I was determined not to make that mistake again. Before I got involved with somebody else I had to be sure in my mind that there was more to them than that. I had to dig a bit deeper. And, no, I wasn't looking for somebody plain. I was just looking for the right woman and that . . . Fran, my love . . . is you.'

She melted just a fraction, still stinging from the not beautiful thing. It might not be true but it would be nice to be told she was beautiful. Nobody had ever said that. Her mother had always said it of Diane – my beautiful treasure – never of her. She didn't care whether or not it was true. What was truth? All she wanted was for somebody to say it. Confidence, she now realized, was a fickle thing. This American notion – which was seeping into the playground here – of constant over-zealous encouragement and praise, was all very well but, ultimately, it was dangerous. Eventually, shortcomings caught up with you and had to be faced.

'You shouldn't do yourself down so much,' John went on gently. 'Your hair is to die for. I want to bury my face in it. It smells wonderful and so do you. I love you and I never thought I'd say that again.'

She raised her head to look at him.

He meant it.

'John. . . .' She managed a smile which he acknowledged with relief. 'All right, I forgive you,' she said. 'Although if you ever call me homely again, I shall kill you.'

'I never did call you that,' he said, turning and switching off the cooker. 'I don't know about you but, suddenly, I'm not hungry. I'd much rather take you to bed.'

For a while after that it had been as if they were on honeymoon. She was sneaking out of Park House at all hours to spend time with John, although sleeping together when the girls were around did not feel right to either of them.

She knew it was a fool's paradise and that, before long, she would have to face the truth. John wanted her to meet the children. He hadn't rushed her, he said, until he was sure of her feelings for him because it wasn't fair on them to present them with a new lady unless she was around to stay.

Oh dear God.

It was Sunday afternoon and love in the afternoon was a bit risqué in her books but they had taken the opportunity of spending time together whilst the girls were out with the lady who baby-sat them occasionally. She had hoped she would be long gone by the time they got back. Now, John had let it slip that they were due back very shortly.

Panic hit her and she busied herself as he drew the curtains, fluffing the duvet and pillows, knowing she was acting like a domestic but she was in such a flutter and she could feel her heart beating in her chest. She needed to get out of here. Fast.

'They'll like you,' he said, coming across and sitting with her on the edge of the bed. 'Stop worrying, sweetheart. They'll see you as just a friend of Daddy's. They don't expect you to be Mum, not yet.'

'Not ever,' she said stonily, biting her lip. She caught a glimpse of herself in the dressing-table mirror, clothes back on, feeling uncomfortable after the afternoon lovemaking. It was fine while it lasted but now it had left a sordid taste in her mouth. She didn't want this hole-in-the-corner stuff. She wanted to be married to him but how could that be? 'I'm sorry, John. I can't do this,' she said. 'I've tried to tell you. I am hopeless with children.'

'You're a teacher.'

'So?' She shrugged helplessly. 'That's other people's children, a completely different set-up. I am not the least maternal. When I was little, I never played with dolls.'

'Boys' toys?'

'No. I was more into jigsaws and books. I still like doing jigsaws. Didn't I tell you?' she asked, feeling her insides flutter, wondering why she was wasting time talking such trivia.

'No, you didn't. I'll get you one for your birthday,' he said, trying to make her smile. 'Look, Frances, I don't know what you're getting so het up about. Lots of women don't consider themselves to be maternal. Julia never did.'

'Quite.'

Julia was hardly a role model, was she? Deserting her children? Little girls at that. She had eventually prised it out of him that Julia had left for a new life in the south of France as the pampered partner of a wealthy and younger businessman. No ties. It suited her perfectly.

'You'll be no worse than Julia,' he said. 'And you never know, you might really take to it.'

'Don't patronize me,' she said, moving her hand away from his. The pleasure she had taken from him, given to him, this afternoon was diminishing and fast. Why couldn't it be just the two of them? Just her and John. She had never felt as comfortable and happy as she did with him, so desired and yes . . . so beautiful.

'I'll leave it to you,' he said, glancing at the clock as it tinkled the hour. 'They'll be on their way back. Mrs Jones took them over to Morecambe for the day. They'll be full of it when they get back. She'll have spoilt them rotten. If you don't want to risk meeting them accidentally then you'd better go now.'

'Thank you. I will,' she said, scurrying round with indecent haste, hating the look in his eyes but not knowing what to do about it. She did not want to meet the children. Simple. She would not know what to say. Children weighed you up and saw right through you. They were not fooled. They would soon cotton on to the fact that she was completely incompetent.

'You need a little more time,' John told her as he said goodbye. 'I'm trying to understand that, Frances, and I'm sorry if I seem to be rushing you.'

'It's not you,' she said unhappily. 'It's me.'

'Perhaps it would be best—' He hesitated. 'Perhaps we should let it stand for a while. Cool things. See how it goes.'

She found herself backing out of the drive at breakneck speed, ridiculously afraid of Mrs Jones and the girls arriving back and block-ing her in, forcing a meeting. Driving the short distance back to Park House, she had to work hard not to cry. Tears would not solve a thing. She was a fool to have let it get to this stage. She should have walked away at the start.

Well done, Frances. She had handled that brilliantly.

She might as well kiss goodbye to John. He had never tried to keep the children secret. She had known from the beginning and it was stupid to pretend otherwise. She had had what she wanted from him. His love. And now she was throwing it back in his face. He was torn between his feelings for her and his children.

But of course there was no real contest.

The poor motherless mites would win every time.

CHAPTER TWELVE

ON the way over to her father's house, Maggie decided to call in at a charity coffee morning organized by one of the fundraising groups she had dealt with when she was north-east area coordinator. The A1 had been the usual nightmare and she needed to stretch her legs.

Strictly speaking, it wasn't her baby any more but it seemed churlish to drive past when she could pop in briefly and maybe say a few official words to the guests. She knew the local group would appreciate that, stuck out here, and it made them feel part of the wider organization, which was important. These volunteers propped it up. If they decided to walk out, give up, the whole thing would split asunder. It was drummed into them, the paid staff, that they had to keep the volunteers happy at all costs.

The village was nestled in the Pennines, looking wonderful today as the sun shone. Thank heavens for that. Maggie knew just what went on in order to produce an event like this and bad weather could really put the skids on it.

'Maggie! How unexpected and how lovely to see you.'

The chairperson of this particular group was an amiable lady well into her seventies, a force however to be reckoned with for she had personally raised thousands of pounds over the years. The coffee morning which, if it was lucky would raise a couple of hundred at most, was well under way and her unexpected arrival was greeted with delight. There was a big poster, balloons and bunting by the front entrance, an arrow directing guests past the stable block to the rear. Maggie was suddenly uncomfortably aware that she wasn't dressed for an occasion like this, not in her travelling gear of jeans and T-shirt. Normally, she would wear a suit, try to look the part. Happily, Mrs Evans seemed not to notice, although she herself was beautifully dressed in a blue silk dress, her hair set in rigid silvery waves.

Irene Evans clapped her hands for attention before introducing her to the assembly. 'This is Maggie Troon, ladies and gentlemen, our area coordinator.'

Smiles and a little muted applause from the guests and ridiculously Maggie felt she ought to give a bow. Renée Evans lived in some style and little tables covered in pretty check cloths were dotted about the large lawn. Coffee or tea and a selection of home-made cakes were on offer, nothing as vulgar as shop-bought biscuits. 'Sadly, Maggie is leaving us to take over the north-west and we shall miss her, won't we, ladies?'

Indeed they would.

And, she realized with a surprised pang, she would miss them too. Take over the north-west? Hardly that. She was a small cog in a big wheel but they did not seem to think so. To them, she was a VIP.

She mingled, good at that, and bought some raffle tickets, hoping to goodness she would not win for they would insist she pocket the prize whatever it was and there were some splendid prizes sitting on the raffle table. These ladies and their husbands had their hands permanently in their pockets and she never ceased to marvel at their devotion to the cause. They knew nothing about her private life but, over the years, she had learned a surprising amount about theirs, the ups and downs, the arrival of grandchildren, the joys and sadness, the occasional loss of one of the members. She was very aware that she was the charity's representative, their personal contact, and as such she knew she was regarded with affection and, for some reason, awe. Quite a few of them were also under the unfortunate impression that she was herself a medical marvel. One person even referred to her as 'Doctor'.

Standing on the terrace, in blazing sunshine, she rustled up her

107

usual little thank-you speech, thanks to the ladies who had got together this marvellous spread, the organization involved, and thanks to everybody for turning up to support them, even a thank you to the sun for shining down on them. A brief word then about what the charity was up to just now, a few encouraging words about new research and so on – not too much and not too technical because then their eyes would glaze over – then a final thank you and that was that. The raffle was drawn and she did not win, having kept her fingers crossed throughout. A little late in the day, a representative from the local paper turned up and they, she and the committee members posed for a photograph.

As she drove off later, she felt a little warm glow at the pleasure her impromptu visit had caused. She was so glad she had taken the trouble to call in. Two hundred and seventy-nine pounds had been raised with Mrs Evans cheerfully adding a further twenty-one pounds to bring it up to a round figure.

If only her visit home could bring about the same amount of joy to her own family but that seemed a forlorn hope. Diane could set sparks flying. The most she could hope for was that they didn't actually come to blows over the next few days.

When she had returned home from John's house that day earlier in the summer, the day when she thought she would never see him again because she had not wanted to meet his children and he had ominously suggested a cooling-off period, Frances noticed the quiet of Park House directly she opened the door.

It was an unnatural silence.

Dropping her car keys on the hall table, she called her father's name and when she got no answer, she knew at once something was wrong and had to steel herself to open the door of his study.

There he was lying on the floor. At first, as she rushed over, calling his name, she thought he was dead. She was ashamed later at how much she had gone to pieces. She was supposed to be a sane, sensible person but her sense had deserted her as she curled up on the floor beside him, cradling his head against her lap, murmuring soothing words. He was out cold and there was so much blood. She had done a first-aid course once upon a time, had to do for school, but, in her panic, all that training went completely out of the window and she waited far too long before she erupted into action.

Stupidly, she did not even think to ring 999.

The first person she thought of to ring was John, babbling incoherently until he told her to take a deep breath and try again.

By the time it had all blown over, Dad back home, not much the worse for wear, crisis averted, she and John were back together, if ever they had been apart, that is, and she had promised she would do what he wanted and meet his little girls.

'Where's Frances?' Maggie asked, struggling with her bags after persuading her father that she could manage them very well herself, thank you. She had parked her little car beside her dad's solid Volvo estate. It pre-dated her mother but was looking as good as ever because he rarely used it.

'Frances is at the supermarket. She's panicking about meals,' he said. 'She's been making lists for days.'

'She shouldn't. We'll all help.'

'You know Frances.'

'How is she?' Maggie asked, a sudden vision of the three of them, her, Frances and Diane in the kitchen. They would be hard pushed to scramble together a decent meal between them. Pity Rupert wasn't here. He would have done them proud.

'She's been out a lot lately. I think she might have a man.' He paused. 'I think it might have all blown over but I daren't bloody ask. She seems a bit down.'

'A man?' Maggie laughed. 'Are you sure? She hasn't said anything to me.'

'She hasn't said anything to me either, not officially. She keeps things to herself.' He smiled and gave her a hug. 'It's good to see you, darling. I expected you for tea. We've got a coffee and walnut cake in especially for you.'

She hadn't the heart to tell him she rarely did coffee and walnut

109

cakes these days. It was sweet of him to have remembered.

'Sorry, I didn't mean to be so late. The journey was awful. There was an enormous tailback on the motorway – an accident, I think – and it was standing traffic for a while. I did try to ring you but you didn't answer.'

'Funny, I've not been out.'

'You're not going deaf, are you?'

'No, I am not. You're as bad as Frances. She's always making me out to be getting past it. I was probably working on the book. I get carried away and don't always hear the phone.'

'For goodness sake, Dad. Why don't you have an extension in your study? Or, better still, a mobile?'

'I can't be bothered. In my experience, things are never so urgent that they can't wait a while. You look very well if a little frazzled, darling,' he added, giving her a quick once-over. 'Sorry about the Dave thing. I never did like him.'

'You never met him,' she huffed, smiling nonetheless.

The house looked good, better than she remembered. She hadn't been home for ages, pre the new cleaner anyway, and it had been looking just a bit sad then. There was a lovely display of flowers in the hall – roses from the garden by the look of it and the place shone in a way it had not on her last visit. This was all presumably the work of Mrs Latham, whom she had not yet met.

Her father insisted on carrying the bags upstairs for her and she let him, worrying however as she followed him up the stairs that he might suddenly overbalance and come flying down on top of her. But no. In fact, he looked good too, lean and as fit as she had seen him for some time.

'Are you taking your pills?' she asked, going across the bedroom at once to look out at the well-remembered view of the hills.

'Don't you start,' he grumbled with a slight smile. 'I *am* taking them if you must know. Bloody nuisance but there you are. So you're coming to stay for a while, I hear?'

'Is that all right, Dad?' She turned to look at him, needing his approval, realizing that she was making rather a lot of assumptions here. 'I'll just stay here for a bit until I get myself sorted out. I'll look for somewhere to rent in town.'

'Don't be silly. You must stay for as long as you like. It's your home just as much as Frances's. Where is the new job based?'

'Officially Carnforth but it covers the whole area,' she said. 'I'm joining a small team. I'll be out and about a lot introducing myself to the groups. And I've got some ideas for bigger events. I'm looking for some volunteers to do a sponsored bungee jump.'

'Don't look at me.'

'Why not?' she teased. 'You keep saying you don't feel old.'

'I like to keep my feet on the ground. When you're ready, let's have a cup of tea. Diane phoned. She's on her way.'

'I'll just unpack first,' she said, still riveted to the view as he left her. She was not looking forward to meeting Diane, an undiluted Diane at that, without Rupert or the children. She always found Rupert a wonderfully restraining influence on her sister. She and Rupert had had a long chat on the phone recently. He had caught her at a good moment when she was just relaxing in front of the television watching a particularly unfunny situation comedy which she was more than happy to switch off. Diane was working late, wining and dining a client, and she could picture Rupert relaxing in turn on *his* sofa, taking advantage of Diane's absence, wearing old paint-splashed jeans, barefoot, of course.

It was all innocent stuff, talk about the children and Diane's damned job. There had been an edge of impatience in his voice, unusual for him, and Maggie wondered how long it would last, the honeymoon that had gone on for over ten years. There had to be give and take, she knew that, but it seemed to her that Rupert was doing all the giving. Diane should not expect him to devote so much time to the children, not when he was trying to paint. They did not paint themselves, these paintings of his, and Diane would do well to remember that.

'Have a word with her when you see her,' he said at last, probably coming to the point of ringing her in the first place. 'She might take notice of you. She was back at work far too soon after the miscarriage. It's taken it out of her far more than having a baby ever did. In fact—' He lowered his voice. 'I'm worried that she's not concentrating on her work and you know how seriously she takes it. She needs a proper break and it will do her good to be up there for a while. Get her to stay for a bit longer than a few days if you can. Everything's under control at this end and they are more than happy for her to take some time off work. Talk to her, Maggie . . . she seems to have got it into her head that she's let *me* down by losing the baby.'

Maggie remembered the conversation now as she put her clothes away in the big old-fashioned wardrobe. As, understandably, she was a bit down herself, she was not sure she was capable of cheering up a sister who was depressed. Diane would very likely bite her head off. Come to think of it, the last time she had spoken to Diane she had sounded quite anxious. She would do her best and maybe it was time they had a heart-to-heart, the sort they had gone in for when they were teenagers together. A year's difference in age was nothing, nothing at all, and Diane had always taken on the role of older sister even though she was not.

As she went downstairs, she could hear a car pulling up outside.

It was Frances. If Dad was right and she had recently been dumped then that would be somebody else in need of consolation.

Maggie put on a determined smile as she went to meet her sister.

CHAPTER THIRTEEN

THERE were flowers in the hall. Goodness, Frances was pushing the boat out. Diane tweaked them into shape, despairing of the vase they sat in.

She was surprised that her father looked so well despite the ghastly baggy shorts and sandals that he seemed to live in during the summer months these days. Her mother would have gone daft. She would have shot him rather than let him out of the house. Mum had always kitted him out in smart three-piece suits for work and equally smart casual gear. Shorts did not enter into the equation even on holiday.

'How long are you thinking of staying?' he asked, even before she had the chance to dump her bags in the hall.

'And a warm welcome to you too,' she said with a smile he ruefully acknowledged. 'I'm only here for a few days, Dad. I can't spare any longer away from work. I can't spare these few days to be honest. God knows what they'll get up to when I'm not there.'

'I didn't ask you to come,' he said grumpily. 'Did Frances?'

'No. I came on my own accord. I wanted to see you,' she added, feeling a touch peeved at his attitude. 'How are you coping?'

'Coping?' He leaned over as she reached up to kiss him. 'Hello, darling,' he said a little belatedly. 'What a lot of bags for a few days.'

'Clothes,' she said. 'You know me. I couldn't decide what to bring. How *are* you coping?' she repeated.

'Superbly,' he said, waving a nonchalant hand. 'I feel fine, never better. I just fainted, that's all, and was unlucky enough to crack my

113

head at the same time. I don't know why everybody is making such an infernal fuss. Why hasn't Rupert come with you? And the children?'

'They wanted to but it was easier for them to stay. I can't take them out of school during term time, not without being thought a very bad mummy indeed.' She pushed a hand through her hair. The effects of the journey were beginning to get to her. 'That drive seems to get longer. Where is everybody? Frances and Maggie? She has arrived, hasn't she? I didn't see her car.'

'They went out again,' he said. 'Frances lost her list and forgot half the stuff at the supermarket. She's in a dream most of the time these days. I suppose she's ready for the end of term.'

'Aren't we all?' Diane said, although in some ways the school holidays coughed up a whole new assortment of problems. 'Where have I been put?'

'Up top,' he said. 'Is that all right? Wendy's made up the bed for you.'

'Wendy?'

'Mrs Latham.' He seemed surprised she had not heard of the woman. 'The cleaning lady.' He eyed her shrewdly as she had known he would eventually. 'Well, Diane, it's good to see you again. You've had your hair cut.'

'Yes.' Self-consciously, she put her hand up to it. 'It will grow again.'

'I missed you all at Christmas. Pulling a solitary cracker with Frances is not much fun. She tried to cook a turkey at that.'

'Oh. You could have easily come down to us,' she said, recognizing the resentment he felt because they had turned down his invitation. 'We went to the cottage. It was lovely. Rupert did the cooking.'

'I don't like travelling at Christmas; the roads are too busy, and I couldn't leave Frances.'

'She could have come, too,' Diane said, with a click of her tongue. 'Rupert cooked a goose big enough to feed the five thousand. Honestly, do you have to have an official invitation, you two? You know you're welcome any time, Dad. The children love to see

Grandpa. You're the only grandparent they've got with Rupert's parents being away.'

'Have you eaten? You could do with fattening up. I hope you're not on a diet. Diets never did anybody any good. Look at your mother. Look at me. I've never been on a diet in my life and—'

'You're just out of hospital,' she reminded him tartly.

'I'll put the kettle on,' he said, seeking a diversion. 'Come down to the kitchen when you're ready. I expect your sisters will be back soon. How long does it take to get some eggs and a few biscuits? Why does it take two of them?'

'They were probably glad of the opportunity to have a chat,' Diane said, not even convincing herself. The three of them had a ropey relationship although, if she leaned towards either of them, it had to be Maggie. Frances was impossible.

Diane took her time. She wasn't in the mood for unpacking her clothes so she left the suitcases standing just inside the room and, stepping thankfully out of her driving shoes, headed for the window seat. She loved the odd shape of this attic room, the way the window seat had been eased into the slight curve. It was a wooden seat with a floral cushion and she knelt on it, looking down onto the garden. A bird's eye view from here and it meant she could take it all in.

At least Frances kept the garden up to scratch. From this angle, it looked wonderful, the lawns clipped, the sides edged, the borders perfect. Opening the window with some difficulty, for the latch was sticking, she let the fresh country air flood in, taking a deep surprised breath as it did so. This was what she missed most. There was just something about brisk northern air that was absent elsewhere, even at her cottage down in Kent. It was sweeter there, balmier.

She took another deep, steadying breath to stop a sudden panic. Her life was set firmly on course and here she was in great danger of sending it onto the rocks. She had to get a grip on herself.

This was still home, Park House, although the links were now tenuous and she was seeing more and more niggling little faults whenever she returned. How long could they seriously expect Father to hang on to it before he looked for something smaller and more manageable? The house was in danger, or would be soon, of becoming a millstone round their necks because it needed money spending on it to stop any further deterioration. Dad could not see it because he was here all the time but she had noted the roof was past its best and most of the windows needed replacing. If it was put on the market that was the first thing a potential buyer would spot. They could jiggle it up in fine clothes, try to disguise it, but ultimately the basics would be its downfall. It was a top-notch property for this part of the world and people who had that sort of money to play with were not easily fooled.

Checking her watch, she saw there was little point in ringing home now because Alice would be in bed and asleep, the older boys hooked on their computer games and Freddie was hopeless on the phone.

Rupert was right. She needed to face facts about their youngest son. She knew in her heart that it wasn't entirely the fault of the teachers at his school, an excellent prep school, incidentally. Freddie had problems; 'learning difficulties', the school had politely called it. She had refused to accept it, closing her mind to it, but it had to be faced. How could it possibly be? She and Rupert were both of above-average intelligence so how could it possibly be? It was a real bummer but unless he perked up they might have to consider resorting to specialist teaching or, better still, a private tutor.

We must talk, Rupert had said ominously. But she didn't want to talk, not about Freddie nor about losing the baby, particularly about that. Away from Rupert, on neutral territory, she could look at things in a new light, consider her recent actions and work out what to do about it. Her father's illness had been a good excuse to come up.

Aside from Candida, there was a big decision looming workwise, the biggest one; namely, should she get out now before she was sacked? She had made a few big bloomers of late and for somebody in her position it was unthinkable and unforgivable. She had let things slide and if one of her underlings had done a similar thing, she would have pulled him up sharp. She did not want Rupert finding out things before she told him and she did not trust Candida. Candida would find a way. Candida was a ferreter.

As for Rupert, he was her rock and maybe it was a cliché but by God, it was true. Without him, she could not function. She could employ the au pair and the cleaner and so on but it was Rupert's constant presence at home that held it all together like Super Glue. She fiercely wanted him to be successful, to have the critics breaking into a sweat and the galleries and private individuals in a panic to buy his paintings although, privately, she sometimes doubted his talent, which was unbelievably disloyal. Maggie thought they were good but then she knew nothing about art either. Rupert professed to be laid-back but lately she had detected an anxiety as his lack of success hit home. That's why she had organized the exhibition early last spring – wine and canapés and a few arty friends – and Rupert had been so thrilled at the result. Watching him putting those little sold stickers beside the paintings had reminded her of the pride the children felt when they were given a gold star at school.

At last, with three paintings sold, he must feel he was contributing something substantial.

She yawned. Rupert was right. She should have come up by train but she liked driving and she would need her own wheels or she would be trapped here. Making her way downstairs, she paused a minute outside Frances's room, before opening the door. Even, presumably, with Mrs Latham's efforts, there was a distinct air of messiness that invariably accompanied her sister. Good heavens, you would think a teacher would be more organized. There was a pile of school books that looked as if they had been dropped from a great height and heaps of paper on the little desk under which there was a predictably overflowing waste-paper basket. There was an assortment of make-up on her dressing table, half used and incredibly tatty, and more than enough clothes lying about.

With a shudder, she picked up a photograph of a younger-looking Frances, at a Christmas party by the look of it, with tinsel in her hair and folds of pale flesh spilling out of a green satin frock. What did she look like? Justine would swoon at the sight. Frankly, even Justine would have her work cut out to make Frances look presentable. Sometimes, and this was something that she couldn't even tell Rupert, sometimes her sister had hairy legs.

Before she could be accused of prying, she went quickly down-stairs to find her father and the welcome pot of tea.

'Before they get back, I just want to say bad luck about the baby, darling,' he said. 'I didn't ring you because Rupert said not to but I was thinking about you. Frances too. We were both very sorry. Rupert sounded upset when I spoke to him but, with hindsight, perhaps it was for the best.'

'Why? Why do you say that?' she asked sharply, reminding herself that just about everybody had said that. Just because she had four children already, they somehow assumed it did not matter.

Taking note of her expression, her father did a rapid bit of back-pedalling before letting the subject drop.

Diane wished she had not been so short with him, not when she had only just arrived, and tried to make up for it by digging in her hand-bag and showing him some recent photographs of the children. Roger, in particular, was developing quite a look of his grandfather, which pleased him no end. He was also showing an aptitude for drawing, not surprising given Rupert's talent.

She kept the conversation going, moving on to discussing a few problems she was having with the cottage in the country. Predictably, that was a mistake because her father had thought it a waste of time and money from the start.

'I told you it wouldn't work.' He shook his head. 'Having a part-time house has always struck me as daft. They're just white elephants in the end. Rupert says you hardly ever have time to get over there.'

Rupert would say that.

Struggling to change the subject, it was a relief when the door opened and Frances and Maggie, laden with supermarket bags, piled in.

They ate a simple meal; tuna salad followed by strawberries and low-fat yoghurt. They ate in the formal dining-room for Father would not eat anywhere else, other than outside in the garden, of course, and it was much too late in the evening for that.

'This is nice,' Frances said, more than once, and they had all smiled in agreement, for what else could they do?

Maggie could not get over how tired Diane looked. *And* she had lost weight she could ill afford to lose but that was probably the after-effects of the miscarriage. She was dressed beautifully, of course, beating the two of them hands down, but the new cropped hair was a surprise. Never, in the history of Diane, had she had hair as short as that. Was it the new look? Some people might get away with it but it sat uneasily on Diane.

'I know,' she said, touching it self-consciously as she caught Maggie's glance. 'It's a mistake. I'm letting it grow again. Anyway, you've got highlights,' she added accusingly. 'It's only Frances who has the same old style.'

'Thanks a lot,' Frances said. 'Meaning I have no sense of adventure, I suppose?'

'Meaning nothing of the bloody kind,' Diane said. 'Don't be so sensitive. It suits you like that. You've got nice hair.'

'Frances knows what's good for her,' Harvey said, topping up the wine glasses, having given Diane a hard look when she swore.

'Is Dad allowed wine, Frances?' Diane asked.

'I wish you wouldn't speak about me as if I wasn't here,' Harvey said, amiably enough. 'Red wine's supposed to be good for you, isn't it? Anyway, it's something I'll make my own decision about, thank you very much.'

'OK.' Diane grimaced, sitting back and letting Frances fuss round, clearing the dishes.

Maggie offered to help but it was refused and Frances disappeared into the kitchen. Harvey excused himself, too, taking his glass with him, saying he wanted to finish off a chapter of his book.

'Was it something I said?' Diane asked as the door closed behind him. 'I do it every time, don't I?'

Maggie smiled. 'Frances takes things to heart much too easily. She has no confidence at all.'

'How does Dad seem to you?' Diane asked, not waiting for an

answer. 'He seems fine to me. In fact, if I didn't know he had had the stroke last year, I'd say he's not looked so well for some time.'

'It wasn't a proper stroke. A proper one causes a lot more damage.'

'I know that but it was a warning and this last little do is worrying. Frances says he is very cavalier with his pills. She reckons that if he was on his own he would forget or not bother.' She sighed, smiling across the table at Maggie. 'How are you, anyway? We were just saying recently that we haven't seen you for absolute ages. Why ever not? The children love seeing you.'

'I love seeing them too.' Maggie was just about to enquire after Freddie then thought better of it. Not yet. 'I'm all right. Break-ups are always a pain, aren't they?'

'They must be.' Diane shot her a sympathetic glance. 'What you need is a makeover. How many times must I tell you to wear things that flatter you? Those cropped trousers—' She shook her head. 'Justine would die a thousand deaths if she saw you in those. I can arrange a personal consultation with her although it will mean you coming down to London.'

'I can't afford it.'

'It's on me.'

'Thanks but I couldn't possibly.'

They looked up as there was a clatter from the kitchen followed by a loud curse.

'I didn't know she knew words like that,' Diane said with a small smile. 'What do you make of her? Dad thinks she has a man.'

Maggie laughed. 'She has but she's not saying much about him. She's trying to work something out, she told me. He has a family apparently.'

'Oh no. Poor Frances. In that case—' Diane shut up abruptly as Frances came back into the room. 'Sorry, we're leaving you to slave away. We shall do everything tomorrow, won't we, Maggie?'

'You'll have to,' Frances said. 'I'm off out tomorrow. I hope you won't think me rude to dash off and leave you when you've only just got here but you do understand, don't you? I'm meeting my . . . my friend.'

'A man?' Diane seized gleefully on that. 'Don't be coy. Tell us all.'

Maggie shot Diane a warning glance. 'You get yourself sorted out, Frances. Of course we don't mind you going off. Diane and I have lots of catching up to do.'

'I'm exhausted.' Frances sighed. 'You won't mind, will you, if I go up?'

The two of them moved into the sitting room after Frances, still apologizing like there was no tomorrow, got herself off to bed.

'She's not the only one. I'm exhausted too,' Diane said. 'That drive has knackered me. But I know I'm in one of those awful moods when I'm too tired to sleep. So I might as well stay up a while.'

'Me too,' Maggie said, stifling a yawn. It was true. Yawns were catching. 'It's been a long day.'

'Cosy, isn't it?' Diane's voice was edged with sarcasm. 'I don't come back up here as often as I should for a simple reason, Maggie. I hate these trips down memory lane. As I drove up and spotted the house, my first thought was, here we go again. I suppose I've skittled up the path far too many times. There are some stones best left unturned, don't you think?'

'What do you mean?' Maggie frowned. 'You had a happy enough childhood surely?'

'Did I? Who's to say?'

'You were Mum's favourite,' Maggie said, wishing she hadn't but it was something that had always rankled.

'Who says? I don't believe that. Mothers have favourites at their peril,' Diane said with a slight smile. 'You share your love out in an absolutely even proportion. I worry about what my own kids will think when they're grown up. I'm never around. Will they think I abandoned them for the sake of my career? Will they think I cared more about work than I did them?'

'Of course not.'

Diane gave her one of her special looks. 'I need to tell you something, Maggie. If I don't tell somebody, I shall explode. Are you up for it?'

121

'What is it?' Maggie settled further into the chair for it looked as if they were in for a long session. They were in the smaller of the reception rooms, the one they had used as a playroom in the old days. The wallpaper was different but somehow the past lurked and she remembered with a jolt the toys spread on the floor and herself spread-eagled amongst them. She had had a doll's house, a three-storey town house, a precious belonging, and had adored playing with the little people who came with it, constantly rearranging their home, putting the dining-room up in the loft and the mummy and daddy's bedroom next to the kitchen. Nothing seemed odd to her but her mother, seeing it, objected and told her crossly that she was being silly. You couldn't have a dining-room up there. How would you get the food to it without it getting cold?

She hadn't considered that but, to please Mummy, had changed it anyway.

Alice had the doll's house now and the same elderly little dolls seemed happy enough with their move to London. She played with it, with Alice, whenever she visited and if Alice chose to put the dining-room up in the loft, as she did, she never said a word.

'Problems?' she prompted Diane gently, as she seemed reluctant to proceed.

'You could say that. The thing is, Maggie . . .' she hesitated. 'I'm afraid I'm in a bit of a fix.'

'Not you and Rupert—?' Maggie felt cold. If *they* split up, that was it, she would never ever believe in the sanctity of marriage again.

Diane tried a smile. 'The fact is I've dug myself into a hole at work and I might have to resign.'

'Resign?'

She nodded. 'After fifteen years. It will break my heart, Maggie.'

'Is it getting too much for you?' Maggie asked. She was not entirely surprised at the news, not after Rupert's concerns. 'I'm sure everybody will understand if it is. Perhaps you could reorganize your week? Work fewer hours? Part-time maybe.'

Diane huffed. 'Part-time? I would lose all my credibility. And what the hell would we do for money? Our outgoings are huge, Maggie.

You have no idea. And neither has Rupert. He lives in cloud-cuckoo-land where money is concerned. The truth is we live a little above our means. We took on a ridiculous mortgage to buy the house and we stretched ourselves to buy the cottage. I'm considering selling it. It was a mistake because we never have the time to visit and places go off if you don't keep them aired and used. I hate to say it but Dad was probably right about that. We could rent it out but I don't want strangers wandering round it. As for the credit cards, well . . . they are astronomical.'

'Good heavens, Diane, don't tell me you owe a lot of money?'

'A bit. It's not desperate yet but it's all finely balanced. I know . . .' she gave a wry smile. 'You earn a lot less and you manage. Don't rub it in. Added to that, I've just been emotionally exhausted these last few months. And I am physically very tired. The worrying thing is I'm making mistakes at work and, if they came to light, it will do my career prospects no good at all. I never make mistakes at work. I'm in great danger of losing us one of our major clients if I don't sort a few things out.'

'I'm sure you're worrying about nothing. And, if it comes to the worst, you can find another job that isn't quite so challenging and so demanding of you. With your experience, you'll walk into another job.'

Diane ignored that. 'If I resign, I shall say I am resigning so that I can spend more time with my family,' she went on, her smile faltering. 'Isn't that what they always say? Complete and utter crap, of course. The truth, certainly in my case, is just a little different. My home life is very nearly past the point of no return,' she added, with a desperate shake of her head.

Maggie stared at her. 'Why? What's happened? Is it Freddie?'

Diane frowned, shaking her head. 'Why do you say that? Why should it be because of him? He's perfectly all right,' she said, her defensive attitude speaking volumes. 'He's not autistic if that's what you are suggesting.'

'Not at all,' Maggie said hastily.

'I should hope not,' Diane said, giving her a frosty look. 'Children develop at different rates, that's all, and it's dangerous to compare one with another. We were spoilt with Roger and Philip being bright as buttons and we have to be careful not to make too much of it. No, no, it's not about Freddie.'

'What then?' Maggie persisted.

Diane kicked her shoes off and tucked her legs underneath her as Maggie waited for the confession to step up a gear. 'Rupert is the only reason I've been able to do this job,' she said. 'You know what it's been like. We're very broad-based and have to do a lot of liaising with our American parent company so I have to be prepared to pack my bags at a moment's notice and catch a flight to New York.'

'I used to envy you that.'

'You needn't. One long flight, a couple of meetings and a long flight back. It's not a holiday. Anyway, the point is, I can only do that because he's there as a back-up. You can't always rely on paid staff but, by God, I can rely on him. He loves me to bits, Maggie, and he's not a bit jealous of my success as some men would be.'

'I know. You're very lucky,' Maggie said, thinking for an inexplicable moment of last year's Christmas card of the Buckman family group, a photograph of the six of them in their home. Rupert, as proud as punch, arm round Diane, and just looking at it had made her choke with emotion. It all seemed so perfect, maybe too perfect.

'So, what with worrying about work and people finding out about the mess I've made, there's also been the miscarriage to face up to.' Diane shifted in the chair and started to twist her rings round and round her finger, a sure sign of agitation.

Maggie held her breath. Rupert was right. It was tearing her apart.

'I lost it. I lost the baby,' she said, eyes filled with tears. 'It was only ten weeks and they called it a spontaneous abortion. I didn't try to make it happen, Maggie. I really didn't.'

'I know. . . .' Awash with compassion, Maggie rose and went across to her, crouching down in front of the sofa. She had rarely seen Diane like this. Diane never let herself go. 'I know, Diane. And you should let yourself grieve about it. Don't bottle it up. Rupert's worrying that you're doing that. There's nothing wrong with having a good cry. I wept buckets when Dave told me he was leaving. The bastard,' she finished, trying in vain to make Diane smile.

'I lost it,' Diane repeated, looking lost herself.

'Rupert doesn't blame you for that,' Maggie told her. She wanted to give her sister a cuddle but Diane's tense nature had always resisted such obvious displays of affection. She settled for holding her hand instead. 'It's not your fault. How can it be? It was just one of those things. And if you really want another one, then why don't you try again after a while?'

'Oh, Maggie, how can you be so naive? Did it ever occur to you just why I wasn't exactly thrilled to be having another baby? I thought you of all people would understand. You know me. I love being pregnant so why was I less than thrilled? Have I really got to spell it out?'

'I should think it's obvious. You have four children already. That's enough for most people.'

'No. Five would be good. I love having babies and being pregnant. The thing is, it wasn't Rupert's.'

'What do you mean?' Maggie gave a nervous laugh. 'How can it not be Rupert's?'

'Too easily.' Diane's lip was trembling now. 'I'm sorry to spring this on you but I have to tell somebody.'

'Not Rupert's?' Maggie was stunned, still trying to take in the implications.

'No. And now, perhaps, you might understand my problem?'

CHAPTER FOURTEEN

THERE WAS A SILENCE

O N the mantelpiece, the clock's tick suddenly became noticeable. A French gilt-bronze and white-marble clock, it was horrific, beloved of their mother, tolerated by their father, but something that none of them would fight over when the time came.

Diane sighed. 'Say something, Maggie, for God's sake.'

'I can't believe it. Is this a joke?'

'Would I joke about something like this?'

'But you and Rupert have always seemed so perfect together. You seem the ideal couple.'

'I've been having an affair with a colleague.'

'Obviously . . .' Maggie could not help being tight-lipped for Diane had just – in a single sentence – destroyed her own stout belief in love and romance. Oh yes, it had floundered a little over the past years, but she was an optimist and still firmly believed in the institution, with Diane and Rupert the supreme example of married bliss.

'Don't look like that. Please.'

'What do you expect?' Maggie dragged her gaze away from her very pale-faced sister; found she was staring instead at a framed picture of her mother. They were everywhere in the house, as if she was still keeping a watchful eye on them, which was ironic considering she and Dad had been close to a split once upon a time. He thought they didn't know but they did. Her father was a very patient man because her mother must have been hell on earth to live with. Ratty, jealous, brittle. So far as she knew, Dad had never strayed but he could hardly be blamed if he had. And now, looking at her mother's photograph, Maggie was just grateful that she wasn't really in the room, listening in, for Diane was her little angel and could certainly do no wrong in her mother's eyes.

'You're shocked?' Diane asked, seeming surprised, as if Maggie was overreacting.

'Of course I'm shocked,' she said. 'What do you expect?'

'Promise you won't tell Dad.' It was a little girl plea, reminding Maggie that Diane was her baby sister still, only a year younger but that year weighed heavily now. The two of them, so close in age, used to have a little conspiracy going, usually directed against Frances.

'I have no intention of telling him.'

'Thank you. I know I can rely on you. Please don't breathe a word to Frances either. She won't understand.'

'I'm not sure I understand. How long has it been going on?'

'For nearly a year,' Diane said, casting her eyes down. 'I'm not proud, Maggie. I hate myself for it. I've come close to telling Rupert everything once or twice but something stopped me.'

'Thank goodness. You mustn't tell him,' Maggie said. 'He must never know.'

'It can't go on as it is. It's coming to a head, Maggie, I know it is. The point is how can I go on working with Leo, day after day, how can I? There's this sizzle between us. We try our best to be businesslike in front of others but I can't help thinking that it shows, that everybody knows. Candida is ferreting about. She smells blood. Mercifully, Shirley is the soul of discretion. She wouldn't say a word even if she was stretched on the rack.'

'So *she* knows, then?' Maggie sighed. 'What about this man? This Leo? I suppose he's married too?'

Diane nodded. 'And how. His wife's called Dorcas of all things and she's still in the States. I think their marriage is pretty shaky but then I would say that, wouldn't I? He's very attractive.' She gave a half laugh. 'I know it's no excuse but he created a real buzz when he first arrived. The other guys are just so nerdy and so very English and here he was, American with a deep velvety voice, handsome as hell, the answer to any woman's prayer. Aside from the looks, he's highly regarded by everybody who matters. He's our chief media executive and not only is he full of creative ideas for our clients, he's also a skilled negotiator and he can close a contract like nobody's business. We all expect him to take over when Harry retires. Harry thinks the sun shines out of him. He's the son he never had.'

'And you had an affair with *him*? I don't know how you have the cheek to call me naïve!' Maggie said. 'You must have known what you were doing.'

'Of course I knew. Ridiculous, isn't it? I'm an intelligent woman and I should know better. What can I say? Intelligent or not, I'm still a woman.'

'With a husband and four children.'

'I know. Don't rub it in.' Diane gave her a hard look. 'We were working very hard together on a project for a particularly sensitive client and Leo asked me out to dinner. I told myself there was no harm in it. It was purely professional and we had a lot to get through. He had given me this brief for the client and we had worked our arses off to get it up to speed. We had come up with this fantastic idea for a presentation. The thing is we had tried to get this client before and been pipped at the post and Leo was determined that wouldn't happen again. The dinner was purely about work and I do it all the time, Maggie. Sometimes you work much better in a convivial atmosphere. You get some of your best ideas then. I phoned Rupert to tell him about it.' She sighed and Maggie made to stop her, not sure she wanted to hear this but Diane was determined to tell her. 'Just after we had finished our starters, I found myself forgetting the business in hand and just sitting there, watching him, listening to his voice. It's seductive even when he's talking about mundane matters. I know I was looking good. You can't go out to a restaurant like that without looking your best. I had this discreet but utterly fabulous black number on and these gorgeous shoes . . . just a few glittery straps and huge heels. I had worked it out that I could manage about a dozen steps at most before I fell over. They were worth it, though. Every penny.'

Maggie shook her head in disbelief. Here we go – it was exciting confession time, as if they were seventeen and sixteen again. She recalled she had once told Diane all when she had a crush on a boy in the sixth form. She had sworn her to silence but the next time they met him Diane had gone all flirty with him, doing it just for fun. Maggie had vowed never to talk to her about boys again but of course she had, for Diane had a keen eye where boys were concerned. The most recent confession about Dave had, however, produced a luke-warm reaction and a request for Maggie to take a deep breath next time before she fell in love. To think she had actually asked for Diane's advice, believing her to be the ultimate steady-as-you-go wife and mother.

'I should never have gone back to his apartment for a coffee,' Diane said now. 'Why would I do that? That was one big mistake and I think I knew it. Even in the taxi, we were both buzzing with excitement and it was nothing to do with work. He took my hand as he helped me out and I just melted.'

'Diane!' Maggie shook her head. 'How old are you?'

Diane ignored her. 'He's renting this gorgeous apartment with views to die for. As soon as he took my wrap and led me over to the window to look out onto the city, I'd had it. Sinatra love songs, low lights, yet another glass of wine . . . I was just dizzy with excitement.'

'That's enough. I get the message,' Maggie said sharply, seeing Diane's eyes going misty at the memory, dreading further details. 'Does Rupert have any idea?'

'You must be joking,' she said with a shudder. 'He trusts me implicitly. We've always been straight with one another. Until now, that is.'

'Are you sure the baby was Leo's and not Rupert's?'

'Would it make a difference? Yes, I am sure it was Leo's but Rupert and I—' she hesitated, showing some sign of sensitivity.

Maggie nodded, understanding that she had made sure that Rupert need have no doubts. 'Oh Diane, what were you thinking of?'

'I know. I've behaved like an absolute cow. And I'm sorry but it's too late. Rupert never suspected a thing but then why should he? He was pleased as punch as usual and he thought my reservations were simply because, yet again, it was not planned and it was number five. Eyebrows start to rise when you have five children. It's regarded as being greedy. What on earth shall I do, Maggie?'

'I don't know. Give me chance to think. You've sprung this on me. I think I need to sleep on it.'

'Sorry, I've landed you in it. The point is, if I resign, and I don't see what else I can do, what will happen then? What will I tell Rupert?'

'You'll think of something. I think he might be rather relieved. He keeps saying that you're under far too much strain, that you need to take it easy. You can just say it's all getting too stressful.'

'Normally, I thrive on it. Rupert doesn't understand what my work means to me.'

'Under the circumstances—' Maggie hesitated. 'Having a miscarriage might have been no bad thing.'

'I knew you were going to say that.' Diane leaned forward, head in hands. 'No. It wasn't like that. All right, I admit that at first I wanted to lose it because that would be the easy way out but, once I got used to the idea, I was fine about it. I thought it wouldn't matter. I would never ever tell Rupert. After all, family resemblances are fleeting affairs, don't you think? Do either of us look remotely like Frances?'

'Your children have all got something of Rupert in them,' Maggie said. 'So that wouldn't have worked long-term.'

'I told myself he would never suspect. I can't believe now that I imagined I would get away with it. How could I watch Leo's baby grow up and not say anything? It was laughable. But then I *was* pregnant and you do get some funny ideas. Your mind goes slightly off-centre.'

'What about Leo? Did you tell him?'

'Too right I did.'

'And. . . ?'

'He was surprised but OK about it.'

'Good for him.'

Diane gave her a look. 'Please don't hate him. He was prepared to stand by me. Prepared to admit to being the father. Even prepared to leave Dorcas. He doesn't particularly want children but—' she shrugged. 'He wasn't going to abandon his child if that's what you're thinking. On the other hand, if I wanted to keep it from Rupert he would have gone along with that idea too.'

'Are you trying to convince me that he's an honourable man?'

'Not just that. He loves me.' She managed a thin smile. 'If Harry gets wind of it, we'll both be for the chop. He's from the Bible belt and very puritanical and absolutely would not tolerate an adulterous liaison within the company. He has a Bible on his desk, Maggie, and says grace before a meal. I ask you, what chance would we have? As for Leo's wife, well ... I don't think she'll be in the market for a quick and easy divorce.'

'Nor should she be,' Maggie said, still feeling a tightness in her chest, still needing to make it perfectly clear where she stood.

'She doesn't need any money from him. She's an heiress,' Diane continued, with an exasperated glance her way. 'This posting to London for Leo was only for a year initially and she refused to come with him. She's an ice-cold customer from all accounts.'

'From Leo's accounts. So, as Harry's golden boy, he must be earning a lot of money?'

'Oh yes. But, if the truth came out, he wouldn't be able to hold onto the job and Harry has a lot of influence. As for his wife, well, she would turn all manner of screws.'

'For God's sake, Diane!' Maggie's exasperation spilled over. 'You're the other woman here and don't forget it. Don't make her out to be a monster. You've never even met her.'

Diane's face froze over. 'I knew I would get no sympathy from you.'

'Well, tough. Do you expect me to congratulate you?' Maggie sighed. 'Look, don't let's argue. The thing is these things go on all the time. The statistics about office affairs are incredible. I think you're overreacting.'

'I'm not. If Harry finds out, we're dead ducks. Both of us.'

'Hell. What sort of business are you in, Diane?'

'Successful,' she said. 'But there's a fine line between success and failure so there's a lot of backstabbing.'

'Resign then. I don't know what your problem is. As I said, other people will be falling over themselves to employ somebody with your experience.'

'Not so. I've been putting out feelers ever since it happened and it isn't like that. In my line, there has to be a believable reason for moving on and I haven't got a good enough one. The spending more time with the family line has had its day. It wouldn't wash with them because they know what I'm like. Anyway, it would filter out, the real reason. I might as well stand in the middle of Trafalgar Square with a bloody loud-hailer.'

'Why doesn't *he* resign then? He could say his wife was pining for him back in the States.'

'He's offered to do that but I've said no. I don't want him to go back permanently.'

'But he will have to. This can't carry on. You still want to see him, don't you?' Maggie said as it dawned. 'Haven't you any sense at all? For goodness sake, walk away from him now before it's too late. If you don't stop it right now then Rupert is bound to find out sooner or later.'

'I'm trying,' Diane said. 'I'm really trying. I'm trying for the sake of the children.'

'And for Rupert, too, I hope.'

Diane nodded. 'Well, yes, but the truth is I've fallen out of love with him, Maggie. It's been happening gradually, ever since Alice was born. Long before Leo came on the scene.'

'Fallen out of love?'

'Yes. You fall in love so why can't you fall out of it? I thought it wouldn't matter, his not being successful with his paintings, but it does, Maggie. He has no drive. If it was me doing the painting, I'd have been exhibiting in the Tate Gallery by now.'

'Oh, don't be so pathetic. This isn't a game, it's life. Don't you realize this is just a big girl crush that you're having on this man?

Nothing more. You love Rupert.'

'Don't even begin to tell me who I love. You talk as if you're the world's expert.'

'You did ask for my advice.'

'Sorry. I don't know why. As if you could produce a magic wand and everything would suddenly be all right again.'

'Pull yourself together and don't panic,' Maggie told her, even though she was close to it herself. She could not bear the thought of Rupert finding out about this. She loved him as much as she could love a brother-in-law. She loved him because he was so nice and uncomplicated and such a good husband and dad. The children worshipped him and he must be protected at all costs. 'And for heaven's sake, don't tell Rupert.'

Diane raised her head, looking heavenwards with a huge sigh. 'Try to understand, Maggie. I know it was wrong but it was exciting at the time. I haven't had that sort of excitement in my life for a long time. Snatching a few hours together, both of us supposed to be somewhere else. Shirley covered for me.'

'That woman deserves a medal for loyalty beyond the call of duty,' Maggie said. She had never met this Shirley but on the odd occasion she had tried to contact Diane at work, she had the impression that Shirley was the sort of woman who would pin her to the floor rather than interrupt Diane at a critical meeting.

'I know. I'm lucky to have her. I'm lucky to have Rupert too. I wish I'd never met Leo but I have and I can't put the clock back. I know it's hopeless but I adore him,' she said. 'Crazy, isn't it? I've never felt like this before. I've never felt like this with Rupert, not even in the best of times. And Leo feels the same. He says why don't we just give everything up and go off together, just the two of us, and damn the consequences.'

'And leave Rupert and the children? Are you completely mad? You have to get away from that office. You have no choice. Let's be practical about this and we'll work something out. How much of a drop in salary can you afford to take?'

'Hardly anything. I've told you about our financial commitments.

133

They are terrifying.'

'What about Rupert? His paintings are taking off at last,' Maggie said, trying to think of something positive. 'He tells me he has a commission now from this dealer in the States and that must be worth a lot. And he says that once the word gets round, the sky's the limit. I've never seen him in such a buoyant mood before.'

'Oh, Maggie—' Diane shook her head. 'That's another thing. There is no American dealer. He's an invention of mine. I felt so sorry for Rupert, failing time after time, so I bought the paintings myself.'

CHAPTER FIFTEEN

F RANCES made sure she was out of the house next morning before her sisters were up. The two of them had stayed up very late. She knew that because she had heard them coming to bed eventually and checked the time.

It was half past midnight. What on earth had they found to talk about for so long? She felt a bit guilty for sidling off to bed and leaving them but she had got herself into such a silly state about today that she had known she would be rotten company. She had also worried that Diane would somehow wheedle it all out of her and start to offer advice. Polly was starting to do the same and, although it was well meant, she did not want to listen to it, however sensible it might be. Ultimately, if she was going to make a mess of her life, then she wanted to be solely responsible.

Today was the day and, as she snatched a piece of toast and marmalade for breakfast, it felt like the last meal before execution. Her stomach was playing up but she knew that was just nerves. Nevertheless, it still felt as if a clutch of butterflies were fluttering about inside.

She was going to meet his girls. After agreeing to do so some time ago, she could not put it off any longer. She worried about what to wear and how to do her hair. She didn't want to appear too formal for them, looking like a schoolteacher, but at the same time she didn't want to look a scruff, which she was more than capable of looking when she was kitted out in casual gear. She did not care for her clothes, she knew that, just hunging everything in the wash at the same temperature and hoping for the best and often not bothering to iron things when a shake and a smooth over with her hands did the trick. Diane had given up on her, not even bothering now to make suggestions.

On the way to the supermarket yesterday, she had told Maggie about John. At least, she had told her a little about John. If Maggie was surprised that a man could possibly be interested in her, she had kindly not shown it.

'I don't know that I should be advising you,' she said. 'Not with my track record, but I generally go with my feelings. Unfortunately, that means you get stung sometimes but it's always fun while it lasts. Don't take it too seriously. Enjoy it.'

Maggie had probably discussed it with Diane and Frances's greatest wish just now was to have some good news for them. By some sort of miracle, she would bond instantly with his children and all the worries would vanish.

She was meeting John first thing in town and they were spending some time together before the big event and he had reserved a table for lunch at a slightly more upmarket venue than their usual one. Frances knew she was blowing this up out of all proportion. Gracious me, as Polly had said, all she had to do was be herself and not try too hard. If they didn't like her, they didn't like her and that was all there was to it. At the same time, she couldn't be more nervous if she had been meeting the Queen.

Maggie had suggested she take some sweeties along.

'I don't like bribes,' Frances had said. 'And they'll see through that straightaway.'

Maggie laughed. 'No, they won't. Never underestimate the power of a bribe. Children are such innocents. Sweets are sweets. Take them some hair slides then. Just something little. There's no need to go over the top. And relax, Frances, for goodness sake. They're only children. They aren't going to bite you.'

'Who are you?' the middle one asked.

'She's Daddy's friend,' her sister Victoria told her, holding onto the little one's hand protectively.

'That's right,' Frances said. Her mouth felt dry and the butterflies had moved up to her chest. John had abandoned her, deliberately and callously she felt, having gone to get fish and chips, a special treat, for tea. He had been gone a while, long enough to have caught the fish himself in Morecambe Bay, and it irritated her that he had left her alone with them like this, throwing her in at the deep end. What on earth did he hope would happen? Did he seriously expect everything to slot into place? Like Maggie, like Polly, John was supremely optimistic about the outcome of this, laughing at her anxiety, telling her she was worrying about nothing. His little girls were not some sort of interviewing panel, trying to catch her out. They were simply little girls and wore their hearts on their sleeves.

Frances was not sure about that. The female sex was born devious. You only had to look at the way the girls ran rings round the boys in the classroom to see that.

Did John think that, when he got back, she would be sitting on the sofa surrounded by this trio of small girls, all of them happy and smiling, a study in mother and children perfection? To Frances, it was the most unlikely scenario. Now, confronted by the three of them, she felt as if she was an actress on stage who had momentarily forgotten her lines. She needed a prompt, a maternal prompt from somewhere.

'Are you Frances?' Victoria asked, not waiting for an answer. 'Do you have another name?'

'Amelia. Frances Amelia Troon,' she said carefully. The middle name was unfortunate, the initials spelling out FAT, but she was sure it was unintentional.

'Daddy's called John Edward.'

'Yes, I know,' Frances said, forcing a smile even though the muscles in her face felt frozen. 'And you are Victoria, Isobel and Eleanor, aren't you?'

'Which is your very favourite name?' Victoria asked. 'In the whole wide world?'

'Well. . . .' Frances struggled as they waited, looking intently at her.

'Don't you know?' Victoria seemed to have a monopoly on this conversation. 'Mine is Samantha.'

'I'm having a baby,' Isobel butted in, pointing to the teddy she had stuffed up her top. 'When the clock goes six.'

'Lovely,' Frances said, wondering when she would be able to string more than two words together. What was wrong with her? What did you say to little children? The children she taught were from eleven to sixteen, some of them going on forty, so she had no idea. The primary school teachers she knew all seemed to be built in the same mould and she was most certainly out of a different one.

The smallest girl, Eleanor, slight with dark curly hair, was wearing a fairy costume complete with wings, and her legs, encased in silvery tights, were clamped together. She also wore pink-framed glasses, which Frances could see were incredibly smeary.

'Do you need a wee?' Victoria asked, shaking her head and looking back at Frances with an exasperated expression as Eleanor denied it vehemently. 'She always waits until the very last minute. Do you know where our bathroom is?'

'Yes.'

'Are you very old?' Isobel asked, shouted down at once by Victoria, who said it was rude to ask ladies that.

'Quite old,' Frances replied, feeling a sudden unexpected stir of amusement mixing with the anxiety.

'The baby's coming,' Isobel announced, pulling the teddy out and giving a great yell as she did so.

Where had she learnt that?

'It's a girl,' she said, dropping it on the floor as she lost interest. Coming to sit beside Frances, she looked carefully at her before asking what *her* baby was called.

'I don't have one,' Frances said, making room for her. She could see in the child's face something of John and something else too, something that reminded her that this little being was a product of John and Julia's one-time love for each other. It was as if a pain pierced her chest suddenly.

'*Why* don't you have a baby?'

Stumped, she smiled instead. It was exactly the same with her niece, Alice. She was hopeless at small children talk. Maggie could do it. Maggie could say things to make them laugh. Maggie caught them up and cuddled them in a perfectly natural way. She wished she could do the same.

'Our mummy went away,' Victoria told her and, behind the big child-eyes, Frances could sense the sadness. 'She didn't love us any more.'

'I'm sure she does,' Frances said, shocked by the straight words. 'It's just that sometimes some ladies . . .' she paused, irritated that she was about to dig herself into a hole.

'Some ladies what. . . ?'

How could she explain it when she did not even know herself what had prompted Julia to leave them, other than her falling in love with this other man?

'Are you going to be our new mummy?'

Ah. The big one.

Eleanor had asked the question, dancing round now, hands firmly between her little legs.

The question fluttered around but, panicking as to how to answer it, Frances hastily grabbed the offered diversion.

'Do you need the bathroom, Eleanor?'

For some reason, they were in the sitting room, the room where there were no toys, John's private room, and she didn't think he would appreciate it if she allowed the child to wet the beautiful deep-pile cream carpet. She was nearly five, too old to be doing that, perhaps, but maybe the loss of her mummy was having some effect. 'Come with me,' she said firmly.

'No.' Eleanor adjusted her glasses with one hand and stayed put.

'You can have *my* baby then,' Isobel said with great generosity, her mind obviously still on the unfortunate fact of Frances not having one of her own. She picked up the discarded teddy and cradled it in her arms. 'It's called Daisy.'

'That's a lovely name. Look, I'm going to the bathroom. Who wants to come with me?'

139

They all did.

They went to the nearest one, a little cloakroom that just housed a lavatory and a washbasin. For four of them, plus the new baby Daisy, it was a tight squeeze.

'You can go first, Frances,' Victoria said magnanimously. 'If you're desperate.'

No. After you. . . .' Again a nudge of amusement caught at her and, as it did, some of her nerves disappeared. If she could see the funny side of all this then maybe there was a glimmer of hope.

After the children had washed their little hands and the teddy's paws had been pretend-washed, they toddled off to their room whilst Frances, feeling frazzled, went into the kitchen to get biscuits and juice for them. With fish and chips due any minute, she wasn't sure about the wisdom of biscuits but what the heck. . . .

She bustled around, feeling rather proud of herself.

Maybe she could do it after all.

And then came the scream from above.

Earlier that morning, Harvey heard Wendy pottering about on the landing as he dressed. He hated oversleeping but he also hated setting the alarm – a throwback to having to get up for work – and he had no idea why he had allowed himself to be shunted from waking dream to waking dream this morning.

Angela had featured in the last one, a starring role, and Wendy had had a walk-on part at some point – a cameo, he thought they called it. He was watching in the wings, as you do in dreams, looking at the two of them as they faced each other for some sort of confrontation, one that never materialized because he woke up properly then.

He wondered just how the two ladies would have squared up to each other in real life, not that it would have ever come about when Angela was alive. He had been remarkably circumspect, he now real-ized, and, even though the thought of having a bit of a fling might have crossed his mind, he had never done anything about it.

Angela would not have liked Wendy.

Just about to put on the old shorts he had worn yesterday, he tossed them aside and looked for something smarter. He had seen Diane eyeing them up last night and knew exactly what she was thinking. She was so like her mother and not just in looks. He had the feeling that it wouldn't have taken much for Angela to walk out on them, the lot of them, without too much of a backward glance. He called that being selfish and Diane had that same selfish streak. Like Angela, she always looked so clean and pressed, as if she was wearing her clothes for the very first time. Frances's clothes looked lived in but Maggie had turned a new leaf, so she told him, now that she had got rid of that bloody Dave whom he had never met and whom he hated for making his daughter unhappy.

His daughters got on his nerves, to be honest. They interfered, tried to do things for him that he was more than capable of doing himself. He had caught Diane nosing through his pill box last night and it was on the tip of his tongue to remind her that she might occasionally remember to take her own particular pill, the one he assumed she took to prevent pregnancies, but he had wisely kept his mouth shut. The subject of the baby seemed a closed shop with her being so damned touchy about it.

What the hell was Wendy up to out there? He could hear her moving things and he hoped she wasn't trying to shift the sideboard that sat out on the landing because it was deceptively heavy and she might put her back out. Diane had muttered something about insurance liability and he hadn't a clue about that. He just didn't want Wendy hurting herself, that was all.

Dressed eventually, taking a comical age to decide what to wear, he opened the door to find Wendy still outside, polishing the big sideboard, her back to him, going at it like there was no tomorrow. The air reeked of artificial lavender.

'Good morning, Wendy. Are my daughters round or have I got you to myself?'

She turned, giving him a nervous smile. 'Frances left a note. She's gone out for the day and the others have gone into town,' she said. 'They said they would have lunch out. Maggie's left you a salad in the fridge.'

141

He nodded. That sounded a bundle of fun.

She stuffed the duster in her pocket before tucking a strand of hair back into place, avoiding looking at him directly. She was, he noticed, wearing pale blue jeans and a darker blue top and, when he drew nearer, he noticed a trace of perfume, something more subtle than the lavender of the spray polish. 'It's nice for you, Harvey, isn't it, having all your family here for once?'

He noted with pleased surprise the easy way his name had slipped out.

'Wendy . . . while we've got the chance, we need to talk.'

'Ssh. I'll make us a cup of tea,' she said, seeming to think that was the answer to everything. 'It is time for my break,' she added, glancing at the nearest clock – the Vienna wall clock – as if he cared tuppence whether or not she was due an official break.

Going down to the kitchen, Diane's knockout scent lingered on the stairs and he marvelled a moment at the way his youngest daughter coped with her busy life. She was a go-getter was Diane. How she held down an important job and brought up a large family at the same time was beyond him. Four children, very nearly five. Three had been more than enough for Angela and she hadn't even worked outside the home. Diane's conception, so soon after Maggie, had been an unpleasant surprise but she had rallied round surprisingly well, convinced it was a boy. He hadn't been around at the birth, not like Rupert, who had been there every single time for Diane, but Rupert and Diane were different, a bloody good twosome and still going strong.

Wendy sat opposite him at the kitchen table, pouring their tea from a warmed pot, pushing the sugar bowl his way. He looked smart this morning, trousers out of the press, his short-sleeved white shirt unbuttoned at the neck. She had seen photographs of him about the house, as a young man, and he had been very handsome once upon a time. Looks didn't really matter, not that much. What mattered to her was the man himself, and she liked what she saw and also liked what she could not see, the kind heart of the man.

Tom would have liked him.

'Look, I—' she paused, not knowing how to say it. She was terribly out of practice with this. Since his proposal, the little warm feeling had heated up, and just now, as he had opened his door, she had felt a distinct flutter in her heart.

'Wendy, listen to me.'

She liked the decisive note in his voice. If there had been a fault with Tom, it was the way he always let her make the decisions when sometimes she yearned to be told what to do. Harvey reached for her hand, held it, and looked into her eyes. The message he was sending her was embarrassingly clear cut.

'No, don't look away,' he said quietly. 'I'm sorry I upset you, going at it like a bull in a china shop, but I meant what I said. Let's forget all this nonsense about you working for me. We could have met anywhere but we happened to meet here. You're a lovely lady, Wendy. I don't know about you but I'm feeling quite relaxed about it all, this second-time-around business. It's just an extension of being friends. There's no pressure on us. That's how I see it.'

She was not sure. 'Just friendship?' she said. 'It's got to mean more than that if I'm to marry you.'

She heard him catch his breath. 'OK. I'll show you what it means. Come here,' he said, raising her to her feet. 'Come close to me.'

'Here? Now?' She looked round in alarm. 'Good heavens, Harvey, what are you thinking of?'

'This.' he touched her face and smiled. 'That feels good. I want to kiss you. Will you let me?'

She laughed for it had felt good to her too. 'Nobody's asked permission to kiss me before,' she said. 'They've generally just done it. That was when I was young, of course. After you've been married for years, you don't do it so much. You take all that sort of stuff as read. And we would have to take it slowly, let me get used to the idea.'

'Is that a yes?' he asked, giving her hand a squeeze. 'Is it a yes, my darling?'

She had thought about it, lain awake last night particularly think-

143

ing about it, perhaps been rather cold and clinical in weighing up the options. She would never have considered it at all if she hadn't had a few very nice feelings for him. As it was, marrying Harvey would solve her problems at a stroke. She could move in here, to this lovely house, and she would never have to worry again about the future. Other than Moira at the shop, she had nobody to talk to about it. She had very nearly told Moira but had pulled up at the last minute because she knew she would make her own mind up and she didn't want Moira putting her off and telling her that she was making one big mistake. This way, she had only herself to blame.

'Yes,' she said quickly before she could change her mind. 'If you're quite sure, Harvey. What will people say? After all, I am your cleaner. They might think I'm marrying you for your money.'

'They can think what they bloody well like,' he said and, wrapped in his arms, she relaxed at last. It was different from being in Tom's arms but that was how it should be. Tom had been Tom and this was Harvey. She hadn't been held so close by a man like this for some time and it felt wonderful. She was fed up with doing things herself all the time. She was the sort of woman who needed somebody to care for her. Frances treated this man, her father, as if he was old and frail and, holding her close like this, he felt anything but. He was strong and she leaned gratefully into him, in no rush to be kissed. Time enough for that.

But Harvey had other ideas and, as he tilted up her face, she saw the triumph in his. His kiss was gentle, fleeting as a first kiss should be.

'Marrying me for my money, eh?' he asked in a low voice. 'When I could swear, Wendy, that you love me maybe just the teeniest bit already. And we have all the time in the world left to us.'

'Let's not talk about love, not just yet,' she said, a sharp memory surfacing of Tom and the first time *he* had kissed her. Tom had never called her his darling either because it wasn't a word he used.

The front door slammed and they leapt apart as if they were teenagers, assuming an air of propriety by resuming their seats at the table.

Hastily, Wendy fluffed her hair, hoping she didn't look too flushed. She exchanged a little smile with him, reaching forward quickly to wipe away a tiny smudge of her pink lipstick that had lodged on his mouth.

'Leave it with me,' Harvey told her. 'I'll pick the moment to tell them.'

CHAPTER SIXTEEN

ELEANOR, glasses askew, was on her way downstairs, leaving a little trail of bloody handprints on the wall. She had tripped and fallen on the edge of a table – just like Father – and cut her head above the eye. Blood was everywhere, although Eleanor herself seemed more concerned about the state of the fairy dress.

Frances took charge, pushing down her initial panic. This time there would be no dallying about, she thought, as she ran to get a towel from the bathroom. So by the time John arrived back with the fish and chips, Frances was murmuring comforting words to a grief-stricken Eleanor, having successfully stemmed the blood flow with a towel whilst the other girls were busy covering teddy with bandages.

Calm as you like, John whipped into action. Examining the wound, he would take Eleanor to casualty, he said, as he thought it needed a couple of stitches. Could she hold the fort? No, she could not. She had held more forts over the years than the entire cavalry put together and she was coming with him, they were all going together.

'It might take some time,' John warned her. 'The last time we had to wait nearly an hour to be seen.'

The last time? She did not enquire, intent on looking after Eleanor, whose eyes had lit up at the idea of a visit to hospital for stitches. By the time she had been seen and the wound glued up, Frances had calmed down too. She spent the time in the waiting area reading to the other girls from a book she had grabbed on the way out. Intrigued by the comings and goings of the accident and emergency department,

146

they behaved very well. In fact, an elderly lady sitting nearby took the trouble of complimenting Frances.

'It's so refreshing to see well-behaved children,' she told her with a smile. 'You are to be congratulated, Mummy.'

Hey, hang on ... but she was gone and Frances found she was smiling, bathed in a glory that she didn't feel she was entirely due.

'I'm sorry,' she told John on the way home. 'I'm so sorry. You must think me completely useless. You leave me with them for five minutes and this happens.'

'Don't blame yourself. I should have warned you that Eleanor's accident prone.'

'Oh dear, is she really?' Frances swivelled in her seat so that she could observe the wounded soldier sitting in the middle, a wounded soldier who now looked particularly pleased with herself. 'That plaster looks very smart,' she said. 'You mustn't get it wet, though.'

'We'll need a new pair of glasses, of course, but that's nothing new,' John said in a muttered aside. 'So, no harm done except to the fish and chips. They'll be stone cold. What shall we do for supper, girls?'

They ended up at a burger joint, her first time ever, and it all seemed so cosy to be playing the mother role in this family set-up that for a moment Frances was seduced, before common sense took over.

Back at John's, with the girls tearing off to get their nurses' outfits on to play hospitals, she made her excuses. She ought to get back. Diane and Maggie needed looking after and she felt guilty about leaving them alone all day when they had only just arrived. As a hostess, she was failing miserably in her duties.

John kissed her goodbye, reiterating that she wasn't to blame herself for what happened.

It wasn't that, although the nerves she had suppressed were now kicking in as an afterthought. She was a bit shaken up as she wasn't good with blood but the reality had to be faced. If she married John and, although he had not actually proposed, he seemed to take it as read that she would, then this would be her life, constantly fetching and carrying, putting the children first, losing herself in the process.

She couldn't begin to contemplate how much her life would change. With most women, with Diane, for example, the change was gradual as babies were born, which must give you time to adjust and adapt but in her case it would be instantaneous.

She had to be sure for they could not be let down a second time, this ready-made family of little girls, whom she thought were still eyeing her up before they came to any conclusions. On her way out, she had popped upstairs to say goodbye and been greeted by complete nonchalance, although at the last moment Eleanor, changed into pyjamas, had given her a cheery wave and a smile, oblivious now to the fuss she had caused.

She was in a sober frame of mind when she returned home.

Earlier in the day, Maggie picked up a message on her mobile from Rupert.

'Call me. Don't tell Diane,' it said.

Not used to cryptic texts, she clicked it off, glancing at Diane across the café table. It wasn't a café either of them remembered but then there wasn't much about town that they remembered. It was odd going back to the town where you were a child. It was all different and yet somehow the same, seen through older and wiser eyes. The people seemed different too, give or take the familiar accent, hurrying as if there was no tomorrow but then that was the bustle of today. Ever more frantic. The feel of the place was the same, though: sombre, hilly and, for a city, small.

'You're quiet,' Diane said.

'I've got a lot to think about,' Maggie said. 'I took a long time to get to sleep thinking about what you told me. Diane, how could you be such a fool?'

'Oh, for goodness' sake, don't be like that. Help me out, please. It's done and I regret it. I'm trying to make amends now.' She sighed, picking at the salad she had ordered. 'Frankly, I don't know what we're doing up here. It's claustrophobic and don't ask me why. I know you don't like London but I do. I can't imagine why you've chosen to come back to live here. At least you had Newcastle on your doorstep and from what I remember of that, it's a lively enough city. But here? What are you thinking about?'

'I'm thinking about the future. After Dave, I need a move. I can't afford to live down south and, strange as it may seem to you, I like it here. I can take or leave cities.'

'This is one,' Diane remarked drily.

'Well, yes, but you know what I mean. And the important thing is I'll be able to help Frances out a little with Dad. I know he seems all right at the moment but he's not getting any younger and, if there are two of us here, it's bound to help.'

'True. I'm sorry I can't help out more but you do understand my situation? I've had a word with Dr McGowan and he's pleased with Dad's progress. Of course he can't be one hundred per cent sure there won't be a recurrence of his problem but that's life. None of us can be sure, can we? I didn't tell you but I could easily have been killed on the motorway the other day. A lorry cut me up.'

'Oh no. That must have been horrible.'

'It was. My life flashed before my eyes, although it didn't throw up any answers to my problem. I still can't decide what to do next. Should I get out now before the truth gets out?'

'You obviously don't want to resign but be realistic. Staying there will just create problems.'

'Yes, but Leo will be back in the States before long. If I can just hang on in there a bit longer then I have nothing to worry about. Temptation removed. We shall have to be strong, both of us. We're not seeing each other except in the normal course of business and then we just have to do our best not to look at each other.'

'It's up to you then,' Maggie said, knowing that her advice would go unheeded as it always did. She wasn't sure why Diane had told her about it all because in the end she would simply do what she wanted.

'Excuse me. . . .'

They looked up into a face Maggie recognized immediately, even if it was a few years since she had last set eyes on him.

'If it isn't Mags Troon,' he said cheerfully. 'I thought it was you. You don't look a day older.'

Smoothy. Opposite her, she could see Diane dipping instantly into flirt mode. Honestly, you would think after four children and a recent affair, she might have some sense of sobriety left.

'I take it you're here for the reunion on Friday?'

'What reunion's that?' she asked as, with a quick query in his eyes, he sat down at their table, before ordering a coffee from a hovering waitress.

'The school one, of course,' he said, glancing at Diane. 'Hi, Di. Are you both here for it?'

'You must be joking,' Diane said, sending him one of her looks, for she hated the abbreviation of her name. 'I'm trying to put a name to your face,' she added coolly. 'Mark somebody, isn't it?'

'It is. Mark Broughton. Hello, there. . . .' Rather pointedly, he turned to Maggie. 'Good to see you again. Long time no see.'

Maggie smiled, hoping he had not heard Diane's exasperated sigh.

'I heard you'd moved away. London, wasn't it?'

'No. That's me,' Diane said, peeved that he wasn't paying her more attention. 'Maggie's been living in the north-east but she's moving back, would you believe?'

'Oh, that's great. I'll see more of you then. I like to get up to the Lakes whenever I can. I'm into sailing. Are you interested?'

'No. I don't do water sports.'

She caught Diane's sisterly look, found herself taking in the older version of the Mark Broughton she had once known. She wondered what had happened to Trisha. Had he married her? Should she ask?

This was hopeless. If Mark wanted a private word with her, Diane was having none of it, sitting there like a very stubborn gooseberry. Realizing that, Mark, after a few more pleasantries, made a quick getaway although not before he had given Maggie details of the reunion, which was to be held in a couple of days' time at a hotel on the outskirts of town. She wouldn't need a ticket, he said, as the take-up rate this year was on the low side, but she should ring the organizer to let her know.

'Fancy meeting up with him?' Diane mused on the way back. 'He was head boy, wasn't he? Didn't he go to Oxford? He always had a nice way with him. I fancied him myself once upon a time. I'm surprised he hasn't moved on. You went out together for a while, didn't you?'

'You know damned well we did.' Maggie gave her a wry smile. 'You seem to remember more about him than I do.'

'I never knew he called you Mags.'

'Awful, isn't it?' She smiled a little. 'Considering he dumped me once upon a time, I was quite pleased to see him. He's worn well, don't you think?'

'Very well. No wedding ring. You should have asked him if he was married. What's the point of you going to this reunion if he turns up with a wife in tow? Bit slow there, weren't you?'

'I have no intention of getting involved with him,' Maggie said. 'I've grown up a bit since then. It was just teenage stuff.'

'That's the problem with this returning to roots business. You're bound to meet up with old friends whether you like it or not. School reunion!' she laughed. 'Can you imagine it? If I didn't have to get myself home, I would think about going just for a laugh. What did it say on his card? He did give you his business card, didn't he?'

'No.'

'He did have rather an affluent look about him,' Diane said thought-fully. 'Quality shirt. Discreet gold cufflinks. Rolex. Good shoes.'

Maggie sighed. How the hell had she noticed his *shoes*?

'If he is available, you could do worse, Maggie. I know you're not over Dave yet but sometimes it's better not to hang around too long.'

Maggie laughed. 'Thanks for the advice.'

'Who am I to give advice?' Diane said with a rueful smile. 'But surely you noticed that he didn't give me a second's glance? It was you, you, you. Wasn't he going to study law?'

He was.

At the last count, Mark Broughton had got the best exam results possible and had gone off to his chosen college. Was he now a lawyer? Was he married or engaged?

She had to confess to just a touch of curiosity.

CHAPTER SEVENTEEN

T HEY found Father and Mrs Latham in the kitchen, just finishing off a cup of tea by the look of it.

'I see you're having a break, Mrs Latham,' Diane said, an accusatory note in her voice, plonking her bag on the table. 'Everything all right, Dad?'

'Absolutely fine.'

Maggie thought he looked a little cagey and wondered for a minute if he was not feeling well, scared to tell them, although he looked very bright. She was twitchy as hell at the moment for him but, if it was possible, it was as if he was fitter now than he had ever been. He had lost that haunted look, too, the one he had taken up during her mother's illness and never quite shaken off.

Declining coffee and cake, leaving Mrs Latham bustling round after Diane, who had slumped into a chair at the table, she escaped into her room, remembering Rupert's message and giving him a call.

'What's the panic?'

'Hi, Maggie. You haven't said anything to Diane?'

'No. You asked me not to. It's not one of the children, is it?' she asked, the horrible thought hitting her.

'No, no, they're all right. It's work,' he said. 'I know she's only been gone five minutes but all hell's broken loose at work. The shit is just about to hit the fan, as Diane would say.'

'Why?' She felt her heart race. 'What's happened?'

'Shirley rang me. She's Diane's secretary. She knew that Diane didn't want to be disturbed but she thought I should know what was happening. Has Diane mentioned a woman called Candida?'

'Candyfloss?'

'That's her. It would seem she's taking full advantage of Diane being away. She's making out that Diane's messed up big-time with one of the clients. I don't know the ins and outs but it's an important contract worth a cool million. Now Shirley knows what's what. She admits to me that there was a problem but it's in the process of being resolved. However, she has to be very careful just now for it was something of a botch-up. Very untypical of Diane but I suppose we should all be allowed one mistake.'

'Don't you believe it, Rupert,' Maggie said, smiling a little at his naïvety. He was almost too laid-back for words and she felt the smallest irritation at the way he just let the world slide by. If he had been paying more attention, for heaven's sake, they wouldn't be in this mess. How on earth had he allowed Diane to wriggle out of his grasp?

'Shirley thinks Diane ought to get herself back as soon as she can. To be honest, I'm not keen on her doing that. She needs this break and I think Shirley is just overreacting.'

'What a bunch of mean-minded idiots! Can't Diane have a few days off without all this happening? What does this Piers bloke say about it? Surely she can rely on him to defend her?'

Rupert laughed. 'You've obviously never met the man. He's a fence sitter.'

'But she's worked there for years, Rupert, surely nobody's going to take this Candida woman seriously?'

'My sentiments exactly, although I know she's got under Diane's skin and she does sound a bitch. The worst thing is . . .' he hesitated. 'I hardly know how to tell you this but she's acting like a little girl in the playground trying to stir up trouble.'

'One of those, eh? Little girls like that never change, Rupert.'

'I thought not. Aside from the business fiasco, on a more personal level, she's sending out a rumour that Diane . . . Diane, mark you . . . has been having an affair with one of the guys at work. As Shirley says, it's ludicrous. Candida's not exactly naming names but she's making it pretty clear who she means. He's called Lionel . . . a big noise. He's American, I think. Diane has mentioned him.'

'Leo,' she corrected him and could have bitten her tongue off.

'Leo. then,' he said, the fact that she knew his name and must therefore have been talking to Diane about him, not seeming to register. 'And that's where I saw red, Maggie. She can't do that. She can't spread malicious gossip about my wife and get away with it. So, don't tell Diane, but I'm going in tomorrow to sort a few things out. Can you imagine what this guy will think if he gets to know of it? He's a devout Catholic, Shirley tells me, so he would no more have an affair than I would. I've got to step in before it gets out of hand and if it causes trouble for little Miss Candida then she has asked for it.'

'Now, hang on, Rupert—' Agitated, Maggie walked over to the window. Everything looked the same out there. Her sister's marriage was in grave danger of imminent collapse but nothing had changed out in the garden, the summer flowers soaking up the sunshine, the lawns looking a little parched. 'Don't be hasty.'

'Hasty?'

'Can't you see?' She thought quickly. 'A jealous husband storming in and creating havoc is just what Candida wants. What she's been saying will soon be forgotten but you making a scene won't be. Diane will never forgive you for that.'

'But if I don't, it will look like I don't care,' he said heatedly. 'Look, I have to defend Diane. I can't have people thinking this of her.'

'Trust me, Rupert,' she said, feeling such a heel to be saying such a thing to him. In his innocence or possible stupidity, he did trust her, just as he trusted his supposedly loyal wife. At that moment, she could cheerfully have strangled Diane. 'It will make matters worse. Stay away. Lie low. If you like, I'll talk to Diane before you do; try to prepare her for it.'

'Will you?' He sounded strangely relieved as if his heart had not really been in creating a scene in the first place. He was too gentle a man for that. He never raised his voice, not even to the boys when they were misbehaving. It suddenly occurred that perhaps that was the cause of it all. He was *too* gentle for Diane; maybe she needed somebody with a bit more fire in his belly. 'I think Shirley's panicking,' he went on. 'She's having a lot of domestic problems as well, poor soul, and I'm sworn to silence about them. She's a pain, frankly, and I don't know why Diane keeps inviting her here for supper. It's one damned thing after another with Shirley.'

'That's probably it,' Maggie reassured him, desperate now to get him off the phone before she really put her foot in it. 'Leave it with me. Diane's missing you and the children,' she added.

'Is she?'

'She certainly is. She will be ringing later, expect.'

'I don't think so. I told her not to unless it was an emergency. I told her to try and relax and forget about us for a few days. She must concentrate on herself. We'll still be here when she gets back.'

She noted the wistful note as she snapped off the connection. Candida had somehow managed to latch onto the truth. Unless she had gathered together some proof, Leo and Diane had only one option: to brazen it out.

Her handbag had fallen on its side and she picked it up, seeing the scrap of paper Mark had handed her, the one with the reunion details plus his own phone number. With Diane being there today, it had not been easy to conduct any meaningful conversation, but she had to admit to a certain feeling of warmth at seeing him again. His eyes and smile had once had the power to send tingles down her spine in true romantic tradition.

And today, eons later, they had done exactly the same.

The bastard.

Harvey had inconveniently disappeared, leaving Wendy alone in the kitchen with Diane. Wendy was reminded of Angela. This daughter had her mother's colouring, her skin pale and lightly freckled, her hair cut very short, a screamingly expensive cut, and it made Wendy instinctively put a hand up to her own hair, wondering if the same old style she had had for years had seen its day.

'You have four little children then, Mrs Buckman?' she asked, desperate to start a conversation. 'How lovely. Three boys and a girl, isn't it?'

'Yes.'

'Do you have a photograph?'

'Not in this bag, I don't think.' Diane scrabbled about ineffectually. 'No. They're upstairs. I'll show you later.' She clicked her bag shut, half smiling. 'How do you find my father these days, Mrs Latham? Is he recovering well in your opinion?'

Surprised to be asked, Wendy nodded. 'He's as fit as any man of his age,' she said carefully. 'Fitter than some.'

'That's good to know. We need to make sure that he stays that way; that there isn't a recurrence of his problem.'

We? Wendy wasn't sure whom she met by 'we'.

'I have a busy life,' Diane went on quickly. 'There's not a lot I can do to help once I get home. I have my own problems.'

'Frances is very good with him and now Maggie is back that will help,' Wendy said, trying to be encouraging.

'You think so?' Diane gave a short laugh. She was a tense sort of woman, Wendy thought, one of those who kept thin from worry, which she had always thought was not healthy. She hadn't seen her with her children but it was hard to think of her as a mother of four. There must be two sides to her. 'Tell me, Mrs Latham,' Diane continued. 'May I ask if you are satisfied with your conditions of employment? Has Frances sorted out your hours properly? Do you have a coffee break slotted in?'

'Well . . . I don't know as such but I usually make myself a cup of tea or coffee when I've finished. I'm usually ready for it before I face the journey back and sometimes I have a bit of a wait for the bus.'

'Bus?' Diane frowned. 'Haven't you a car?'

'I don't drive.'

'Don't you? I thought everybody drove these days.'

'Not me. Anyway, I have to take the bus home and then I have a ten-minute walk at the other end. Not that I mind,' she added quickly. 'After all, I knew what was what when I applied for the job and walking never did anybody any harm.'

'I agree. Unfortunately, I never walk,' Diane said. 'A company driver takes me into work and the most walking I do is between my office and the lift. I will have to remedy it. I have a gym membership but I never have the time to go.'

'I wouldn't worry,' Wendy said. 'You probably get more than enough exercise looking after your children.'

'I don't look after them. I have an au pair who does that. My husband is a great help also.'

Wendy nodded, as if she understood all about the complexities of childminding. If they had had children she imagined her Tom would have been worse than useless.

'What about holidays?' Diane changed tack briskly. 'Has Frances discussed holiday entitlements with you? Has she drawn up a proper working contract?'

'Not as such. It's all very informal,' Wendy said, worried that she might be getting Frances into trouble. This lady here looked much more on the ball. 'I haven't had a holiday for a while but I usually take the bank holidays off. She pays me half then.'

'I'll draw up a contract. It's best to make it official,' Diane said. 'How does she pay you? Cash or cheque?'

'She gives me a cheque at the end of the month. It's all above board,' she said, feeling Diane was getting at her, suggesting that she was getting under-the-counter money and not declaring it. As if she would do that.

'Very well.' Diane smiled. 'Do carry on with whatever it is you were doing before I interrupted you. I must say the floors are looking good. Well done.'

'I was just going to start on the kitchen surfaces,' Wendy said. 'I like to give them a good going over.'

'Don't mind me,' Diane said, reaching for the newspaper.

Self-consciously, feeling she was being watched, Wendy ran some hot water, tipped in some disinfectant and started wiping the tops down. The silence, aside from the occasional rustle of the paper, was awkward and she wondered if she should say something about the weather but decided against it. Be like that, then. Diane treated her like staff in a way that even Frances did not. Even if, strictly speaking, she *was* staff, it irked. She must make allowances, for Diane had recently lost a baby and that must be dreadful for her and she was probably used to speaking to subordinates at work like they were no better than specks of dirt on the floor. For two pins, she felt like telling her to stuff the parquet floors and, even more mischievously, she was sorely tempted to tell her that her father had proposed marriage. Goodness, that would wipe the condescending smile off her beautifully made-up face.

She decided this woman hadn't an ounce of her dad in her. If she had a softer side, she was keeping it well hidden.

Outside the window, the trees were completely still for there wasn't a breath of wind today. Tom would have given his all for a garden like this. They had only had a patch at the tied cottage and they couldn't even plant what they liked because his lordship kept a keen eye on it. No dahlias, he had said. Frances kept this garden looking good although, if she got the chance, she would like to make a few changes, add a herb bed just outside this window so that she could pick fresh herbs whenever she wanted. Harvey didn't eat well enough. She had seen the stock of frozen dinners in the freezer and a man shouldn't be living off that sort of stuff. They were all very well to have in for emergencies but as a general rule. . . .

'So you live in town, Mrs Latham? Alone?' Diane broke the silence.

Wendy paused, the damp cloth in her hand. 'My husband died a while back and we had to leave the cottage we were in so I just rent a little place down by the canal.'

'How sad. I'm sorry you lost your husband. You must miss him?'

Well, well, there was the softer side emerging at last.

She nodded. She really didn't want to get on to this topic.

'Do you have family?'

'No,' she said. 'There was just the two of us. We never minded,' she added hastily, not wanting Diane to take pity on her. 'We were happy enough.'

'Were you? Whilst I wouldn't change things for the world,' Diane said, in a surprising confessional tone, 'sometimes I wonder about the wisdom of having a family. It's expected, isn't it, but sometimes it's as if you get forced into it. Children are a constant worry. I expect I shall still be worrying about them when they are grown up.'

'I'm sure you will.' Wendy had finished and was just putting things back in place. The clock in the hall struck the hour and she looked up, realizing she was running late and might miss her bus at this rate.

She must have said as much because Diane immediately offered to run her home.

It was a nice gesture, unexpected, but she would not be taking her up on it.

CHAPTER EIGHTEEN

FROM the window of her room, Diane could see Mrs Latham and her father strolling in the garden. Had the dratted woman missed her bus after all? Honestly, she had offered to give her a lift but she had refused point-blank. She was not sure what to make of Mrs Latham. She seemed a bit shy of conversing with her as was the way with some varieties of cleaners, yet at the same time she had a secretive air about her, oddly confident.

And what on earth was she doing out there with Father, chatting for all the world as if they were friends? Dad had no idea how to deal with staff. You had to keep one step removed or it would never work.

She sighed. She had done it now, well and truly, in telling Maggie all. But she had needed to do it because it had been too much holding it all in. How many times had she very nearly confessed to Rupert? Each time she had stopped herself at the last minute, unable to visualize the shock on his face, hardly daring to contemplate the sadness and disbelief he would feel. He looked at her sometimes with a puppy-dog devotion that she now felt uncomfortable with.

She recalled coming back home after time spent with Leo, having to pop into the bathroom first before she confronted Rupert, splashing cold water on her face, but nothing could hide the sparkle, love sparkle, in her eyes that came just after making love. She hadn't been able to look Rupert in the eye, amazed he hadn't noticed.

He trusted her too much, that was his trouble. He had put her on a pedestal from the start and never once, in his eyes, had she toppled off. Being practically perfect was a terrible burden to bear.

Sitting down at the little desk in the corner of the room, she sat a moment, penning her resignation letter in her head. Before she committed it to paper, to Piers, she needed to be sure she had considered all the options. It wasn't quite true what she had told Maggie about other jobs. There were other jobs out there offering very nearly as much money but she just didn't want to leave the one she had. And there was Leo to consider. He had offered to arrange a transfer back to the States sooner rather than later, if that's what she wanted, making it clear it was not what he wanted. He was fed up with this hole-in-the-corner stuff, perfectly ready to bring it all out into the open.

She couldn't do that. Not yet. Perhaps never. They were both of them taking an enormous risk with their jobs and their families but, despite it all, even the fact that his wife would make life difficult if not impossible for him, Leo still wanted Diane.

Leo lived in a fantasy land. He wanted to live far away from Dorcas in California somewhere next to the Pacific. A gorgeous house, warm sunshine, ocean views, he painted a wonderful picture. Breakfast on the terrace. A swimming pool. Just the two of them.

He seemed to dismiss Rupert and the children as things she would willingly discard, just so she could be with him. The arrogance of the man! She had so much more to lose than he did. The very fact that she was even thinking about doing it was appalling. What sort of mother would do such a thing? A callous, uncaring one, that's who, and she would lose everybody's sympathy in a single shot.

She did not even think Frances would be sympathetic, Frances who had little time for little children. Frances would think of loyalty and so on. Didn't Frances understand that you only had one chance of true happiness in life and sometimes it meant that unpalatable choices had to be faced? Sometimes you had to get rid of excess baggage along the way. How could she think of her children, her babies, as excess baggage? The very thought made her cringe.

Her hand trailing listlessly across the desk, Diane's attention was caught by some books in a small pile. Oh look . . . there was her copy of *Sense and Sensibility* that her mother had once given her for her birthday. What was it doing here? She recalled she had lent it to Frances, who had presumably never returned it, which was typical of her. Picking it up, she opened it and stared at the inscription. It was written by her mother in her unmistakable handwriting and Diane sighed, running her hand across the words as her mother would have done all those years ago. 'To my darling Diane on her birthday. Love forever – Mummy'.

Guilt surfaced, rising fast. At the last, with her mother in the hospice waiting to die, Frances had telephoned to say it was nearly time and she had said she would come at once. Why she had then dallied she did not know to this day but dallied she had, hanging around at home with Rupert hovering, waiting to drive her up. By the time they arrived, it was too late. Her mother was dead and it was Frances and her father who had stayed with her during those last hours, Frances who happened to be there at the very last.

At the very last, she, Diane, had failed her mother.

What would her mother have to say about all this?

Her mother would be horrified. Her mother had a thing about duty and she would never have deserted them. If it came to the worst, a divorce, then it might be Rupert who got custody of her children for he was without doubt the better parent, the carer, and if it got nasty ... she could not imagine it getting nasty but Rupert was a fighter where his kids were concerned. What if he refused her access? Would living with Leo ever make up for that? Would she regret doing it for the rest of her life? And yet if she did not spend the rest of her life with Leo, would she also regret that? Half of it was sex, of course. It had become predictable with Rupert, a routine, but with Leo it was all brand new and exciting. And yet, given time, would that, too, become routine?

Going onto the landing beside the bedroom, she found herself automatically straightening a picture on the wall. There were none of Rupert's paintings here but then Rupert did not like the idea of people feeling they had to have one of them just because he was related. This particular picture was a stinker, a hunting scene, fit only for the charity shop, but she straightened it anyway. Below the painting, there was a chest of drawers. The top drawer still stuck as it had for years and she tugged at it. When anybody lost anything in this house, they stuck it in this chest and, taking a quick look, she saw it was still full of lost property: old calculators, pencils, a pack of cards, a camera, some batteries and a few light bulbs.

The normality of this – for she had similar drawers at home – helped calm a sudden panic and she took a deep breath as she closed the drawer, trapping the lost things once again. She slid her hand over the polished top of the chest, thinking that Mrs Latham was certainly doing her job coming up to this neglected area of the house, when she stopped suddenly.

There was something missing.

Where were the three dolls?

Frances tried her best to sneak into the house but Diane waylaid her on the stairs.

'Frances . . . you're back. Come on through. We're having a cup of tea.'

Maggie was in the sitting room, a magazine on her lap, looking up as Frances came through.

'How did your day go?' she asked.

Frances sighed. She didn't want to go all through it, the trip to the hospital and everything. 'It was all right,' she said, sitting down and realizing how tired she was.

'Only all right?' Maggie gave her a sympathetic smile.

'Guess who we met in town?' Diane asked, doing something for once and pouring Frances a cup of tea. Her sisters had tried, Frances noted, getting out the best teapot and cups. 'Do you remember Mark Broughton?'

'Frances won't remember him,' Maggie said, shooting her an irritated glance. 'She was away at college when I knew Mark.'

'One of your old boyfriends?' Frances guessed. 'It can hardly be a surprise. A lot of people have stayed around here. That's what will happen now that you're back. You're bound to meet up with old friends. Whether you want to or not.'

'That's exactly what I told her,' Diane said. 'One of the penalties.'

'Not necessarily a penalty.' Maggie sat there, blushing. 'As a matter of fact, meeting him has set me thinking. I might go to the reunion after all. Just to catch up with people.'

'Huh.' Diane laughed. 'We know the real reason, don't we, Frances? She's intrigued as to what Mark is doing these days. You wouldn't be teaching one of his children, would you, by any chance?' she asked, flashing a mischievous smile Maggie's way.

Frances considered the question seriously. 'I don't teach anybody called Broughton but that's not to say he doesn't have children. Is he married?'

'We don't know. That's why she's going to the reunion. She wants to find out. If you ask me, he looked fairly interested in her.'

'Fairly?' Maggie huffed. 'Fairly isn't good enough. Will you stop it? I wish you'd stop making me out to be desperate, Diane. I'm not. I am curious, I admit, but it doesn't matter to me whether he's married or not.'

'Really.' Diane yawned. 'By the way, you won't have to put up with me much longer. I'm off home on Thursday.'

'Gracious me, that was a flying visit,' Frances said with a frown. 'Hardly worth your while.'

'I have a family, for God's sake,' Diane said. 'I'm not like you. And I have to get back to work. We aren't all in the lucky position of having six weeks bloody holiday.'

Frances sighed. 'You don't know the half of it, Diane. We might not earn as much as you do but we work just as hard.'

'You have no idea the hours I put in, have you? Yes, I do get paid a lot but my God they wring me dry.'

'I'd like to see you face a class of hard-faced thirteen-year-olds,' Frances said. 'And I do *not* have six weeks free time either. I have an awful lot to get through before term starts again. Lesson plans don't write themselves.'

'You two.' Maggie laughed.

'OK.' Diane gave a conciliatory shrug. 'Just teasing. I know how touchy you teachers are. You've still got six weeks holiday, though, whichever way you look at it. Are you going away anywhere?'

'As a matter of fact I am,' Frances said. Diane was not to know but she had just made the decision for her. 'I'm going on holiday with John – that's my boyfriend – and his children.' She was instantly sorry about the use of the word *boyfriend*; saw the amused looks her sisters exchanged.

'Oh. So it's serious, then?' Diane did not attempt to hide her surprise. 'I hope you know what you're doing. Taking on another man's family is not going to be easy. Is it, Maggie?'

'Don't drag me into it.' Maggie smiled at Frances. 'Go for it. If you love him then you'll get by.'

But was *getting by* good enough?

CHAPTER NINETEEN

H ARVEY grabbed Wendy directly she was through the door and told her he had called a meeting in his study for eleven o'clock.

'A meeting? With the girls?'

He nodded. 'I've got to tell them today. Diane's going home earlier than she thought and she has to know before she goes or she'll never forgive me.'

'Oh Harvey . . .' she knew it had to be done but she was dreading it.

'They'll have to know sooner or later,' he said with a little laugh.

'I know that but . . .' she bit her lip. 'But it will be such a shock for them. Daughters never think their fathers are . . . you know . . . capable of getting married again.'

'You're not pregnant,' he said with a grin. 'That would be more of a shock.'

She hid a smile. 'All right. I'll be there at eleven,' she said. 'Shall I bring some tea and biscuits in?'

He shook his head. 'No. We'll just get it over with.'

She knew he was more agitated than he was letting on but he was right. She just hoped they would be all right about it. She wasn't too worried about Frances and Maggie but she had an awful feeling about Diane.

Harvey seemed at a loose end, trailing after her as she opened the door of the cupboard where they kept the cleaning stuff.

'What the hell are you doing?'

'What do you think I'm doing?' She could talk to him like this, cheekily. 'I'm not sitting round doing nothing for the next hour. I can have the downstairs rooms done by then.'

He left her to it and she busied around although her mind was not on the job in hand. It would have to do for now, she thought, as the clock headed towards eleven.

She was back in the study with Harvey in good time, waiting for them to arrive. Frances had been out somewhere and they heard her car and hurried footsteps. Maggie and Diane had been in the sitting room, talking quietly together. She and Harvey exchanged a slightly worried smile and he reached for her hand, stilling a sudden trembling. He squeezed it as the door opened and they came through. Wendy knew that the holding of hands would tell them everything they needed to know without a word being said.

'Sit down, girls,' Harvey said. 'This is all very convenient, you all being here. Wendy and I have something to tell you.'

'So I see. . . .' Diane sat down in a great flurry of indignation, glaring at Wendy as she did so. Ignoring a warning look from her sisters, she carried on, her voice shrill. 'What the hell have you been up to?' she asked. 'Because if you think you can squirm your way into this family, Mrs Latham, you can think again.'

There was a moment's shocked silence as the awful words seemed to smash against the walls and reverberate, with Maggie and Frances frowning at their sister. Diane's face was flushed in spite of the cool toning-down powder she habitually wore. Wendy felt the pressure of Harvey's hand in hers, even as she fought to slip away.

'Shut up, Diane,' he said, his voice strong and firm. 'And have the decency to hear me out.'

Diane was rigid in her chair whilst Maggie and Frances seemed struck dumb, gazing, not at their father, but at Wendy.

'As you may have gathered,' Harvey continued, 'I've asked Wendy to marry me and happily she has agreed. My mind's made up and it doesn't matter what any of you think. However, I'd rather you were pleased for us.'

The silence shook and it was Diane who broke it with a brusque question, one that came out of the blue, completely unrelated to the matter in hand. Across the room, Wendy could sense the waves of animosity heading her way. She had known it. This was not going to be an easy ride.

'I'd like to know where the dolls have got to, Mrs Latham?' Diane said. 'I trust you know the ones I'm talking about. The pot dolls that sit on the chest on the upper landing. There are three of them and they are rather special.'

Wendy knew that. It had been hate at first sight. They made her skin crawl. Horrible things, they were, with eyes that followed you round. Pale pot heads, weird hair and crushed linen clothes. However, she was always careful with them, terrified of breaking them, for they were on the list of valuables Frances had mentioned.

Beside her, she heard Harvey's sharp intake of breath. She shushed him with a little shake of her head. She opted for a calm reply, looking directly at Diane. 'I don't do that landing every week,' she said. 'But they were certainly there last time I did it. Frances was saying something about putting them up in the loft . . .' she glanced at Frances. 'For safe-keeping.'

'As a matter . . .' Frances was wriggling in her chair. 'I—'

'That's quite enough, Wendy,' Harvey said, interrupting Frances by holding up his hand. 'There's no need for you to make excuses. And I'm surprised at you, Diane, for having the effrontery to suggest that Wendy might have taken them. I can't believe that's what you're saying.'

'It's exactly what I'm saying,' Diane said crisply. 'It's happened to me before. Things have gone missing in mysterious circumstances. Staff today are notoriously unreliable.'

'Apologize for that remark.' Harvey's voice was not raised. 'Apologize right now, Diane Troon.'

'Buckman.' She had now gone pale, lips pursed, eyes stingingly angry.

'Buckman, then. Apologize.'

Wendy glanced at him anxiously. It was sweet of him to defend her honour but she really didn't need him to do that. She could look after herself, thank you, and she could certainly deal with Diane. It would give her a certain satisfaction to do it at that. She needed taking down a peg or two.

'Diane.' Maggie frowned at her sister. 'For goodness sake. . . .'

'If the dolls are found, then I will apologize but not before,' Diane said. 'And stop treating me like a little girl, Dad.'

'Why shouldn't I? You're behaving like one.' Harvey said, and as Wendy saw a throbbing vein in his neck, she worried for him. He ought not to be upset like this and it was enough to make her round on Diane.

She shook his hand away. She could do this herself but she had to hold onto her temper. Harvey had yet to see her with her temper roused and she didn't want it to be yet. 'I don't care whether you apologize to me or not,' she said, as icy now as Diane. For the first time, with Harvey at her side, she felt the power of her new position in this household. 'But I think you should apologize to your father, young lady.'

'Young lady?' Diane laughed. 'You're not a member of this family yet, Mrs Latham, and I wouldn't count your chickens if I were you.'

'Diane. . . !' Harvey exploded, half rising to his feet until Wendy pulled him back down into his chair.

'Gracious me, what a fuss. Would you all stop it? I know where the dolls are,' Frances said. 'If you'd thought to ask me first, Diane, before you jumped in with both feet, I'd have told you that I have given them to John's daughters.'

'You've done what?' Diane spun round to face her. 'How dare you? They're not toys, for God's sake.'

Maggie giggled, putting her hand over her mouth to quell it as she caught Diane's furious glance.

'I should think that's exactly what they are,' Frances said, standing her ground for once. 'You said you didn't want Alice to have them, otherwise I wouldn't have given them away.'

'Given them away? Are you mad? They are worth a few thousand pounds,' Diane said. 'They're an investment.'

'Don't be so mercenary.' Harvey's voice was ice cold. 'You of all people should know better.'

'In any case, they weren't hers to give away,' Diane continued, sulky now. 'Mummy left them to me.'

'She left you one each,' Harvey said. 'Grow up. I'm glad they've found a good home. What was the point of them sitting on top of a chest giving everybody the willies?'

Maggie gave an uncertain laugh. 'Dad's quite right. They are awful things. If the little girls like them then we should be glad to see the back of them.'

Diane's face was a picture but an apology did not seem to be on the cards and Wendy was not going to insist on one when it was perfectly obvious to them all that Diane had made a mistake. She had flushed again, deeply and uncomfortably, almost to the roots of her hair.

'Look.' Wendy smiled round at them, determined to defuse the situation. Diane had got herself into a state and she wondered how on earth she coped with big business if she got herself into such a ridiculous tizzy about something as unimportant as this. 'Let's all calm down. We've got off to a bit of a bad start, haven't we? But that doesn't mean we can't sort this little misunderstanding out. You're distraught, Diane, with one thing and another and you must be missing your family.'

'I don't know why you bothered to come,' Harvey broke in. 'You've been nothing but trouble ever since you got here. You're touchy as hell and, if you were supposed to be making me feel better, you haven't bloody succeeded. All this damned fuss. . . .'

'Ssh, Harvey. Your father and I. . . .' Wendy looked at them each in turn. 'We are to be married come what may,' she said firmly, realizing now how much she wanted it to happen. All those cold, calculated reasons could go by the board and she might just as well listen to her own heart. It had not been wrong about Tom and it wasn't wrong now. Instinct. Trust it. 'And, as your father says, we want you to be happy for us. Please.'

It was Maggie who made the first move, coming across and giving them both a hug and whispered congratulations. Then it was

Frances's turn, although she felt stiff as a poker, still calling her Mrs Latham when Maggie had smilingly called her Wendy.

That only left Diane.

'Well. . . .' She looked at Diane. This would not be easy and she suspected they would never forget this, that they would never quite be friends but maybe they could go some way towards it eventually. It would help when she met Diane's children. They might be the key.

'Sorry . . . it was an easy mistake. I wasn't to know Frances had taken leave of her senses.'

It was an apology of sorts, wrung out of her but Wendy stilled Harvey's protest with a small smile. The girl was upset. They had to make allowances.

'Diane.' She held out her arms, willing her to come over. Holding Diane briefly in an embrace, Wendy could feel the misery there. Poor child. She had no experience of babies but she guessed how traumatic it had been for her, losing this last one. She was grieving and nobody realized.

'Everything will be all right,' she found herself saying, patting her on the back in an effort to console.

Diane looked at her; tried a brave smile.

'I'm afraid it won't be,' she said.

CHAPTER TWENTY

Harvey had taken Wendy home, Frances had disappeared and Maggie and Diane were sitting in the garden, under the oak tree. Maggie had made them cool drinks and she handed one to Diane now, the ice rattling against the tall glass. It was too pleasant a day to be angry and upset and she hoped that sitting out here in the sun might go some way to soaking up Diane's bitterness. But first, there was something to be said. Diane couldn't get away with behaving like this.

'Don't you ever think before you speak?' Maggie gave her a pained look. 'You made an exhibition of yourself. All that ranting and raving. Accusing her of stealing the dolls? Poor Wendy. I felt quite sorry for her. I thought, under the circumstances, she behaved remarkably well.'

Diane shrugged. 'Don't go on about it. I admit I made a mistake. I apologized. OK. But at the time 1 believed it to be the truth and I wasn't going to shirk saying it. I don't believe in holding back.'

'Obviously. Are you like this at the office? Going in with a machine-gun?'

'No. I'm sure of my facts there,' she said, smiling ruefully. 'Sorry again. I did go at it, didn't I? Oh hell. Once I get started, I can't stop myself and I know I said some awful things. I'm cringing now. I wouldn't have said it if Rupert had been there. He keeps me in check. I don't think she's the sort to hold a grudge, do you, otherwise we'll be banned for evermore. I see her as a kindly soul. Simple but kind.'

'There you go again. I think you're being unfair. She's a bright woman. Lots of women clean for a living. Stop being such a snob.'

'It's not that. Well, maybe it is.'

'There's more to Wendy than you think. She's very keen on quilting.'

'Really?' Diane was singularly unimpressed.

'If she makes Dad happy then that's all that matters.' Maggie glanced round, at the calmness of the garden. She loved it here and she dreaded the time when they would sell it. With a bit of luck, Dad and Wendy would keep it going for a while yet. She hoped it would be long enough for her to bring her own children here. First, of course, there was the small matter of finding a suitable man to father them.

'You might be a lady of leisure, Maggie, but I can't sit around much longer. I've got to get home,' Diane said, glancing at her watch. 'I'm going as soon as I'm packed. I've decided I need to talk to Leo before I do anything else.'

'Look, Diane . . . I've got something to tell you.' Maggie saw the sudden flare-up in her sister's eyes. 'Rupert contacted me.'

'When?'

'Does it matter? Shirley had been in touch with him to tell him what was happening.'

'What *is* happening? I hope you didn't say anything. You promised, Maggie.'

'No. He knew already. At least . . .' Quickly she related what Rupert had said, how she had persuaded him not to have it out with Candida.

'Thank God for that.' Diane bit her lip. 'Talking to you has cleared my mind a bit.'

'I can't think why.'

Diane stretched out her bare suntanned legs, red wedge sandals dangling from her feet. 'I've been giving this serious thought and I think Leo and I shall probably sit it out, deny everything if necessary. After all, what proof does she have? It's all hearsay. How could she know? I've told you, we were very discreet.'

173

'Discreet or not, there's always the risk of it coming out. Wasn't that part of the thrill for you both?' Maggie asked, feeling almost nauseous at the callous way her sister had gone about things. She wasn't a prude, goodness knows, but the sordid aspect of all this kept coming back to her. For all sorts of reasons, she had never had an affair with a married man.

'Haven't you ever been tempted by a man at the office?' Diane asked, seeming to read her mind. 'Come on, admit it.'

'No . . . well, yes, I suppose so. But I have more sense than you.'

Diane eased herself up, slipped her shoes on. 'Let me know how things go with Dad and Frances. And, I suppose, on the bright side, now that he's got dear Mrs Latham to look after his every need, he really doesn't need us any longer. But I hope he's not going to go the whole hog, cut us out of the equation and leave her everything in his will.'

'I couldn't give a toss if he does. That's never crossed my mind. It's all about money and possessions with you, isn't it?' Maggie said. If Diane was like this at work, she could understand why Candida wanted rid of her. She might even do the same if she was in Candida's shoes. 'What's wrong with you? Where's your compassion gone these days?'

'You have your head in the sand,' Diane said coolly. 'You see the romance in the situation when it's very likely calculated. I bet she had her eye on him from the word go. It happens all the time. Young woman meets elderly frail man, flatters him, marries him and bags the lot.'

'That's not true. Wendy's not exactly young and I wouldn't call Dad old and frail either. You've seen them together. She obviously thinks the world of him and he adores her. He didn't even look at Mum like that.'

'But he's had a stroke or as near as and he could have another and next time he might not be so lucky. The will could be up for grabs then.'

'Diane! Can you hear yourself? What's the matter with you? You don't need the money.'

'It's the bloody injustice.'

Maggie sighed, weary of it all. For two pins she could hit her. 'Get yourself home,' she said. 'And sort yourself out and do be careful. I don't want to hear that you and Rupert are splitting up.'

Diane paused, pulling at the belt on her dress, having the grace to look suddenly ashamed. Her eyes were bright, too, and she gave a little shudder as she fought for control. 'I'm sorry, Maggie. I've been an absolute bitch these last few days, haven't I? This is not me. I'm not as bad as this. It's only because I'm scared shitless. That's why. I always turn aggressive when I'm frightened and I can't think straight just now.'

'Do be careful driving back,' Maggie said, worried for her. 'It's a long journey and you had that fright on the way here.'

'I will be careful.'

Awkwardly, they embraced, Maggie patting Diane's back as she had done when she was little. Whenever she fell over, Diane used to make the most enormous fuss and it was often Maggie she ran to.

'Say goodbye to Dad for me and good luck,' Diane said, putting a finger to her lips. 'I want to make a quick getaway before they realize. I'll let you know what happens.'

And with that, she was gone.

Polly's aunt was dead.

Polly asked Frances to accompany her to the funeral. It would be a slim turn-out and Frances was happy to oblige, recognizing that, although the event had been anticipated, Polly was still upset by it.

Afterwards, with the other few guests despatched, she and Polly had a meal together in a nearby pub. Polly's eyes were still red-rimmed, threatening yet more tears. 'Honestly, this is awful,' she said, dabbing at them with a tissue. 'I never thought I was the sort to go to pieces but she was such a lovely lady. She ought to have been a wife, a mother, had a big family, but she never married. She lost the love of her life during the war and she once told me that no other man could compete with him. Isn't that so romantic? And so pointless.'

'What will you do now?' Frances asked. 'Will you move to France?'

'It's early days,' Polly said. 'I was the sole beneficiary of her will but somehow that's not important any more. It's funny – you can have a dream for a long time when there's no real chance of it happening and then, when it can happen, it no longer seems such a good idea.'

'You're too young to retire. You'd have to start a new career.'

'I could do that. The trouble is I don't know what.'

Frances found herself wishing that Polly would stay around. She found her a sympathetic listener, somebody she would be able to turn to for whatever reason, somebody who understood her. She had been a bit short on friends like Polly over the years, proper friends. She would have Maggie around from now on, too, but there were some things you could talk to a friend about and not necessarily a sister, a baby sister at that.

She told Polly about her father and Mrs Latham.

'Good for him,' Polly said. 'I like your father and I did think he had a rakish look about him. Getting married again, eh? What did I tell you? I like the sound of Mrs Latham.'

'It's a bit difficult for all of us coming to terms with it,' Frances said. 'She was an excellent cleaner but I suppose I never thought of her as anything other than that. I'm worried now that I was a bit short with her sometimes. Needless to say, my mother would not have liked her.'

'But she's not here any more, is she? And you wouldn't have wanted him to marry a copy-cat of your mother, would you? I think it's healthier this way. At least he's not marrying Mrs Latham because she reminds him of your mother.'

'I suppose I'll have to think about moving out. I can't see myself living in a house with newlyweds.'

They exchanged a small smile. 'So, will you be moving in with John?'

'He hasn't asked yet.'

'That's not what I said.' Polly picked up the dessert menu. 'Shall we go the whole hog and order a pudding? Aunt Jenny was a great one for puddings. We can toast her over a sticky toffee one.'

They were onto coffee and mints and the mood had lightened

considerably before Polly brought up the thorny subject of John again. 'Don't get drawn into it simply because it happens to be convenient at the moment,' she warned. 'That's no reason. You must think it through very carefully, Frances. If the children are going to be too much for you then you must break it off now. Children like that, kids from a broken relationship, are especially vulnerable. They must not be hurt twice.'

'I do know that.'

'Good.' Polly did not look particularly confident but moved on. 'Did your sister forgive you for giving away her dolls?' she said, for Frances had blurted out the whole sorry tale. 'My God, that was a mistake.'

'They weren't *her* dolls, we had one each.'

Polly smiled but said nothing.

'I don't know if she will ever forgive me but I don't much care. It was a disaster from start to finish. I don't know why she bothered to visit. She's very uptight just now. I was only trying to do something for John's children and they do like them. They're very proud of them. None of us ever liked them but they do. So Diane will have to learn to live with it.'

'I hope you don't mind me saying but that sister of yours sounds a bitch,' Polly said. 'Never mind all the excuses. I know lots of women in her position with a fantastic job and a big family and not only do they manage to cope, they also manage to be very pleasant people. There's no excuse for her at all.'

'She can't help it. It's just the way she is,' Frances said. She was uncomfortable with Polly's observations, true or not. When she got home, she had to concede that the atmosphere was more relaxed now that Diane was gone. There was always a circle of panic round Diane and whatever it was that was bothering her, and she was sure it was something other than the recent miscarriage, she was not in the mood for telling Frances.

She had told Maggie, however, and that hurt.

CHAPTER TWENTY-ONE

T HE journey back from the north remained a complete mystery. How she had ever got back when she had no memory of the actual trip was very worrying. Her mind had been in such turmoil but what kept bobbing to the surface, refusing to go away, was that what she wanted more than anything was to be with Leo. Never mind that what she was planning to do would alienate just about everybody except Leo, she was still prepared to do it. She loved him so very much. Spending the rest of her life resenting the children and Rupert for keeping her away from him was no longer an option. Rupert would get over it. The children would scarcely notice. Frankly, they might be better off without her. One day they might understand and this way, a clean break, was surely better than suffering a childhood of simmering long-term maternal resentment.

These last few days had been just what she needed to work things out, although with so much on her mind, her judgement had been clouded and she wished now she had thought twice before she had put her foot in it with the Wendy fracas. It would, she knew, never be forgotten.

Together, she and Leo could wriggle out of this potential time-bomb of a situation at the office. She and Leo were a formidable combination and they could easily silence Candida. Taking out a contract on her would be by far the best option but since that was clearly a crazy notion, they would have to resort to more subtle means. She and Leo had talked about setting up their own company

A PERFECT MOTHER

in the States, on the west coast somewhere far away from Dorcas, but it would be better if they did that without the stigma of being sacked from their present occupations, for that sort of thing had a habit of surfacing in the corporate world. It was essential that they exited with grace and dignity. Any hint of a seedy connection and it could all backfire on them.

To her chagrin, only underlining her guilt, Rupert was delighted to see her back, fussing over her, taking her bags, insisting she sat down and took the weight off her feet. Over a cup of coffee, she reported on the current state of affairs at Park House; her father's ridiculous affair with the cleaner, Maggie wallowing in some sort of nostalgic dream and Frances in grave danger of taking on a ready-made family.

'She'll be fine,' Rupert said. 'Not many women could hang a sign round their neck saying "perfect mother" could they?'

'I certainly couldn't.'

'The kids are fine,' he said and she realized, with a pang, she hadn't asked about them.

'Apart from them, what's been happening this end?' she asked.

'Not much.'

So she wasn't to be told yet about Candida and the rumours. It suited her not to talk about it just now. She needed to talk to Shirley and Leo. She wanted to talk to him right now, hear the delight in his voice when she told him of her decision.

The fall-out would be immense but they had to stand firm. Once it was done, a blissful, happy, successful future loomed.

'Oh. We didn't expect you back so soon,' Candida looked up from the filing cabinet in Diane's office. What the hell was Candida doing in *her* office? 'I have a meeting shortly with Piers. Have you sorted your domestic problem out?'

'Yes.' Diane threw down her bag. 'Where's Shirley?'

'Now there's the thing.' Candida smiled, her blue eyes wide and innocent. She was wearing a cream fitted suit with a short skirt, totally impractical and utterly beautiful. For once, Diane felt frumpy in her navy one. 'It wasn't my idea but the general consensus was that we needed a switch round with the girls. Stagnating a bit, don't you think? And James's secretary is on maternity leave so Shirley's gone over to help him out rather than have him stuck with a temp. We've got Louise on board at this end now. Once we reached the decision, there was no point in hanging about.'

'We'll see about that,' Diane said, so taken aback that she could scarcely think straight. God, she'd only been gone a few days and already the knives were out, the first person to be stabbed in the back obviously Shirley. Pathetic or not, she felt she could not function properly without Shirley. They held each other's hand and had stood shoulder to shoulder for years. They were a bloody good team and Shirley was one of Alice's godmothers, for heaven's sake. She was a friend now as well as a work colleague. 'Take a seat that side of the desk, Candida. We need to talk.'

'You'll have to be quick. Piers doesn't like to be kept waiting.' She glanced at her watch, a chunky masculine one that sat oddly on her very slender wrist. 'What can I do for you, Diane?'

'You can tell me why you're rummaging about in *my* office for a start?'

'Collecting some files,' Candida replied coolly. 'Life has to go on even when you're not here.'

'My God, you've been quick off the mark.' Diane drummed irritated fingers on her desk.

'As I said, we were under the impression that you were taking at least a week off.'

Diane let that pass. 'What's this I hear about some silly rumours that you've been putting about?'

'Rumours? I can't think what you're talking about.'

'Don't pretend. You can stop telling porky pies right now and put Harry straight. Have the rumours about me and Leo reached him yet?' Diane stopped the finger drumming in an attempt to appear more relaxed. 'And another thing – how dare you heap the blame on me for the mess *you* landed us in with the Janey account?'

'Porky pies?' Candida seemed worryingly cool. 'You can tell you have children. As to the rumours about you and Leo, I honestly do not know what you are talking about.' Her hair, damn her to hell, seemed extra long and gorgeous today, her lip gloss extra shiny, her eyes extra sparkly. 'However, on the work front, I must say, Diane, I can't believe you've got away with it for so long. I'm not taking *any* responsibility for the Janey account. That's your baby and just one example of slipshod work and, when it came to a head, I felt it was my duty to inform Piers of the shortcomings. It's up to him if he takes it any further. We're not a charitable organization, for Christ's sake. It's for the good of the company and that, I'm afraid, has to take precedence over my personal feelings. Believe me, it's not personal. I like you.'

Diane gave a short, disbelieving laugh. 'Really?'

'Yes. In fact, I'll go so far as to say that I admire the way you cope with work and all those children of yours. But it has to be said that sometimes it must be hard for you to know where your priorities lie. I, on the other hand, am fully committed to the job.' Her eyes were keen, triumphant. 'I intend to remain single and do not intend to lumber myself with children. Piers is not unsympathetic. He understands your problems as a working mother but at the end of the day. . . .'

'Stop right there.' Diane had been mesmerized for a moment, watching Candida spouting forth, barely taking it in. 'What shortcomings?' she asked, wondering why it was taking so long to drag her mind back into work-mode.

'This business with the Janey account,' Candida began gently. 'I know they've been our clients for a million years but we can't afford to be complacent. We've got into a hell of a mess with the latest sponsorship deal, missing deadlines and so on, and I've had to bend over backwards to get it sorted. Did you oversee the presentation we made?' she carried on smoothly, as Diane struggled to remember it. 'Obviously not, because, if you had bothered to check, you would have seen that Chris was about to make an unholy mess of it. Our team were amateurish and the rival company was polished and on the ball. Creatively, they beat us hands down. There's no loyalty these days, Diane, and it was necessary to arrange a personal meeting with

Joe Campbell to try and smooth things over, get him to give us another chance, remind him of our past strengths.'

'He's *my* client!' Diane exploded. 'How dare you call a meeting with my client without my knowing?'

'I'm sorry but he had made a complaint about you,' Candida continued, her voice still irritatingly gentle, making Diane, with her raised tones, sound like a fishwife. 'And Piers authorized me to deal with it. It took a lot of persuasion for Joe to drop his complaint. He felt you had been a bit gung-ho, Diane, in your dealings with his juniors and that you were guilty of not briefing them properly. You kept people waiting. You were guilty, I'm afraid, of a lot of palming off and he's not the sort of man to be palmed off. If we had lost this account, Harry would have gone berserk. Anyway . . .' she flicked at her hair, moistened her red lips with her tongue. 'I had dinner with him and—'

'Harry?'

'Joe Campbell.'

'You slept with him?' Diane asked icily.

'No,' she said, equally cold now. 'I most certainly did not. What do you take me for? I am not in the habit of mixing business with pleasure. That is a very dangerous thing to do, as you well know.'

'OK. I accept that there may have been a few hiccups recently but that's because I've been snowed under. I regret that and I will see it does not happen again. I will have words with Chris for a start. It's time he stood on his own two feet and accepted some responsibility. I will follow the complaint through personally and thank you for bringing it to my attention,' she said magnanimously. 'However, my private life is my own concern,' she went on, aware of her frail position, knowing the only way out was to attack. 'I object to you spreading ridiculous rumours about me and Leo. I await your apology,' she finished grandly, feeling her heart thud as she caught the look in Candida's eyes.

There was no apology, merely a bemused look followed by a toss of the glorious hair, and she was gone.

*

Shirley, in an agitated state, caught up with her outside the office, apologizing for something that was not her fault.

'It's all right, Shirley,' Diane said with an attempt at a smile. 'Everything will be fine.'

'There's a letter for you.' Shirley glanced round conspiratorially and passed the white envelope to her. 'It's from Leo. He said to make sure you got it personally.'

'Thank you.' She slipped it into her bag. She was summoned to see Piers in twenty minutes and, as Candida said, he hated to be kept waiting. Once Shirley was gone, she went up to Piers's floor, stepping into the Ladies first to refresh her make-up. Unable to wait a minute longer, she read Leo's letter in private, sitting on the loo.

She sat in Piers's office in a dazed state, Leo's words bouncing about in her head. 'Dear Diane', it began – not my dearest, my darling, my lovely . . . all the things he had once called her. It was typewritten at that, *typewritten*, as if anything more was needed to outline the formality of it.

It would seem that Leo was returning to the States permanently and would not be seeing her again in the foreseeable future. As to the rumours he had heard . . . well, he was denying them vehemently and trusted she would do the same. How do these things get started? He then had the cheek to finish the letter by adding the words 'your trusted friend and colleague, Leo'. His flamboyant signature, 'Leo', filled the rest of the page.

It was a carefully worded letter. Perfectly innocent, nothing incriminating. He couldn't have made a better job of it if he had drafted it with the aid of a lawyer. There was no mention of the time they had spent together, the wonderful times when they had toasted each other with champagne, wallowing in each other and in their dangerous liaison.

'. . . and your persistent maternity leaves.'

'What? What did you say?' She looked across the desk at Piers. Through the window behind his desk, the city sprawled in a heat haze, visibility not good, and with the air-conditioning set high, it felt suddenly cool and she shivered in her linen suit and camisole top. She found herself looking at her hands, trying to keep them steady, her rings, the ones Rupert had given her, very firmly on her finger. Leo had promised her a diamond the size of a pea but it had never materialized and now never would.

'I sympathize, Diane, I really do, for after all I am a father too but *my* wife stays at home and looks after the children.'

'I am fully entitled to maternity leave and it's not as if I take advantage of it. Some of the men in my department have had more time off with a head cold,' she finished, seeing his eyes flash with annoyance because it was not far from the truth. 'Be careful what you say.'

'We've felt for some time that you were in danger of losing it,' he went on as, mesmerized by him as she had been by Candida, she found herself looking at his mouth as he spoke. She wondered about his wife, who seemed such a normal soul, rather nice if a little cowed. She had never noticed before how blubbery Piers's lips were. It must be like kissing a fish, holding a snake. There was something reptilian about Piers. And he was still talking, weighing his words as if this was carefully rehearsed as it undoubtedly was. 'As to the personal rumours that are circulating, well . . . I take those with a pinch of salt. Leo is an honourable man and he assures me they are false so this decision has nothing whatsoever to do with them.'

'Lies!' she said, stung into action.

'Be that as it may.' He glanced at her and she shut up. 'We would respectfully ask that you take a leave of absence for a while to sort things out. Sick leave. After all, you never took time off after your unfortunate . . . er, miscarriage. After six months or so, you will be welcomed back with open arms. Candida will take over for the moment and when you return we'll find something very exciting for you. Full pay, of course. We'll call it a sabbatical. You've earned it, Diane. You've put in lots of extra hours over the years and never taken your full holiday quota. Take some time off now. Enjoy the kids.'

'Like hell, Piers,' she said. 'Sabbatical, my arse.'

'Really, Diane.' He pulled a face. 'Let's not be childish about this.'

'You'll have my letter of resignation tomorrow.'

'There's no need to be hasty,' Piers said, although she could feel the waves of relief from across the desk. She had walked right into the trap, she now realized, but at the moment she could not care less. Candida could have the job. The only person she felt remotely sorry for was Shirley, who would be lost without her.

'As to Shirley . . .' she tried a smile, hoping to appeal to his better nature, if he had one, that was. 'I want you to give me your word that you will take care of her.'

'Will do,' he said shortly, already dismissing her. Job done, presumably. 'We'll be very generous to you, Diane. You've been a loyal employee for many years. We shall miss you.'

'For heaven's sake, I don't have to listen to this crap,' she said.

He looked pained but manfully carried on. 'We appreciate your efforts in the past to secure us clients and we are sorry that it's ended like this. You'll have our letter of recommendation as soon as we process your resignation.'

Dazed, she gathered her personal belongings from her desk, mercifully not meeting anybody on the way out, especially not Candida, which was just as well because the way she was feeling she could have cheerfully cut her throat. Mind you, she did have a sneaking admiration for the naked ambition that had driven her to it. The girl would go far.

Deep down, she knew the truth, the truth being that she had known all along that she was putting her job on the line by dallying with Leo. She had chosen to play a very dangerous game and she was a fool to think that he had ever loved her. She might have known he would drop her like a ton of bricks if the going got tough and to think she had even considered leaving Rupert and the children for a rat like him.

There was nowhere to go to have a cry and she desperately wanted to cry. How could he do that to her? Had she really read it all wrong? He had said he loved her and she had believed him.

She was not yet ready to return home. She had a letter of resignation to pen but she ought to have discussed it with Rupert first.

Principles were all very well but they did not put bread on the table. The last thing she wanted was to be forced to go crawling back to Piers, apologizing, begging for her job back. She would rather cut her fingers off, one by one.

Armed with some totally unnecessary purchases and some sweets for the kids – what the hell! – she went home eventually for there was a limit as to how long she could spend drinking a latte in a café.

Nearing the house, she dreaded breaking the news to Rupert but it would have to be done.

CHAPTER TWENTY-TWO

GOING to a school reunion was a seriously crass idea, Maggie decided, as she drove herself there. It was so much better to let the past go, to move on, and she was worried now that she might stir up a hornets' nest if Trisha was there with Mark, married to him at that. They, she and Trisha, had been on non-speaking terms at the last, passionately disliking each other as only fired-up teenagers can do.

So, what the hell was she thinking of in turning up tonight? After much soul-searching, her curiosity had got the better of her and she had rung the number Mark had given her, spoken to an excitable woman whose name she vaguely remembered, and she was to collect a ticket from the hotel reception desk.

Tonight, she felt about seventeen again, felt that same ridiculous excitement as she had when she *was* seventeen and getting herself ready for a date with Mark. She was even getting herself ready in the same bedroom, sitting at the same dressing table. Some things had changed. Frances must have persuaded Father to spend some money on a new carpet recently but the room was essentially the same all these years on. Things sat in the same place out of necessity, the bed, the wardrobe and the dressing table that was covered now with her belongings.

Part of her was still seventeen but . . . she considered herself carefully in the mirror. She could not get away from the fact that she was eighteen years older. She wished she could say wiser, too, but she wasn't so sure about that.

She and Mark Broughton had dated for a while when they were in the upper sixth, nothing very serious but, just for that important short time, they were regarded by all and sundry, all the people who mattered to them, as a couple. He had come along to Park House a few times but always as part of the crowd, although her mother had liked him and spotted him out as a potential suitor. She had then proceeded to quiz Maggie on him and he passed the mother test with flying colours because he was from a family she approved of *and* he was going to study law.

'Mum, we're just friends,' she had explained hastily, looking at Diane for support. 'Don't you dare say anything to his mother.'

Diane laughed at that and even her father joined in.

'Leave the child alone,' he said in that amiable and not very assertive manner of his.

She wasn't so sure about the *child* bit. She was seventeen, she thought indignantly, and a woman. In the event, there was no need for her to worry about her mother striking up a friendship with his because, shortly after that, it all came to nothing. Her mistake, if you could call it that, was to refuse to have sex with him and he had promptly gone off with Trisha, a girl who presumably had no such inhibitions. What kind of man did that? Had he just been after her body?

'What happened there?' her mother had asked accusingly. She was not about to confide in her mother but Diane dug it out of her and, for a short time, it was the best time for the two of *them*, with Diane and only Diane offering any sympathy.

His rejection of her had hurt, though, for all sorts of reasons and she still remembered having to steel herself to go into school next day and pretend nothing had happened. She was a fool to harbour any feelings for him still but she had grown up and so had he and things had changed. A boy of seventeen could be excused for acting the way he had, something about peer pressure. She would forgive him. She had liked the way he smiled at her the other day, had felt triumphant that there was a glimmer of interest there. She could still do it.

She was going to look stupid if he turned out to be married to Trisha and a dad. Why had she not asked? She could just have politely enquired without it sounding as if she cared.

Did she care? Or was she just in love with the romantic notion of what might have been? Seeing him again had given her a jolt, shooting her back to the past. What was it about first loves? Romantic they might be but they weren't all they were cracked up to be and that's why they hardly ever worked out in the long run.

Here was the hotel and it was time to sort this out. She backed into a space, waiting a few minutes to compose herself. A few people were going in, none of whom she recognized, and suddenly she felt shy. She had two options. She either went in or drove away.

She was wearing a new red dress and now wished she wasn't because, as in the way of red dresses, you wore it for one reason only, to stand out from the crowd. Diane had helped her choose it the other day, complaining bitterly about the lack of decent shops but managing to find a treasure of a boutique in a hidden side street. The dress was expensive but Diane had insisted she have it, offering to buy it for her. That was Diane. She could be so awkward and downright rude to others but she was still capable of being terrifically generous. Even though it would hit her credit card hard, Maggie had refused the offer, remembering Diane's grumble about her *commitments*. Now, she was having second thoughts about the dress, a silky wraparound, worrying that it was too good for the occasion.

Predictably, most of the women going in were wearing black.

Come on . . . she stepped out; steeled herself.

Clutching her ticket, feeling like a little girl again, she ventured into the bar where the reunion guests were gathering prior to going into the dining-room. To her horror she did not know a soul. Who were these people? Was she at the right reunion? There were a few glances her way, a few smiles, but they were the smiles of strangers.

Glancing round anxiously, she scanned the faces, increasingly desperate, and it was with great relief that she finally spotted somebody she recognized, a guy whose name she instantly recalled: Simon Newell. Round and over the heads of others, they exchanged a glance of recognition and then he made a beeline for her.

'Well, well, if it isn't Maggie Troon?'

'Hello, Simon,' she said, not sure whether he was going to kiss her on the cheek or not. In the event, he just stretched out his hand and she was grateful for that. He had a firm handshake and looked at her directly, which was nice.

'I haven't seen you at one of these dos before,' he said with a smile. His eyes were very nearly on a level with hers but that could be the spanking heels on the shoes she had borrowed from Diane. Comfortingly, Simon looked much the same, still had the same sticking-out ears that had earned him a predictable nickname. To be honest, he had never made much of an impact on her, a quiet scholarly type, with four older sisters, she seemed to recall. 'Contact lenses,' he said, pointing towards his eyes. 'In case you were wondering. . . .'

'Oh. No, not really.' She smiled back, realizing that there had in fact been something missing.

'I hope it's not because I'm vain,' he said worriedly. 'But I do a lot of outdoorsy stuff and glasses are just not practical. Anyway . . .' he seemed a little awkward and she remembered he had been shy, too, a shyness he had endearingly not quite grown out of. 'It's great to see you. What brings you up here? Visiting your parents?'

'My father,' she said. 'Mum died some years ago.'

'Oh, sorry. You lose track.'

'I'm moving back to the area,' she said, finding herself suddenly close to him as somebody jostled her. She couldn't put a name to his aftershave but he smelt clean, as if he had just stepped out of the shower. 'Dad's not been well and it's time I helped my sister Frances out a little. But that's not the only reason,' she said, glad to see that he was listening intently. 'I suppose I was just ready to come back. I miss it.'

'I know the feeling. I was away for a while but something about home draws you back, doesn't it? We, all of us, live within a twenty-mile radius now. My sisters are all married and I'm an uncle ten times over. Uncle Simon,' he added earnestly and unnecessarily so that she found herself smiling.

'I've got nephews and a niece, too,' she said.

'How did you hear about this?'

'I bumped into Mark Broughton in town and he mentioned it.'

'Oh yes, Mark usually comes along. He's done well for himself.'

'Has he?' She was just about to interrogate him further when she thought better of it. Simon seemed so pleased to see her that it seemed not quite right to be showing interest in another man.

This could be embarrassing, she thought, as he shouldered his way to the bar to get their drinks. She could hardly dump this poor man when Mark arrived and she didn't know what was happening with the seating plan, if indeed there was one. Looking round, her mood settling, she did now recognize one or two people but they either didn't recognize her or weren't bothered enough to come across. She had an uneasy feeling that, if Diane had come along, she would have attracted a little admiring crowd by now.

Miraculously, they found a quiet corner to have their drink. Simon was conservatively dressed, wearing a grey suit with a pale blue shirt and dark tie. To her amusement, she found herself doing a Diane and glancing at his shoes, which were black leather. They looked OK to her.

'I often wondered what had happened to you, Maggie,' Simon said, watching her closely as she sipped her glass of white wine. 'You were in my history group.'

'That's right,' she said. 'You went on to do history at university, didn't you?'

He nodded, offering no further information. 'I asked after you last year. Somebody said you lived in London and did something glamorous in the city.'

'That's my sister Diane. You remember Diane? She was in the year below us.'

'Redhead?'

She nodded. 'She's the mother of my nephews and niece,' she said. 'People are always mixing us up. I can't think why. We don't look much alike.'

'You're prettier,' he said with a little smile.

'I work for a charity,' she told him, surprised and pleased about the 'you're prettier'. 'I enjoy it although I wish it paid more. I'm going to struggle to buy a house even here. I shall probably rent for a while.'

'I'm just thinking about buying myself. It's a four-bedroom on a new estate. Planning for the future,' he added.

'Good for you,' she said, hoping they weren't going to get into a very grown-up discussion about mortgage rates and so on. 'Are you married? Sorry. It's as well to get things straight, isn't it? I'm not.'

'Nor am I. Still on the look-out,' he said. 'My mother and my sisters despair. They've had the hats ready for years.'

'I split up with my boyfriend recently so I'm not in the market at the moment for anything else,' she said, needing to make things absolutely clear. 'Unless . . .' she looked away, willing Mark Broughton to appear.

'Expecting someone?' Simon asked, casually enough, but she caught the slightest of disappointments in his face. Unlike Dave, this man showed his emotions. She would know exactly where she stood with this man. 'There's a list on the wall over there of the people expected to be here. Do you want me to check it for you? Everybody's listed by year. Somebody in our year, I take it? Or is it Mark? Had you arranged to meet him?' he paused. 'He married Trisha, you know?'

'Did he?' Something sizzled inside.

'They separated a couple of years ago,' he went on, twirling his glass, trying to look nonchalant. 'It's OK, Maggie, don't think I'm trying to monopolize you. If you want to shoot off, that's fine by me. Oh, talk of the devil, there he is, just come in. Off you go. We'll catch up later.'

'No. I'm all right here.' She had just spotted Mark too – jeans and a casual suede jacket – and suddenly it did not matter much whether

192

or not she spoke to him again. She had felt the slightest feeling of satisfaction to know that the marriage had failed, a satisfaction predictably followed by guilt. So, with Trisha out of the equation, Mark was free but suddenly, inexplicably, she was no longer interested in him.

She did not want to abandon Simon. She wanted to know more about him. She liked what she saw on the surface but thank goodness there was nothing to remind her of Dave. His slight reserve appealed to her, that and his sympathetic air. He was not so mind-bogglingly attractive as Dave but she was not going to be swayed by looks. She wondered what he did for a living. Diane would have found that out by now.

A bell jangled.

Just like school.

One of their old schoolteachers had appeared from nowhere, standing with a microphone at the entrance to the dining room. There was a little self-conscious cheer before she spoke.

'Good evening, boys and girls . . .' she said with a little laugh.

'Good evening, Miss Marsh.'

A few giggles.

Ah. It was to be like that, was it?

'The last thing we want is a stampede into the dining-room,' she said. 'So if you could please form an orderly queue and check where you are to be seated *before* you come in and . . .' she smiled broadly. 'If there's any nonsense, I shall have to insist you come in two by two in a crocodile.'

Maggie glanced at Simon, exchanged a rueful smile with him. The two of them went back a very long way, to primary school. She recalled him vaguely even then.

'I was never your partner in a crocodile, Simon Newell,' she told him as the queue, strangely subdued by Miss Marsh's strident tones, shuffled forward.

'No, but I always wanted you to be,' he said, his sidelong glance warm. 'I can't tell you how nice it is to see you again, Maggie.'

She wondered what this man did now; decided it really didn't matter.

Later, she was to wonder how on earth he had wangled it so that, surprise surprise, they just happened to be sitting next to each other.

Much later, when they were talking about the first time they met up again, he would tell her.

CHAPTER TWENTY-THREE

S CHOOL was over for another term and the long summer holidays stretched ahead for Frances. They had not heard from Diane since she returned home – at least, she had not, although she suspected Diane had been in touch with Maggie. Why was she always excluded from their little games?

It did not matter. Dad and Mrs Latham were wasting no time and the wedding date was fixed already. It was going to be difficult adjusting to Mrs Latham being her stepmother and, at her age, she supposed she would never quite reconcile herself to that. She was being as gracious as she could about it all; bearing in mind that her father looked very contented these days.

It also meant that she felt an urgent need to get on with her preparations to leave home. Her dad had said there was no rush for either of them to leave, her and Maggie, and Mrs Latham – she really could not get used to calling her Wendy as she had asked – Mrs Latham insisted that they must stay for as long as they liked. The house was huge and there would be no problem. They could happily co-exist together, she said, but Frances was not so sure. It had been just her and Dad for so long that she could not help it feeling like an intrusion, no matter how nice Mrs Latham was being.

'Where is he taking you? Anywhere exciting?' Maggie asked, watching as Frances packed her holiday bags.

'The seaside,' Frances told her with a wry smile. 'Devon, actually.

He's rented a cottage by the sea.'

'Sounds good.'

'I don't know about that. It's self-catering,' Frances said. 'John says he's going to do the cooking.'

'Lucky you.' Maggie grinned. 'That's what I'm looking for. A man who can cook.'

'A bucket and spade holiday.' Frances sat down suddenly, heavily, on the bed. 'I don't know if I can face it.'

'Oh, come on, you'll enjoy it. It's for the kids. And the forecast is very good. Sand and sunshine, what more could you want?' Maggie sighed, coming across to sit beside her. 'Frances, you've got to get over this. I know it's not what you would have planned but these things happen. You don't always fall in love with the man you imagined you would.'

'How did it go with Mark Broughton?' Frances perked up a little, knowing that Maggie was right. The best-laid plans and all that . . . a dream of a nice quiet life shattered.

'Do you know, I went right off him,' Maggie said. 'But I had a very good time with Simon Newell. You won't remember him. He was another of the sixth-form crowd. It was good fun, the reunion, once we all got together. I hardly recognized some of them. Some of the girls have really gone to seed. Sorry . . .' she grimaced. 'Katie Walsh has a daughter who's seventeen, for heaven's sake. It made me feel ancient.'

'Simon Newell?' Frances was thoughtful. 'Didn't he have identical twin sisters? They were in my year. I see them quite regularly. They still look exactly alike,' she added, smiling as she realized the absurdity of the remark. 'I can do a bit of detective work if you like?'

'No. For heaven's sake, no,' Maggie said. 'I'll find out in due course. He did history with me and I'm trying to remember what else he did and where he went to after that.'

'So you are meeting him again?'

'Yes, I certainly am. We're meeting for lunch tomorrow,' Maggie said happily. 'It's all happening for us, isn't it? You and your John.

Dad and Wendy. Me and Simon. Pity about Diane though. . . .'

Frances shot her a glance. 'Why? What's happening with Diane? I feel very left out. She never tells me anything. It's as if I can't be trusted with a secret and that really gets me. What's wrong with her? She's not ill, is she?'

It occurred that if she was it would be very Diane-like to keep a stiff upper lip and not breathe a word. Remembering their mother and how quickly her illness had taken hold, coming as it did out of nowhere, was enough to send a little flutter of fear zipping round her body. They didn't get on, heaven knows, but there were the children and Rupert to consider. . . .

'I promised I wouldn't tell,' Maggie said, looking doubtful. 'But I always felt it was mean of her not to tell you too. I understand that she might not want to tell Dad because he would go completely daft but you would understand . . . as much as I do, anyway.'

'They're splitting up?'

'I hope not.' Maggie sighed. 'The thing is. . . .'

'She's having an affair?' Frances said flatly, as it dawned. She waited a moment until she knew from Maggie's expression that she had it right. 'Don't worry, you've not told me. I've guessed. I might have known. What is the matter with her? And surely she can't be serious about it? What about the children?'

'It's tearing her apart,' Maggie said. 'That's why she was in such a mood. I've told her to be careful, to think about it, not to get carried away and most of all not to tell Rupert.'

'Does she imagine for a minute that he doesn't know?'

Maggie looked at her oddly. 'I never thought of that. I assume he doesn't. If he does, then he's playing it very cool.'

'Why on earth didn't she talk to me? It's as if I don't exist.'

'Do *you* talk to her?'

'No.'

'Then you should. I can't do it for you, Frances.'

Maggie was right. Infuriating but there it was. Frances lugged the bag across the floor, dumped it by the door. 'This sort of thing causes heartache all round, for everybody. Look at me; I'm trying to pick up the pieces after Julia left John. Trying to repair the damage. . . .' She paused, realizing that this was the first time she had thought of it in that way. 'Diane's a fool,' she added. 'And I suppose she didn't tell me because I would have said as much. The trouble with Diane is that the truth hurts too much sometimes. She behaves like a spoilt little girl. That's her problem. She's always got what she wanted. She just clicks her fingers and there it is . . . a fantastic job, a man like Rupert, children, everything on a plate.'

'Leave Diane to me,' Maggie told her, glancing at her watch. 'Let me help you with the bags or you'll never get to John's. And stop looking as though you're heading for the scaffold. Try to enjoy it, Frances.'

'I will. And good luck with Simon. He sounds a really nice man.'

'He is.' Maggie looked dreamily past her. 'Would you believe it? I've been scouring the country for him and here he is, right under my feet.'

'Careful. You've only just met him.'

'Yes, but I've known him since I was five. It's not quite the same.'

Maggie looked so pretty standing there, her hair tousled, her face clear of make-up, and suddenly Frances was so very glad that she was back for good. Even if they would not be living together for much longer, they would be within easy reach of each other and that mattered. Diane was better at a distance, her problems far removed, but she felt relieved that Maggie would be around to help her out if she needed it.

John had rented a cottage on the north Devon coast which was one hectic journey on the first weekend of the school holidays down the M6 and M5. With all the services jam-packed with fractious families, it promised to be a journey from hell. On balance, Frances thought she might have preferred a long-haul flight trapped in economy beside a *talker*.

On Polly's advice, she had bought a book on how to survive a family journey, taking it to heart, studying it as intently as one of her college textbooks, arming herself with some games and puzzles that were intended to keep little minds fully occupied. It worked after a fashion and John was impressed by her ingenuity but, as the miles flipped by, tempers flared and boredom soared.

Boredom equalled quarrels and noise, the sort of noise that always made her want to retreat in horror. John, concentrating on driving through Saturday morning traffic on the awful Birmingham portion of the motorway, was, of necessity, leaving the discipline to her. This seemed a bit off given that she did not want to rock the boat of the tender relationship she was just forging with his three little sweeties or rather, at this moment, the three little horrors. With John surprisingly calm and relaxed, she did not want to take on the role of bad cop but she feared it would have to be done.

Drawing in her breath sharply as some idiot in a caravan swerved in front of them, the caravan lurching from side to side, she did her own swerving to stare at the children. Enough was enough.

'Quiet,' she ordered, in her best schoolteacher voice, the one normally reserved for 4H. She looked at each of them in turn. 'Quiet. Or Daddy will have an accident and we'll all end up in hospital.'

'Hospital?' Eleanor perked up, interested.

'Dead,' Frances added, seeing three pair of eyes widen.

'Frances—' She heard the warning note in John's voice but it was too late to unsay it and the girls were looking at her now with some alarm. Quiet though.

'I know. Let's have a sing-song,' John said. 'Frances's turn to start.'

'Singing what?' she asked, her mind completely blank.

'Any damned thing,' he said, voice low.

'OK. Let's go,' she said, thinking and coming up with 'Old McDonald Had A Farm', relieved when, after a moment, they all joined in with their raucous little voices. Following that, she was on a roll, effortlessly digging deep into her repertoire of nursery songs.

'Fran, you do surprise me. Is there no end to your talents?' John asked with a smile as she paused for breath.

'It's a gift,' she said, feeling a little light-headed, enjoying this now she was in the swing of things. 'We'll do "A Spoonful Of Sugar" and this time Daddy will join in,' she added wickedly. The miles had sped by thank goodness, and they were now approaching the end of the M5 and would soon be at their turn-off.

'No way. I don't sing,' he said firmly, checking the sign and moving in.

'Don't you? You look the part, John. I can just see you striding round the stage singing in an opera. Now you've destroyed my illusions.'

'What's illusions?' Victoria piped up.

'Illusions?' Frances sighed as, signalling to leave the junction, John left her to it. 'An illusion is when you think something is real and then you find it's not.'

'Like when Mummy says she's coming home and then she doesn't?'

Frances heard John mutter something, not sure if she should try a diversion or answer the question. The question hung in the air and she decided she would get no help from him. She had noticed that John inclined to the diversion as often as not when tricky questions arose. This time, it deserved an answer of sorts.

'I am sure your mummy loves you all,' she said, turning in her seat to face the three of them. The younger ones were sleepy and not very interested but Victoria's eyes were bright and she wanted desperately to give some consolation. Looking at her, looking at all three of them, she knew with a certainty that, even though she rated herself as zilch in the maternal stakes, she could not have done it. Julia had done it. Diane might be going to but she – if these were her children – she could not do it. Nevertheless, she was not going to fall into the trap of turning them against their mother. 'She can't always be here but she still loves you. And Daddy loves you too. And so do I,' she added valiantly. 'We all do.'

Everybody lapsed into silence after that, even John, and Frances was left to ponder on what she had just said. Now she had well and truly done it. The simple truth beginning to worm its way into her heart was this. These little beings were John's and she loved him, so by definition, she must love them too. At first, she had just been

'Daddy's friend' to them but now she was something else. It was rapidly and chaotically heading for the moment when, even though she was not yet related in any way, she would not be able, physically, to leave them.

'Nearly there,' John said. 'When we arrive, we'll just give them a quick meal, get them to bed and then we can relax. Just the two of us. How about that?'

'Sounds wonderful,' she said, although the quick meal and into bed he suggested for the girls sounded as if it would be some considerable time before they could indulge in 'just the two of us' time.

The cottage was not far off the beaten track, cosy and warm, the beach a stone's throw away, but that was for tomorrow. True to his word, John had a meal organized for the children very quickly, give or take finding his way round a new kitchen and, once they had eaten, Eleanor was first to go up the little winding stairs to the upper floor and bed.

Frances read her a story, tucking her up with the toy rabbit she had brought with her. The pot dolls had remained at home, one at the head of each bed. Carefully, Frances took the little glasses from her and placed them on the bedside table. There was still a mark beside her eye from the cut but it was fading.

'Please will you leave the light on,' she requested and Frances nodded, turning to look at the child who was now so sleepy she could scarcely keep her eyes open. Gently, she reached down and smoothed back her hair, feeling a fondness for her, very nearly amounting to an ache in her heart. The two of them were developing a bond that didn't yet exist between the others. The other girls were older and more wary; perhaps they had been hurt that important bit more. How could Julia have left them? How could she? And now her sister was contemplating doing the same. If she did, if Diane left Rupert and her children, she would never forgive her.

'Night night, sweetheart,' she said softly, leaning over to plant a little kiss on her forehead. Why had she ever worried? Maggie was right. They were only children and children wore their hearts on their sleeve. 'Sweet dreams.'

'Night night, Frances,' the little voice responded through a big yawn.

John was in the doorway, smiling his Daddy smile.

He raised his eyebrows, looking at her with a sort of triumph.

'Don't dare say a word,' she warned him as she slid past.

CHAPTER TWENTY-FOUR

DIANE quietly opened the door of her house.

After a day like she had had, this was the moment, she thought ruefully, when she would discover Rupert in bed with the au pair and then her world really would be turned upside-down.

Not that she wouldn't deserve it. She did not deserve somebody like Rupert and she could trust him, which was a damned sight more than he could her. How could she have done it? Risked losing all this for a cheap thrill with a man whom she now realized was simply missing his wife. With excitement singularly missing from her life, she had been ripe for an affair and Leo had guessed as much. She wanted so much to hate him for what he had done but could not quite bring herself to do it. She could have said no. It wasn't all his fault.

As she passed the sitting-room, the au pair appeared with her coat on just about to go and pick up the children. Anticipating the question, Diane declined picking them up herself, not wanting to disrupt the routine and needing a private moment with her husband anyway.

Rupert was up in his studio. He was barefoot as usual, wearing old faded torn jeans and a baggy shirt, looking terrific as always. He was the sort of man, like her father, who would age well. A panic kicked in as she realized she was less likely to do that herself; once her looks were gone, where would that leave her?

'I've resigned,' she told him, kicking off her shoes and collapsing onto the old sofa he kept up here. The room smelt of turpentine and paint and she could not see what he was working on. Canvases were stacked around the room. Oh, what a waste of time and effort. The world was full of would-be artists. 'I couldn't bring myself to work for such a corrupt outfit a minute longer.'

Rupert wiped the brush, popped it in the jar, as calm as you like.

'Cup of tea or something stronger?'

'A cup of tea would be lovely.' She stretched out her legs, exhausted by the day's events, as he busied about at the sink in the corner. 'What are you working on? Can I see?'

'If you like. It's another of my signature pieces,' he added with such an odd note in his voice that she looked up in surprise. It was unlike him to be sarcastic.

'You did hear what I said, Rupert? I've resigned.' She looked up at him as he handed her a cup of tea. Weak. No milk. No sugar. Just as she liked it but then, after all these years together, he knew these things. 'With hindsight, it was probably hasty but Piers looked so bloody smug I wanted to wipe the smile off his face.'

'You did the right thing. It's been getting to you lately. I can't believe those stupid rumours either.' He sat down on the floor at her feet, the movement quick and graceful.

'You know about them?' she asked carefully.

'Of course. Shirley told me. We laughed about it. I mean to say, Diane, with me at your disposal what the hell would you be wanting with another guy? The idea is ludicrous.'

She nodded. 'Look, I don't want you worrying. I've had a sort of provisional offer of another job,' she said, needing to tell him that even if it was not true. 'So we'll be fine.'

'We will indeed be fine,' he said. 'Hey, don't get upset about it.'

She tried to stem the tears that had been threatening for hours now. She did not cry. It was not in her nature to cry. She had not even cried when she lost the baby. A great well of emotion had shifted somewhere inside but she had not actually cried.

She had not kept the letter. She had popped it through the shredder and the strips lay in the basket now in her office, or rather in Candida's office.

'We need to talk.' Rupert got up and sat beside her. Gently, he removed the cup from her hand and placed it on the floor. Then, he put his arm round her and drew her close. 'Have we time to talk before the kids get back?'

'Oh God, you're not going to go all serious on me, are you?'

'This is serious, darling. As serious as it gets. You've kept us going these last few years, Diane, and I'm proud of you for doing that.'

'It's nothing,' she said, not sure what he was getting at. 'I love the work. And it's great that you're here for the children.'

'I see our marriage as a partnership.'

She nodded, moving away and looking at him. He had a speck of paint on his cheek and she rubbed at it, making it worse. 'I do too,' she said, smiling a little at his earnestness.

'You could say I've ended up with the short straw, being at home, taking the bulk of the responsibility for the children, shopping, supervising, all that stuff, but I have enjoyed it. I have the best of both worlds. I still have time to do my painting.'

'Thank God for that. And that's why it works so well. We both enjoy what we do. Doing the domestic bit would drive me insane.'

'Things change though,' he went on. 'You need a break and this is the perfect opportunity. There's no need to go rushing into another job. Relax for a few months. Spend some time with Freddie. Freddie needs you to spend time with him.'

'I know.' She thought of her littlest boy and sighed. To think she had thought of leaving him. Could she have gone through with it? If that letter from Leo had been a come-away-with-me letter, could she have done it? 'But that's all very well, Rupert. We need money to function. There's this house, the cottage and all our other commitments.'

'There are several options,' he said. 'We can always sell the cottage. It hardly seems worth while to me. If we want to go to the country for the weekend, we could always book in somewhere.'

'Six of us?'

'Why not? It would be cheaper than running the cottage anyway. We've only been three times this past year. And, if it comes to it, we could sell this place, too, get something smaller further out.'

She frowned. 'No. That's the thin end of the wedge and there's no need to panic. I might start up on my own. Why not? I have the contacts. I could do it. After all, I resigned so that makes it OK.'

'No.' Rupert said firmly. 'Absolutely not.'

'What did you say?'

'Take a job if you must,' he said. 'But it's my turn now, Diane. My paintings are selling at long last.'

How could she tell him the truth?

'Selling *properly*,' he went on. 'To real people.'

He knew. He didn't need to spell it out.

'Look, I only—'

He put up his hand to stop her. God, what was wrong with him today? She had never seen him like this.

'When I was doing the school run I met up with Tamsin Marlow, Jessica's mummy.'

'Oh yes . . .' Diane recalled her. A touch bohemian and one of those rare women who could get away with that. 'And. . . ?'

'She runs her own business supplying original artwork and accessories for hotels and company reception areas and so on. A bit in your line, I suppose?'

'Hardly.' Diane sniffed. She was getting the drift of this already, was not sure she approved of Rupert becoming entangled – albeit in a dodgy-sounding business sense – with the said Tamsin. Tamsin had a very lazy, sexy look about her and no husband or partner as she recalled. 'And I suppose she wants some of your paintings to display?'

'Exactly. She operates a rotation system. There's one company in particular, branches nationwide, that are particularly taken with them. They think they tie in very well with their corporate image. Anyway, I've got a commission. And that's not all,' he finished triumphantly. 'As well as that, I'm starting up with Heather in interior design now that I've got my diploma.'

'Diploma?'

'I did tell you, Diane,' he said softly. 'Obviously, you weren't listening. I've been doing this diploma for over a year now. Two afternoons a week.'

Vaguely, something surfaced in her mind. Maybe he had mentioned it but she had scarcely taken it in. But then she paid scant attention to his daily life, more than happy to have it all ticking along.

'Congratulations,' she said.

'Well, thank you,' he smiled. 'They don't give them away, you know. I had to work for it. Anyway, you know Heather from school.'

'Samantha's mummy.' She stared at him. What was this? Was it some sort of undercover network of working mums who were dead set on pinching her husband for their own gains? She brought Heather to mind. A little dark-haired woman, sharp featured, neatly dressed, definitely not a threat.

'She's been doing it for a while but she's been struggling with it. She's brilliant with clients and her speciality is fabrics but she thinks we will work well as a team with me providing the eye for colour and shapes. She's on a high just now. She's landed this job to do up a house top to bottom for a Saudi businessman. She thinks we should pop one of my paintings on the wall as a present to him and you never know, the word might spread. It's his London retreat and he wants it ready by Christmas. We have to furnish it down to the smallest accessories. He just wants to walk into it. He's told us what he doesn't want so that's a help but even with money no object, it's a bit of a tall order to get it right – but we'll do it.'

'*How* will we do it?' she asked sarcastically. 'How will you find the time, Rupert?'

'I will find the time,' he said.

'Commercial art?' she said with a sniff. 'You always said you would never do it.'

'That's the artist in me,' he said. 'We're talking practicality now, Diane. If I'm to support the family then I have to grit my teeth and do it. And I need more than one outlet as a back-up. If Heather and I get it wrong then we'll be blasted into space.'

Rupert was in a complete sizzle. Looking at him, she tried to match his excitement for he had waited a long time for this, for a kind of success.

207

Going down to meet the children, she had to face facts, the facts being that, rather than being pleased for him, she was incredibly irritated. If he climbed onto this bandwagon, becoming involved in not one but two businesses fronted by two ambitious women, started earning serious money, where would that leave them and their relationship? Could she cope with role reversal?

She wanted things to stay exactly as they were. She was the successful one and Rupert stayed home. She did not want *his* career to blossom.

She was jealous.

CHAPTER TWENTY-FIVE

P REPARING for the drive back up north, Frances slipped the ring on her finger, holding her hand out and admiring the glitter of the diamond. True, she and John had not had much time for themselves, but they had had some truly memorable times this past week dotted amongst the not so good. But then she knew every family had those moments and she was new to all this.

As John pointed out, things were different these days and the so-called perfect family unit was rarer now than the dysfunctional one. Was that true? True or not, she saw what he was trying to say. She was not the only woman doing this, falling in love with a man with a ready-made family. Step-families were becoming the norm. Not only had she survived this week away but in a strange way she had enjoyed it. When you had a family depending on you, it certainly made you appreciate the time you did manage to conjure up for yourself. Late at night, with the children in bed, they could at last spend time together and that easy companionship was not something to be lightly thrown away. In some ways, to her, it was as good as the sex.

'You've been a tough nut to crack,' John said, coming up behind her and putting his arms round her. 'You got it into your head that you're hopeless with children when you're just fine. You got it into your head that you have to be the perfect mother and there's no such thing. And you're not doing this on your own either. You've got me. Remember?'

She nodded. She trusted him.

'About the wedding,' she said. 'Do you think I'm getting a bit long in the tooth for a full-blown wedding dress?'

'No. You'll look fantastic and the girls have got it into their heads that they want to be princesses for the day.'

'We shouldn't have told them just yet,' she said, glad he'd said that, because she wanted to wear a proper dress. 'I'll ask Maggie to help me choose something. I hope I can find one that's flattering, something that doesn't make me look like a complete bridal disaster.'

'Will you stop it, Fran? You will look lovely to me whatever you wear.'

'Thanks.' She smiled up at him. 'I think I should ring home. Break the news that we're engaged. I'd like to give them time to think about it before we get back.'

There were a few raised eyebrows as Wendy had known there would be, a few muttered comments about landing on her feet, but her conscience was clear no matter what people might think. She was marrying Harvey because she loved him and that was that.

They were to be married at a country house hotel, quietly, with just family present. She had bought a suit in peach silk and a feathery fascinator in place of a hat. It gave her a younger look, she thought, she *hoped*. Harvey would look wonderful in a dark suit with a red rose in his lapel. After spending one night at the hotel, they were off to Paris for a few days and then it would be back to Park House as its mistress, although she would still be the cleaner as she had no intention of employing another woman to do it. She had a problem with cleaners generally. They never got into the corners like she did.

Hot on their heels, wasting no time either, Frances would be marrying her John. John's three little girls, added to Diane's brood, meant Wendy was a brand new grandmother to seven children. Just think of all the spoiling she could do. It was a dream come true.

'Two weddings this year already! Isn't that astonishing?' Maggie said, checking her appearance in the hotel mirror. With two fingers directed at Diane's fashion guru, she had chosen a suit in her favourite olive colour. She liked it, Simon liked it, so what the hell?

'Will you make it three?' Frances was beside her, looking at her fondly. 'Wouldn't that be fantastic?'

She laughed. 'Sometime but not this year. Simon's mother's very keen on him getting married and it's putting us both off.'

'She'll get her way. You're doomed.' Frances fastened the buttons on her going-away outfit and contemplated her reflection grimly.

'Why did I choose pink?' she asked. 'Not my colour. Why can't I get it right? Look at Diane – doesn't she look marvellous?'

'Great,' Maggie agreed, marvelling at how happy Frances had finally allowed herself to be and how marvellous *she* looked these days. What a worrier! Contrary to her own belief, she was good with John's children, not over-enthusiastic but maybe that was as well. Children accepted people for what they were and they could cope with far more than you gave them credit for.

Sometime this weekend, when she had the chance, she wanted to grab a word with Diane. Find out what the hell was going on these days. Shortly after her return to London following her few days up here back in summer, there had been a hurried phone call from Diane acquainting her succinctly with the facts; her resignation and Leo's disappearance, insisting she did not want to hold a post-mortem about either of them.

Today, the Buckman family certainly looked the part, pretty nearly perfect, and, if she hadn't heard it from Diane's own lips, it was hard to imagine that, a few months ago, it had been on the verge of complete collapse.

In the event, it was Diane who collared her.

'I never thought we'd live to see today,' she said, a little shake of her head aimed Frances's way. 'How did she do it? A man like that? I could fancy him myself if I wasn't so very happily married.'

Maggie shot a glance at her. Was there a hint of sarcasm or was she being neurotic in even thinking such a thing?

'So you're taking a break from work, Diane? I never thought I'd live to see that either.'

'It's Rupert. He insists. He's suddenly become very assertive,

211

Maggie. It's bizarre, frankly. He's a different man and I'm not sure I like it.'

'He's having some success at last,' Maggie said. 'He deserves it. And you should try to be pleased for him.'

'Is it so obvious?' She smiled a little. 'I liked things the way they were and I'm not sure who I am any more. I certainly don't want to be thought of as just Rupert's wife.'

'Why not? He's been *just* your husband for long enough. Give yourself a break. Freddie needs you around for a little while,' Maggie pointed out gently. 'If you're not around now to sort things out, you'll regret it.'

'What do you know about it?' That familiar aggression was never far from the surface. 'When you have kids of your own then I might listen to you. Are you getting together with Simon?'

'Yes. We're moving in together. I don't know that I'm particularly bothered about getting married.'

'Ah. I see. You've changed your tune. Have I put you off?'

'No. It's not that. There's no rush.'

'They seem to be holding it together,' Diane said, looking up as she heard their father's laugh. He was standing beside his new wife, his hand at her waist. 'He's moved Mum's photographs. Have you noticed? Or perhaps Mrs Latham moved them?'

'She's Mrs Troon now and do try to call her Wendy.' Maggie glanced sharply at her. Would she ever change? She had been barely sociable at Dad and Wendy's wedding, cool in a mint green delight of a dress. It didn't matter how uptight Diane was, how shaky her life was, she always got the clothes spot on.

'I wish Mum was here,' Maggie said as the thought struck. 'Obviously it wouldn't have been a good idea for her to be at Dad and Wendy's but I wish she was here for Frances's wedding.'

'You say the daftest things but I think I know what you mean.' Diane sighed. 'I let Mummy down, Maggie. At the last, I let her down. I could have got here if I'd shifted myself but instead I messed about to make sure that I would be too bloody late. It was only because I was scared. She thought I had made it. Did you know that?

She thought Frances was me.' Her eyes filled with tears. 'She wasn't a happy woman, was she? I could never get through to her, never understand why.'

Like mother, like daughter, Maggie thought.

Diane sniffed. 'Bugger. It's weddings. They do this to me.'

'I'll come and visit soon,' Maggie promised her. 'Relax. It's working out, Diane. Did Rupert ever suspect?'

'I'm not sure.' Diane was blinking furiously. 'Rupert wants to try for another baby.'

'Oh. Do you?'

She shrugged. 'I don't think so. You can't have a baby as a solution to your problems. After Leo went away—' her voice caught. 'I wish you'd met him. You would have liked him. Everybody likes Leo. I can't believe he did it, Maggie. After all the things he said to me. I thought he loved me. How could I have got it so wrong?'

Maggie sighed. 'You've got to put him out of your mind, Diane. He made that very clear, didn't he? You must respect his wishes and not get in touch.'

'For two pins, I'd pack all this in tomorrow,' Diane said. 'Just for some time with him. I can't forget him and I never will. So, just piss off, Maggie, if you've nothing else to say.'

'Right, I will—'

'Sorry.' Diane caught her arm, held her back. 'Sorry, sorry. I wish I'd kept the letter. Maybe there was a secret message there . . . in code.'

'Oh, Diane. . . .' Maggie was beginning to revise her opinion about Leo, at least the Leo Diane had built up in her mind. This Leo was not going to go away without a fight, not in Diane's head anyway, but she had to let him go or it would eventually destroy what she and Rupert had.

'Do come and see me soon, Maggie,' Diane said, a pleading note in her voice. 'Don't forget. I don't know where I am with Rupert just now. He's a different man and it's taking me a while to adjust. If I ever do. It's as if I want all these hare-brained schemes of his to go down the pan but that's a dreadful thing to want, isn't it? Just so I can whip back into action myself and save us all from a fate worse than death. A downsize . . .' she laughed but her eyes were bleak. 'I'm trying, Maggie. I am trying. But nothing's simple with me.'

'I know.' Maggie leaned forward, touched her silk sleeve. 'Be happy. Like Frances and Dad. And me. Rupert loves you, Diane. So what if there's been a bit of a blip with you, you'll work it out. And don't forget, you have four lovely children.'

'Don't lecture me, big sister,' Diane said, softening the words with a little smile, regaining her composure as Frances and her husband powered towards them.

Congratulations and kisses followed.

CHAPTER TWENTY-SIX

F ROM the window of his study, Harvey looked out at the autumn garden. Wendy was planning to make some changes to it, busy drawing up little plans and poring through gardening books. At least she had that in common with Angela but, thank goodness, nothing else.

She was his breath of fresh air and he wondered now how on earth he had managed without her. Yesterday, they had been to the park to see the sapling that had been planted in the summer in Tom's memory. Standing there, in that quiet little corner with its sweeping view of the park and bowling green in the distance – Tom had been fond of bowls – he had felt odd, not quite a part of it. He had stood aside and left Wendy to stand awhile with her memories. He knew she was close to tears but he wanted to allow her a private moment, as it were, with Tom. He had no quarrel with Tom. He had never known the man but they must be two of a kind for they had both of them fallen in love with Wendy.

'How old do you feel these days, Harvey?' she had asked, on the way.

'Forty,' he had replied promptly. It was a damned good age.

'Then I feel thirty-five,' she said, a twinkle in her eyes. 'You don't mind coming with me to see the tree?'

'Not at all. As you say, he loved trees.'

'He did.'

'We can plant one at home for him,' he told her. 'Wherever you like in the garden.'

215

'I know that and it's a lovely thought but Tom loved the park. We should plant something for your Angela at home.'

Home? He loved the way she thought of Park House as her home now. He also liked the way she talked about 'his' Angela. There was no malice there and nor should there be.

They were simply two very different women. For all her faults, he had loved Angela once upon a time and must never forget that. And, after all, she had given him his three daughters. On that front, things were looking up. Maggie had found a good man in Simon so there was hope there. Frances, at long bloody last, had found a man who could understand her. As for Diane . . . well, he was beginning to realize more and more that Diane was her mother's daughter. He couldn't do very much about Diane. She would go her own sweet way, whatever happened.

Wendy had stood awhile in that corner of the park, facing the tree, touching it briefly, and then, he could almost see her bracing herself, squaring her shoulders, turning and coming back, smiling and taking *his* hand.

Rupert was out as he frequently was these days so Diane was pleased when Shirley rang to ask if she could pop over.

Diane had thought a lot about the conversation she had with Maggie at Frances's wedding. Clearly, Maggie was fed up with her and, of course, Maggie was right to be. She was being an absolute pain and a half these days and it was a wonder anybody put up with her. She was short with Rupert and the children, short with herself if that was possible. The only way out of this was forward and the only way forward was for her to put Leo firmly to the back of her mind. Preferably in a little closed compartment.

With that very much in mind, she had settled into her new non-working life with aplomb. She couldn't sit around doing nothing and it wasn't long into the new term before the school had grabbed her, delighted to have somebody with her expertise on their parent/teacher books. She would, she knew, be running the show before long. No matter how much you tried to sit back, impatience at other people's incompetence was never far away and already she was looking at some of the parent/teacher goings-on with complete bewilderment. The chairperson just now was not far short of insane, the committee composed of ditherers. God knows they needed a capable hand at the wheel and that was her.

When she was ready, when *she* was ready, she would start up her own PR company and take Shirley with her. She was glad that Rupert was out this evening because he and Shirley had an uneasy relation-ship. Rupert was such a superstitious idiot and just because Shirley's life had been tragic with a capital T, he thought that she was some sort of magnet for it, tragedy striking those nearest and dearest to her at regularly worrying intervals.

'Steer clear of her,' he warned. 'There's no need to get too friendly.'

Diane ignored him. Shirley was lonely and, although she didn't usually take much heed of lame ducks, she made an exception with Shirley simply because, outside of work, she had nobody. So, she had come over for the occasional meal cooked by a reluctant Rupert and Diane had changed the subject when it looked as if it was going to degenerate into tales of woe. They gave each other a kiss on the doorstep and Diane took her coat and hung it up.

'How's work?'

Shirley just shook her head, bundled up in too many bulky clothes as was her custom, following Diane into the sitting room. She was in her early fifties, her hair still dark in a long bob that probably suited her twenty years earlier but seemed to drag her face down now. 'I'm glad you're out of it, Diane. James is quite dreadful to work for.'

'I should imagine he is.' Diane poured them each a drink, a gin and tonic for herself, a sparkling mineral water for Shirley, who did not drink. 'What's the problem?' she asked when they were settled.

'I've done something dreadful and I can't keep it from you a minute longer,' Shirley said, glancing round. 'Are you sure Rupert's out?'

'Yes.' Diane laughed. 'Why? Is it for girls only?'

'You know how much I like Rupert?' Shirley began. 'He's such a charming man. I know he doesn't like me much.'

'Where did you get that idea from?' Diane looked at her. Oh dear. Shirley's usual default demeanour was of a mild agitation, which sometimes surfaced into complete panic. She did not know if she ever relaxed, if she was capable of it, but, if she did, then she had not seen her do so. What the woman needed was a weekend's relaxation at some posh spa hotel and don't think she hadn't thought of treating her to that – going with her, in fact – but she just hadn't found the time yet to do it. Perhaps they might do it soon now that she was a woman of some leisure.

Rupert thought Shirley was a bag of nerves and said he always felt emotionally drained after an evening with her but they had to make allowances. When all about you regularly drop like flies then there was perhaps reason to be ever on the edge.

'This thing with you and Leo—' Shirley sipped her drink. 'It wasn't my business, Diane. He is an attractive man, after all, and you knew what you were doing.'

'Did I? I often wonder.' She smiled, not really wanting to talk about him, this man she was trying hard to forget had ever existed.

'I never said anything to anybody. I really don't know how Candida got to know about it.'

'I don't think she does. Sometimes you can throw an idea at some-body and look for the reaction and that tells you all you need to know. She might have been guessing originally but I don't think I was very clever in the way I reacted. I might as well have had a label round my neck saying guilty as charged.'

'It's all forgotten. I think most people take your side. They see Leo as such a decent sort of man. They can't believe it of you either. With all the children and everything.'

Diane nodded. God, that made her feel terrible.

'I would never have said anything to Rupert either.'

Diane felt the beginnings of irritation. All right, she got the message. She had always known she could trust Shirley and there was really no need for her to keep going on about it.

'Thank you,' she said. 'You are a true friend, Shirley. I shouldn't have asked it of you and I'm sorry now that I did. I know Leo feels the same way.'

'The thing is . . . oh, I don't know how to tell you but I've not been strictly honest with you.' She reached for her voluminous handbag and delved into it, producing a white envelope. 'There. This is for you. From Leo.'

'Another letter?' Diane took it from her.

'The only letter,' Shirley said quietly. 'I know what it says. I opened it to have a look.'

'You did *what*?' She was too astonished to be angry.

'I opened it. I know I shouldn't have but I felt I had to do something. When Leo gave me that . . .' she nodded towards the envelope in Diane's hand. 'I had to know what he had written because I couldn't bear the thought of you leaving Rupert and the children and going off with him and I was worried that you just might decide to do that and so I tried to do something about it, Diane.' She was rushing the words in her agitation and Diane was hard pushed to keep track. 'So, after I read it, I typed the other one, the other letter, forged his signature. It's such a silly squiggle it was easy to forge and I knew you wouldn't look too closely at that. And that's not all . . .' she added, looking searchingly at Diane. 'I typed another one, from you to him. I got you to sign that one.'

'When?'

'Before you went away. There were a heap of letters for you to sign and I just slipped it in. In the letter, I told him that you had decided to stay with Rupert, that it was all over and that he wasn't to try to contact you under any circumstances ever again. I did say that you loved him but you didn't love him enough to leave your family.'

You did that—' It was taking its time to sink in. 'You let me think that he—' She stopped, choked.

'I'd better go.' Shirley stood up, hoisting her bag onto her shoulder. 'If you want to speak to me later—'

'I won't.'

She nodded. 'Look, Diane, I only did it for the best.'

Diane had to clench her fists to stop herself from saying all she

219

wanted to say. The children were upstairs and they might hear. Instead, she said nothing, ignoring Shirley's anguished look and waiting until the door had closed behind her before she read the letter.

My darling Diane

I know you will get this because I trust Shirley to give it to you. As you will know by now, I am moved back to the States and I can't see myself coming back to Europe. Not ever. You know me, I'm a home bird. I told Dorcas about us and what do you know? – it was no great surprise, she suspected all along I was having an affair. Her reaction was so odd. Can I say this but it was as if it was a relief to her? We've talked for the first time in years, I guess, and, not surprisingly, we've decided to divorce. It's as amicable as it can get. Financially she doesn't need me and she's being generous in that. As she says, she should never have bothered to get married. She's happier on her own and that's why she chose not to come to London with me. Whenever I went away, she was fine without me and she resented my coming back. She came as close as close to wishing us well.

I miss you so much. I can't believe how much I miss you but I know that it's harder for you with your family. You can't just walk away from them so I'm trying to understand, my darling. I'm in California and it is so different on the west coast but I've got contacts – you know me – and my business will be off the ground shortly. I've got a wonderful house here by the ocean. It's close to heaven but it's not heaven yet because you're there and I'm here.

I've talked to Harry. I couldn't be honest with Harry, he's too much of an innocent, and I didn't want to get you into trouble back there so I denied the rumours as you must do too. He didn't take them seriously. They have nothing on us. The only person who knows the truth is Shirley and we know we can trust her.

Don't you worry about me, I will be OK. I'll get by. The business will keep me busy and when I'm busy I can't think too much. More than anything in this world, Diane, I want you here with me. I want you to be part of the business because you're the best and I want you to be part of my life just because I love you.

If you say the word then this is it. I will respect your wishes and I won't ever contact you again.

Goodbye, my darling.

Leo

A few weeks later, from the window of her house in London, Diane watched the children playing in the garden. It was a cold day but they were wrapped up well. Roger seemed to be in charge of whatever it was they were doing because the other three were standing in front of him listening intently.

The double-glazed window shut out all sound and Diane could not hear what was being said.

Rupert was out, working on the house for the Saudi businessman and wouldn't be back until late. By the time he *was* back, she would be gone. She could not, at the last, tell him to his face, so this morning, as he left, he had simply dropped a kiss on top of her head and shot off with a 'see you later'. No backward glance but then he wasn't to know, was he?

Her bags were packed and she was waiting now for the taxi to take her to the airport. Anxiously, she checked once again that she had her documents, closing the clasp on her bag and hugging the bag to her as she watched her children for what might be the last time.

She felt wretched. She would not be sure if she could go through with this until she stepped on the plane. Even then, it wouldn't be too late. She could step right back on another one.

'The taxi's here, Mrs Buckman,' the au pair called from downstairs. 'I've told him you won't be a minute.'

Just at that moment, as if somebody had cued them in, the children looked up towards her, towards the window, and she ducked behind the curtain, letting it fall. Then, she went downstairs where the au pair was fussing with her bags. In the bags there were some photographs and some little mementos of the children, the most poignant being their little name labels that they had worn in hospital. Roger. Philip. Freddie. Alice.

'Have a nice trip,' the au pair said with a nervous smile. 'Are you all right, Mrs Buckman?'

Diane nodded, not trusting herself to speak. For a moment, as the au pair scuttled back into the kitchen, she found she could not move. Physically, she was unable to move. She was positioned so that she could check her reflection in the hall mirror. Her hair was growing, thank God, and she had gained a little weight of late so that her face did not look so drawn. She looked good in her travelling clothes. They were all brand new and beautiful. A winter, white, loosely-cut trouser suit and a matching long fur-trimmed coat. From now on, she need not worry about dirty marks from little fingers.

She took a deep breath, knowing that she must not lose it now. Come on, one foot in front of the other. That's all it took. Climbing into the taxi, she ignored the taxi driver's cheerful greeting.

'Gatwick, madam?'

She grunted and he took that for confirmation, setting off, signalling immediately to take the right turn at the bottom of the road. In the back, Diane had to put her hand over her mouth and hold it tightly there to stifle the agonized wail that was starting up deep inside. Stop, she wanted to tell him. Take me back, she wanted to say.

The moment passed and by the time they arrived at the airport, she had regained a modicum of control.

Leo would be waiting at the other end.

Maggie and Simon were moved into their house just before Christmas. It was rather a modest house on a modest estate but it suited them. It was conveniently close to the motorway junction, a good base for Maggie's travelling and Simon's work at the university. They, neither of them, had much in the way of serious furniture so they were starting from scratch.

Frances was one of the first people to visit, popping over on her own for coffee. 'Where's Simon?' she asked, after dutifully admiring the house.

'Gone to get a Christmas tree,' Maggie told her. 'I've given him strict instructions. Nice and full with a good top for the fairy.'

Frances laughed. She was a changed woman, still inclined to be worried-looking but harassed in a different kind of way now. It was not all plain sailing, she told Maggie, in fact sometimes it was hell on earth, but overall it was . . . well, it was pretty good.

'Come to us for Christmas,' she asked. 'We're a bit more settled than you. I've asked Dad and Wendy too. It will be a real family Christmas. John will be doing the cooking. He's looking forward to it and it will mean so much more this year with the children.'

They looked at each other, remembering Diane.

'What's Rupert doing?' Frances asked, after a moment. 'I haven't rung him. I daren't. I don't know what to say to him.'

'He rang me. He's OK,' Maggie said. 'The au pair's helping out and he spends a lot of time with Tamsin.'

'Oh, do you think. . . ?'

Maggie shook her head. 'No. He's not ready for that. He still thinks she's going to come back.'

They smiled a little, falling silent. They could not get over what Diane had done, leaving Rupert and the children and opting for a new life in the States with Leo. Their father was devastated, absolutely furious with her, and it was just as well he had Wendy there to calm him down and help him through it.

Maggie and Frances were hard pressed to take Diane's side even though she was their sister. It seemed incredible to either of them that Rupert had been in total ignorance of Diane's affair with Leo but perhaps that had been one of the problems.

Even though he did not look it, he was strong underneath and he would be fine. The children would be fine, too, for he would see to that.

'Have you spoken to her?' Frances asked, avoiding saying her name.

Maggie shook her head. She knew that, sooner or later, there would be a call from Diane and she didn't know what she would say until that happened. As Diane had said, repeatedly, Maggie was not a mother so she was in no position to offer advice.

She and Simon were trying hard just now to remedy that, so by the time Diane did get round to getting back in touch, she might be pregnant but it would make no difference to Diane. Advice could be offered, sensible, sane advice, and it could just as easily be ignored. Diane, as had been proved, would do exactly what *she* wanted. As Maggie saw it, it was selfishness of a stupendous degree and unforgivable. Little Alice did not quite understand but the boys did and Rupert was doing his best to cope with that. Following Maggie's suggestion, he had got them a dog, knowing it was scant consolation for losing their mother but, as he had told Maggie, things were not as bad as they might have been.

'How are the girls?' Maggie asked Frances as they sat in the kitchen of her new house looking onto the little garden. She was proud of her kitchen, newly fitted out, very tidy. The garden was postage-stamp size but as she and Simon scarcely possessed one green finger between them, it did not matter.

'The girls are fine.' Frances smiled, pushing at her hair. 'We're very busy. It's the Christmas concerts at school. We're sharing them between us. John is going to Victoria and Isobel's and I'm off to Eleanor's this afternoon.' She checked her watch. 'Mustn't be late. She'll be looking out for me.' She hurriedly finished her coffee and Maggie was amused by the proud mum look she was beginning to develop. Who would have ever thought it? 'Now, don't forget. You're coming to us on Christmas Day and we're all off to Dad's on Boxing Day.'

Maggie nodded, escorting her to the door and waving her off. She thought of last Christmas, which she had spent with an increasingly morose Dave. No joy there. They hadn't been able to drum up an ounce of enthusiasm between them and she had known then it would be their last Christmas together.

This time it was so different.

This time it felt right.

She went back indoors to wait for Simon.

14/01/10

Central Library and
Information Service

NEWPORT COMMUNITY
LEARNING & LIBRARIES

Z573265